To Shar

Double Fantasy

Happy readin'

MARTIN TRACEY

Martin x

Copyright © 2023 Martin Tracey

Martin Tracey has asserted his right under the Copyright, Designs and Patents Act, 1988 to be the author of this work.

All rights reserved.
No part of this publication may be reproduced, stored in or introduced into a retrieval system, or transmitted, in any form, or by any means (electronic, mechanical, photocopying, recording or otherwise) without the prior written permission of the author in line with publishing guidelines.
If you wish to read this work you are kindly advised to purchase a copy. Thank you for respecting the hard work of the author.

All characters and names in this publication, other than those clearly in the public domain, are the product of the author's imagination and any resemblance to persons, living, dead or undead is entirely coincidental.

ISBN: 9798378590223

DEDICATION

For the 97

Also by Martin Tracey

BENEATH THE FLOODLIGHTS
THINGS THEY'LL NEVER SEE

In the Judd Stone Series

MIND GUERRILLA
CLUB 27
LUNAR

ACKNOWLEDGEMENTS

Thanks as ever to my family.
Special thanks to AA Abbott, Louise Dixon, Donna Morfett, and Nigel Howe for ensuring my words made sense.
And last but by no means least…
Dear reader, thanks for reading my words. Without a reader, there is no story to tell.

CHAPTER 1
I'M YOUR MAN

Judd Stone answered his landline telephone after three rings. "Hello."

"Is that you, Stone?"

"Who's this?"

"It's your old mate, Rufus."

"Rufus Tash. Blimey, it's been a while. How's things?"

"Pretty good, thanks mate. How are you?"

"Fair to middling, I guess."

"That good, huh? Listen Judd, I'll cut straight to the chase. I have a proposition for you and you'll be doing your old pal a huge favour if you choose to accept."

"So you call me after all this time because you need something? Nice."

"Not entirely, but I am kind of desperate."

"Thanks, I think! So what is my mission should I wish to accept it?"

"It's a bit of an unusual request."

"Well, you certainly have my attention," said Judd curiously.

"Have you ever wanted to be famous?"

Judd frowned. "Not really."

"OK, let me put it another way. I know that you've always liked your music, right?"

"Yeah, I guess so." Judd wondered where all this was heading.

"The Beatles in particular as I recall."

"Most definitely."

"They were undeniably a great band and they were big in the eighties too."

"Don't you mean the sixties, Rufus? The Beatles were big in the sixties."

"Hell, the Beatles were, are, big in any decade. You know that more than anyone, Judd. Macca's Frog Chorus was in the eighties, right? Oh, and he did all that stuff with Michael Jackson back then as well."

"Yes, OK. Point taken. Although I'm not convinced that the Frog Chorus is the best measure of the capability of The Beatles. But it has its place, I guess. Look, what's this all about, Rufus?"

"I need you to be Andrew Ridgeley for the night."

Judd took the phone from his ear and stared at it in puzzlement, wondering if his old friend had turned to drugs over their lost years. After a shake of the head, he returned to the conversation. "What the hell are you talking about, Rufus? We've gone from The Beatles to Andrew Ridgeley in a millisecond and you need me to be the latter for the night?"

"He has had an accident. Went skiing in Switzerland and broke his arm and both legs. Needless to say, he can't prance around the stage and play his guitar."

"Andrew Ridgeley of Wham!?"

"The very same. Kind of."

"Kind of? This isn't making a lot of sense, Rufus. Have you had a knock on the head, mate?"

"No, of course I haven't. OK, here's the deal. I'm putting on an eighties festival and George Michael won't go on stage without Andrew Ridgeley."

"The same George Michael who died on Christmas Day 2016?"

"No of course not, and that's where the 'kind of' reference comes in. I'm organising a festival of tribute artists. Wham!—or rather Sham!, as the tribute act are better known—are meant to be opening the whole thing. If we stick a black wig on you along with a CHOOSE LIFE T-shirt, you'll really look the part and save the day, Judd."

"Are you nuts? I can play a little bit of guitar, just some basic chords and riffs, but I can't hold my own in a proper concert environment, Rufus."

"There's nothing to worry about. It's all totally OK. There will be a permanent band of core musicians that will play along with all of the tribute acts, to keep things ticking along nicely. I just need you to dance around looking handsome, Judd. I know you can do that. Like I said, George—or rather part-time builder Andrew Baker—is terrified to perform without Andy, or someone pretending to be him at least."

"And what's the name of the usual Ridgeley impersonator? This guy who has hurt himself skiing?"

"George Falmer. He's a chippie. That's how the two of them met and got into this. While working on construction projects together, they would sing along to the obligatory radio, and pretty soon Sham! were born."

"So, George is Andrew and Andrew is George."

"Yeah."

"And a baker is a builder and a farmer is a carpenter."

"Almost, George's surname is spelt with an L not an R in the middle."

"And in their spare time both the brickie and the chippie transform into two musical heartthrobs? Blimey, you couldn't write this stuff."

"Actually, it's more the other way around. They are construction workers in their spare time as they do very well as the tribute act. That was until George Falmer had his skiing accident and we lost our Andrew Ridgeley."

"I have to say that this is probably the most surreal conversation I've ever had, Rufus."

"So, will you do it, Judd?"

Judd wasn't quite sure how to answer. There was a certain attractiveness to the proposition but he'd never done anything like this before. It seemed a little scary. "Why me?"

"Because you are the coolest guy I've ever known, Judd Stone."

"I guess I should be flattered that you asked me Rufus, and in spite of the proverb that flattery gets you everywhere, I really don't think so. Sorry buddy, but it's not for me."

"Come on Judd, you'll be rubbing shoulders with some of the biggest stars of the eighties. The likes of Boy George, Freddie Mercury, Jacko, Prince, Duran Duran, Bowie, Ferry, Bananarama—I know you fancied a couple of them back in the day. Oh, speaking of which, Kim Wilde too and lots more I can't even think of right now."

"But Rufus, they are tribute acts. They are not the real people who sold thousands of hit records. You can distinguish between fantasy and reality, can't you?" Judd remembered how his old pal always had his head in the clouds and often suffered delusions of grandeur.

"Of course I can you sarky bugger. Let me tell you though, these acts are just as good as the real thing if not better. I wouldn't work with them otherwise, would I?"

"Of course, you wouldn't," Judd rolled his eyes. Rufus had always been a bit of a dreamer which led him to exaggerate and be economical with the truth at times. In fact, although he was good, harmless fun, Judd had always considered his friend to be one hell of a prolific bullshitter. It seemed things hadn't changed over the years.

"Come on Buddy, as I said you'd be doing me a massive favour. Oh, Elvis is playing too. He's always a great showman."

"Elvis! He died in 1977."

"Yes, but a version of 'Always on My Mind' charted in 1985 as well as a couple of other releases, so he qualifies."

"It's not for me, Rufus. I'm sorry."

"Come on Judd, I'm desperate."

"And twice you've told me that, Rufus, which doesn't exactly inspire me to help you now, does it? So once again, thanks but no thanks."

"I didn't mean it like that. Besides, in truth, I thought that George Falmer's misfortune presented an ideal opportunity for us to be able to meet up again. It's been too long, Buddy. I think he has done us a favour in a way."

"I'm not so sure that he would see it like that."

"Maybe not, but come on, Judd. You know meeting for a beer or two has been long overdue."

Judd paused for a second, his resolve slightly beginning to wane. "Well I can't argue with that, but I'm just so busy right now."

"Look Judd, even Private Investigators need a holiday. I've already called Diego and Hunter and they're both up for it. It'll be like old times, the four of us back together again. Besides, they said they wouldn't miss you prancing around the stage for all the tea in China."

"Even though I hadn't actually agreed to anything yet?"

"I assumed that you would want to help an old pal out and catch up good and proper with your old buddies. Perhaps you're no longer the Judd Stone that we once knew and loved."

"So you're using guilt-tripping tactics on me now?"

"Come on, Judd. It'll be a laugh. All you need to do is act like Andrew Ridgeley for twenty minutes or so and then once you're off stage it'll be party time. The audience tend to keep their eyes on George anyhow—I mean Andrew…the singer. You know what I mean. So there's no real pressure on your performance."

"Is there going to be a Beatles tribute act?"

"Err, no. I just spoke about them to get your attention

if I'm being honest. It was quite a tenuous link to the eighties really, wasn't it?"

"Yes, it was. So I wouldn't even get to see a tribute act of my favourite band at a festival specifically designed for tribute artists?"

"No, but I am holding the festival in Liverpool, which is the home of your beloved Beatles. You can't fail to have a good time in Liverpool now, can you? Imagine the post-concert booze-up in the likes of The Cavern Club with your old pals. Come on, Judd. What d'ya say?"

The temptation was now simply too much for Judd. He loved the city of Liverpool almost as much as his home city of Birmingham and it would be good to meet up with the boys again. "OK, OK. I must be nuts but I'll do it."

Unbeknownst to Judd, Rufus punched the air. "Good man. I'll meet you at Lime Street Station at two o' clock on Saturday afternoon. You'll be on stage at seven. Cheers Buddy."

The phone went dead. Rufus had finally heard the answer he wanted and there was no turning back for Judd now.

Actually, as daunting as the performance was going to be, Judd was already beginning to think what a great opportunity it would be for him to connect with his old friends. A reunion was certainly well overdue.

It was true that his workload was busy, but he could ask Yasmin—his faithful albeit contrary PA—to reschedule a couple of things for him. Yeah, it would be fun to go to Liverpool.

But then the smile he currently had stretched across his face soon changed when he remembered he already had a commitment for the forthcoming weekend.

Shit. He was meant to be having Billie.

With the phone still in his hand, Judd punched in the numbers that he knew off-by-heart and quickly made a bid to connect with his estranged wife, Brooke.

After a series of rings, Brooke answered.

"Hello."

"Hi Brooke, it's me."

"Hey, Judd."

"Hey. Look, I'm really sorry but something's come up for this weekend."

"You mean something that's more important than caring for your daughter?"

"No of course not, it's just bad timing and unfortunately it can't be rescheduled. I'll make it up to Billie. I'll happily have her for two weekends in a row, or more even."

"No, you won't. If you can't put her first that's your tough luck. Every other weekend is your custody rights, you know that, yet you can't even seem to manage that. Is what you're doing really so important?"

"It's work, Brooke." He closed his eyes with shame as he lied, conscious that it wasn't the first time that he had lied to her. But actually, when he thought about it, perhaps prancing about as one half of Wham! could be considered as work of a sort, so perhaps it wasn't exactly a lie after all. "I can't go into details as it's a very unusual client, but it's very important that I see this through."

"Fine, whatever. Efan and I will take her to the zoo or something."

"Oh yeah, Efan, the wet lettuce."

"Efan is ten times the man you will ever be, Judd, and if Billie starts to see him as more of a father than you, you'll only have yourself to blame."

Brooke's words felt like a dagger going straight into Judd's heart.

"OK, OK, Brooke. I don't want to get into all of this again. I hope Billie enjoys the zoo. I'm really sorry I can't see her this weekend. Please give her a big kiss for me."

Brooke sighed. "OK, I will do. But don't let this become a habit, Judd."

"I won't. You know that Billie is the most important thing in my life."

"Then prove it once in a while. Anyway, we'll see you next time then."

"Thanks, Brooke. I appreciate your understanding."

"Bye then."

"Bye."

The phone went dead with Brooke not hesitating to hang up.

Since separating from Judd, following his one too many love affairs with other women, Brooke had let her guard down with him on just the one occasion. The thing was, that one and only time had been enough for her to fall pregnant. A couple of bottles of Malbec, entwined with flirty conversation of the good old times, had led from one thing to another. She would always fancy him, that was a given, but she didn't want to be with him.

Although Judd had been over the moon with the pregnancy and initially viewed it as perfect reason for the two of them to get back together, Brooke had made it clear that that couldn't happen. She still loved him, probably always would do, but she also hated him for what he had done. She just couldn't see herself ever trusting him again.

Brooke knew of at least two mistresses that had caught Judd's eye, and the type of woman that he had chosen to cheat on her with did little to help his cause. The first woman was one of Birmingham's most notorious gangsters, Gia Talia, and the second was an unhinged and dangerous, narcissistic criminal named Vina Moreno. The fact that he could be attracted to such treacherous and unscrupulous women whilst he was with someone as loyal and caring as her was just too much for Brooke to take.

Nevertheless, she was more than happy that Judd remained a major part of their daughter's life. She insisted on it in fact. They had settled on calling her Billie as a tribute to their dearly departed friend, William. William had been shot and killed on the bank of a Birmingham city centre canal. In the same attack, Crystal, William's wife, had also been killed and Brooke had been seriously injured resulting in her resting in a coma for many months. Judd had also been shot but managed to escape serious injury, which gave him the time and opportunity to cheat on his wife with Vina Moreno as Brooke lay sleeping in intensive care. Judd knew it had been despicable behaviour on his part and he hated himself for it. Yet he still did it.

After forgiving him once for his fling with Gia, Brooke wasn't prepared to forgive him again for his involvement with Vina. especially in such abysmal circumstances.

Judd's hope of a reconciliation was firmly dashed when in waltzed Brooke's knight in shining armour—and prize sap as Judd preferred to think of him—Efan Carruthers. Efan met Brooke when she was about six months pregnant. He soon expressed his undying love for her and offered to take on Billie as his own and provide both Brooke and her daughter with the family stability that was required. And to be fair to the prize sap, which actually didn't help Judd at all, over two years later he was still delivering on his promise.

Judd felt the smug prick was simply too good to be true and one day he would discover a significant chink in Efan's shining armour. But until that moment could be revealed—if it ever could be—Judd had to suck it up and contend with being way behind Efan, in Brooke's eyes.

Judd struggled with the situation on a daily basis. Efan was a used car salesman, for Christ's sake, and who trusts a used car salesman? No wonder he was able to charm the knickers off Brooke, he had crafted an entire career on making people hear what they wanted to hear. To be fair again though, Efan was a bit more than the average car salesman. He was actually the managing director of a famous national car depot project, the sort that provides excellent customer service and extremely reliable used cars that are always less than two years in age.

He was also eight years younger than Judd. Judd hated him.

Judd found himself suddenly needing a friendly voice. Then it became obvious whom he should call next.

If he left out the minor detail that he was standing up his only daughter for the forthcoming weekend, this person would be delighted that he was forming one half of pop duo Wham! and making an appearance at the festival.

For Tilda Chamberlain, sister of his late friend William Chamberlain, was one of the biggest Wham! and George Michael fans on the planet. And she just happened to live in Liverpool.

After a few rings the phone was answered. "Hi Tilda. It's Judd."

"Oh. Hi Judd. How nice to hear from you. How's things?"

"Pretty good, thanks. You're never gonna believe me, Tilda, but guess who I'm going to be this weekend?"

"Judd Stone, I presume?" replied Tilda a little confused.

"Do you remember that television show, where everyday people would transform into pop stars and say the immortal words 'Tonight Matthew I'm going to be…'"

"Yes."

"Well tonight, or rather, this weekend Tilda I'm going to be… Andrew Ridgeley."

CHAPTER 2
GOING DOWN TO LIVERPOOL

Judd was the first departing passenger in line as the train pulled into Liverpool's Lime Street Station. He pressed the button to activate the opening of the doors and simultaneously initiated the accompanying sound of its pneumatic operation. Once safe to do so, he stepped onto the platform and headed towards the row of turnstiles. Choosing one, the machine swallowed his train ticket as he walked on through and he soon began to scan the sea of bobbing heads in search of his old pal Rufus Tash.

It seemed quite fitting that he eventually found his friend standing next to the station's statue of Ken Dodd, Rufus was always capable of bringing a smile to Judd's face even when he didn't necessarily intend to. With his lank hair, comical features and ill-fitting suits, Rufus, was one of life's naturally likeable characters. Even the majority of his legendary bullshits would fetch a smile rather than cause any level of annoyance, which was never actually his intention anyway of course.

As Rufus set about harmlessly trying to impress whoever cared to listen, the inadvertent result would often be an inward or outward giggle at his expense for daring to be so ridiculously economical with the truth.

The two friends greeted one another with a hug and a slap on the back.

"You're looking good, Rufus."

"You too Judd. The perfect replacement for one half of Sham! George Falmer may not get his job back once Andrew Baker claps eyes on you."

"Oh, he will, this is strictly a one-off favour for you Rufus."

"Fair enough. Anyway, it's just so good to see you again Buddy."

"You too. Where are the other two delinquents?"

"One guess."

"The pub."

"Of course, and that'll be the first one heading into town once we go down the steps outside the station."

"No surprise there then. Well lead the way, Rufus."

"It'll be my pleasure, but we can't go too wild with the alcohol, Judd, as much as I know Hunter will try and influence you to drink like a fish. We need you to be compos mentis enough to pull off a half-decent impression of Andrew Ridgeley."

"I'd probably do a better job if I was half-cut to be honest. I'm not quite sure what it is I've let myself in for."

"You'll be fine. I need to introduce you to George, I mean Andrew…you know what I mean. There won't be time for proper rehearsals but at least he can talk you through the set list. I think you're kicking off with 'Wake Me Up Before You Go-Go'."

"A good set opener for sure. I might do better if the audience were a little sleepy rather than awake though. That would stop them seeing any of my dodgy chord changes."

"I've told you, there's no need to worry. You won't be plugged in; the session guitarist will cover you musically."

"Couldn't the session guitarist have just been Andrew

Ridgeley instead?"

"That would never have worked for three reasons. The first being that the session guitarist is the wrong gender. She's a lady."

"Oops, my bad. I really shouldn't assume such things."

"The second, she needs to be independently available for all the other acts, and finally, she is a shy girl and she refuses to step anywhere near the limelight preferring instead to blend into the background. Now quit stressing about it and let's go and meet Hunter and Diego."

Less than five minutes later, Judd and Rufus were inside the pub and snaking their way through the standing drinkers, across the sticky carpet to their mates.

First of all, Judd hugged Hunter. "It's been a long time, man."

"Too long," replied Hunter.

Hunter was as good-looking as he was shallow and his looks hadn't diminished over the years except for the appearance of the odd wrinkle around the eyes. Like Judd, he had aged well. Hunter could easily have been the replacement for Andrew Ridgeley but Rufus didn't need to explain to Judd why he hadn't asked him instead. Hunter was notoriously unreliable and Rufus would have been taking a gamble in reaching out for his help. In fact, they were both a little surprised that he had actually managed to turn up for the reunion at all. Perhaps he had changed over the years and was a little less self-centered than he once was? Only the unfolding of the weekend ahead would tell for sure. In any case, in the main Judd still viewed Hunter as a mate who he could share a laugh and a beer with, not necessarily a good mate, but a mate nonetheless. He was glad to have connected with him once again.

Next, Judd turned to Diego and just about managed to get his arms around the huge frame of his friend. Unlike Hunter, Diego had a heart of gold and was definitely someone who could be relied upon. However, for obvious reasons of a physical nature, he wouldn't have made a good Andrew Ridgeley.

Diego was the size of a bear and as strong as one too, but he was also the proverbial gentle giant.

His real name was Lennox Ferdinand, Diego was just a nickname. Despite the usual origin of the name Diego, he had no Spanish blood running through his veins at all. Instead, he was a first-generation Brit who had been born to Jamaican parents.

His hands were massive, like two huge shovels, and he had the impressive ability to carry two pints of beer in a single hand. This is how his nickname came about as it was considered that to be able to do such a saintly thing, he must have the 'hands of God'. When Argentinian footballer Diego Maradona had been questioned about the time he punched the ball into the net against England – and got away with it to help Argentina run out 2-1 winners in the Mexico hosted 1986 world cup finals – he had simply shrugged and said it had been due to the 'hand of God'.

And so, although not entirely sharing the same definition of the phrase, the nickname stuck with Lennox.

"It's good to see you, Judd."

"Likewise."

"I got you in a lager, Judd," said Hunter.

"Thanks, it's not my poison anymore to be honest but I'll still drink it as you've made the effort. I'm more of a real ale kind of guy, these days."

"Really? Showing your age a bit, there Judd. You were always such a lager lout as I recall. A ruck at the football match followed by a skinful of lager is how I remember you."

"I guess my taste buds grew up. As did I." Judd was a little curt, his days of engaging in football hooliganism were not his idea of fond reminiscing.

"Anyway, let's raise a glass to us whether it be lager or anything else," said Hunter.

"Amen to that," said Judd, much more relaxed.

The four men raised their glasses and brought them together, much like the musketeers would cross swords to portray their camaraderie."

"To us," said Hunter.

"To us," came the unified reply.

"Wait, we are in Liverpool and there are four of us," said Rufus. "Let's try that again. To the fab four."

"To the fab four."

"Reminds me of the time when I met Sir Paul McCartney," said Rufus.

The outrageous comment was duly ignored and instead, honouring the toast, Judd, Diego and Hunter all took a sip of their respective beverages. Sensing it best not to elaborate further, Rufus soon followed suit.

As Diego lowered the glass from his mouth his eyeline was in situ with the television positioned on the pub wall. A news channel was providing a live report that was unfolding in Birmingham. When not showing football or rugby on the screens, the pub always ensured that subtitles were activated to address the inevitable noise that the pub generated through its customers. "Hey Judd, isn't that your place in the background?"

Judd peered up at the screen. "Looks like it. Yes, that's the Rotunda alright. I thought they'd still be reporting on that horrendous earthquake that's happened."

"Yes, that's been a terrible business," said Rufus. "Thousands upon thousands dead."

"They were doing a piece on that, although it seemed to be a repeat of earlier news that I've seen, you know no major updates as far as I could tell. Just filling time. Then they cut away to report live from Brum instead. What can be so important?" asked Diego.

"Actually, it's Birmingham Pride this weekend, so I guess they are just doing the obligatory report. Should be some nicer news than the earthquake for sure," said Judd.

"Except that guy seems to have gatecrashed proceedings," said Rufus, referring to a creepy looking figure who suddenly appeared to interrupt the broadcast.

"He looks like he could be one of the countless manic street preachers that we get on the corner of New Street as it leads into the Bull Ring," said Judd. "And I'm not referring to the Welsh band of the same name."

"Not with a 'I heart Satan' T Shirt he isn't," said Rufus.

"Hey, I've seen this guy before," said Diego. "He keeps rocking up on socials. He gets a mixed reaction but boy does he get a reaction. Loads of 'likes' and 'comments', you know? People seem to find him really entertaining, they video him on their mobile phones and stream his performances. He keeps spouting on about how the second coming of Christ is nigh and how this time it's gonna be a female.

"He says that she must be stopped at all costs so that Satan will finally take his rightful place and rule the world once and for all without opposition. It looks like he has managed to gatecrash a spot on national TV, fair play to him, I guess. Mainstream media is one up on the socials but he's still a nutter."

"So, he's more of a manic street satanist," said Judd.

"Or a satanic street preacher," said Diego.

"Very good," said Judd. "I see what you did there."

The two friends clinked glasses as they laughed.

"Hey, you could get a tribute band called the Satanic Street Preachers to play your eighties music festival, Rufus," announced Diego.

"The bill's full. Anyway, I'd say Satan is already doing a pretty good job considering the wars and catastrophes currently taking place," said Rufus. "And this dude reckons the new JC will arrive in the shape of a woman, you say?"

"Yep," said Diego.

"Then he really is nuts," said Rufus.

"Not necessarily so," said Hunter, who looked agitated by the whole thing. "You don't know what you're talking about, it's no laughing matter."

"Hey, lighten up Hunter. It's just a crazy guy," said

Judd.

Hunter took a drink of his lager, seemingly buying time before he answered. "Yeah, I guess so. This end of days stuff always freaks me out a little, that's all. Sorry for snapping guys."

"Why haven't they cut him off yet?" said Judd. "Why are they even giving him air time?"

"Well, he is entertaining," offered Diego. "I bet they already know that this guy is a big hit on social media so they are letting it run for a bit."

The manic satanic street preacher was wearing dark glasses that completely hid his eyes and his long hair was even darker. The four men watched as he vigorously moved his mouth slightly ahead of the subtitled words that were rapidly appearing on the screen…. "She is coming I tell you; she is coming but she will be stopped. She is a charlatan sent from heaven but she can't rule this world like the foolish believers think she can. Instead, the one true master will take his permanent and rightful seat to control this world. He has already begun his undisputed reign by creating chaos: sending earthquakes and starting wars, things that you report on day in and day out on your TV channel. You call such things Acts of God, how ridiculous, they are obviously acts of the Devil himself. Your God is scared, forced to send his daughter in his form to try and halt the master, but Satan is too powerful and cannot be defeated. Ask yourself this question: Why would your God allow such things to happen? He is losing control…"

"See, he makes a fair point," said Rufus.

"Yeah, there's a lot of shit going on in this world isn't there when you think about it?" offered Diego.

"Sssh, I want to listen," snapped Hunter, which gave the impression that his apology moments earlier had been completely hollow.

The animated face on the screen continued "…The song you sing, 'Jerusalem', you think it tells of the time of

Jesus' missing years when he walked on this green and pleasant land of England, well, it is also a prophecy that the second coming will happen in England when *she* tries to control the world. That prophecy of the song will not come true for we, the disciples of Satan, will ensure that all girls born of the time of the second coming will be stopped. Slaughtered and slain, slaughtered and slain, slaughtered and slain…" The satanic preacher shifted up yet another gear of ferocity, which hadn't seemed possible, as he spat out those final chilling words over and over. The television broadcast was instantly pulled, probably not in good enough time in all honesty. But once the rant had been considered a step too far for the live broadcast, the screen cut to the newsreader back in the studio who began to apologise profusely.

What the news channel producers couldn't do was stop the performance unfolding back on the streets of Birmingham. The perceived Satanist continued to rant and rave whilst a large gaggle of mobile phones captured his every word, highlighting whatever broadcasting control mainstream media thought it may have, in this day and age it needed to give way to the power of social media and the inevitable instant sharing of uncensored videos. Not to mention those witnessing it first-hand in all its 4D glory.

One such person videoing the scene on her phone was a local girl who liked to follow the fashion of Gothic Horror, her style of dress more commonly earning her the label of being a Goth. Kadence, was fascinated by the imagery of Victorian horror and took an avid interest in all things paranormal. However, despite her curiosity in the more unorthodox things in life, she was actually a gentle soul who in reality could never hurt a fly. For example, she was a strict vegan purely on the grounds of her stance on animal rights and ethics.

Most people witnessing the bizarre spectacle in front of them in Birmingham city centre found it hilariously entertaining, dismissing it as a guy who was clearly one sandwich short of a picnic. But Kadence was deeply disturbed at the repeated statement of infant girls being killed and understood that there could be some truth in the claims.

Back in the Liverpool bar, three of the four friends were also laughing and shaking their heads. "What a nutter," said Diego.

"I just need to go to the toilet," said Hunter, who unlike his pals was now appearing increasingly restless. "Here, hold my beer, Diego."

Diego looked at Hunter with a curious stare.

"Please," said Hunter.

"Sure thing."

Hunter made his way towards the Gents toilets.

"What's up with him, he doesn't usually take life so seriously," said Judd.

"I know what you mean, he seemed to take that crazy guy's ramblings very literally," said Diego.

They shrugged and drank their beer.

Once safely locked inside a cubicle, Hunter reached for his mobile phone and made a call. It was answered almost immediately. "Tell me you're in Birmingham today?" asked Hunter.

"Of course, and yes, before you ask, I have just seen the TV report," came the stern reply. "Consider it done."

CHAPTER 3
YOUNG GUNS (GO FOR IT)

An extended exchange of finger clicks and a refrain of "Jitterbug" rang out across the Royal Albert Docks which had been the chosen setting for the eighties festival. To be fair to Rufus and in contrast to his previous history of hollow claims and boasts, this time it seemed that he had managed to host quite an amazing event. There was a decent sized crowd, and although this was a festival of tribute acts the artists were a bunch of very impressive replicas of the real thing.

The evening's backing singers continued to "Jitterbug", and the band occasionally injected some well-placed flurries of various instrumentation that were absent from the original Wham! track. This continued teasing of repeated musical bars went on for almost five minutes in order to heighten the anticipation of the crowd, until George and Andrew, aka Andrew and Judd respectively, appeared in their CHOOSE LIFE T-shirts. George from the left wing of the stage and Andrew (our Judd) from the right.

The reception was amazing and Judd's pre-stage nerves

soon lifted as the afternoon's bellyful of beer (more than initially intended), coupled with the roar of the crowd, helped him transform effortlessly into one of the favourite heartthrobs of the 1980s. Luckily his guitar wasn't plugged in, Rufus being true to his word for once. To be fair to Judd, he looked every inch the part, moving impressively around the stage as he caressed his instrument. He complemented Andrew Baker's thrusting and gyrating very well, who incidentally was almost as charismatic as the real George Michael with his velvety vocals. Not an easy thing to achieve at all.

Liam Gallagher had once described George Michael as a 'modern day Elvis' and when analysing the likeness of tribute artists to the real thing it was probably Elvis and George who were the most difficult to replicate. They both had a certain quality in both their voice and persona that just couldn't be matched. But Andrew Baker came as close as anybody was going to get to the self-titled Singing Greek, and with the security of knowing Judd Stone was behind him as his wingman, he expertly moved through the set list, commanded the stage and the audience's attention alike.

As the crowd clapped and cheered it had to be said that Diego found the whole thing totally hilarious. Even Hunter had lightened up from his earlier mood on seeing Judd's performance. Seeing their old mate prancing around the stage in a wig and trying to look like an eighties' pop star was just too comical to ignore in their eyes. But it was in their eyes only, their perspective skewed by the fact it was their mate who was stepping out of his comfort zone in the name of entertainment. To everyone else Judd was just one half of a tribute act.

As for Hunter's change in mood, Diego had noticed it lift considerably after receiving a text a little earlier in the day. Whatever words had been in the message, it was enough to pull him out of the angst he seemed to be experiencing from the manic street satanist's ramblings of earlier.

Judd didn't care what mickey-taking his mates may be having at his expense, he couldn't see them laughing anyway underneath the bright lights of the stage. He was in his element as he cradled and hugged the white Stratocaster as if it was simply an extension of his body.

Baker sported George Michael's trademark designer stubble and pulled on a biker's jacket for the final songs of the set list: 'I'm Your Man' and 'The Edge of Heaven', but not before delivering a very nice rendition of 'Careless Whisper' with Judd sitting on a stool to mimic the chord changes. Impressively, unlike so many pretenders before him, Baker hadn't bottled the leap of an octave in his voice as he entered the famous chorus of the ballad.

'Freedom' and an ironic performance of 'Last Christmas' on a sunny Liverpool evening completed the Wham! set. Funnily enough, Baker, had chosen not to perform 'Club Tropicana' the smash summer track of the Wham! catalogue, on account he realised that there wouldn't be sufficient time for the required costume change. He and George Falmer would usually wear shorts to perform the song.

There were to be no encores for any of the acts, in order to keep the festival flowing, and Judd surprisingly found his heart sinking as he left the stage. It had been over in a flash yet he felt like he would be on a high from the experience for at least a week.

So, Sham! had successfully opened the eighty's festival on Liverpool's dockland. Next came Durham Durham, a band from the north-east of England who had ventured over to the north-west to pay tribute to one of Wham!'s biggest rivals back in the day – Duran Duran.

Off stage, Andrew Baker gave Judd a big hug. "You were great, Judd. Thanks so much for helping me out there. I couldn't have done it without you."

"Are you kidding," said Judd. "You were sensational."

"I can't go out and do it alone, it's as simple as that. I

get stage fright and feel like chucking up."

"So you'll never go solo like the real George did?"

"Not me, pal. Anyway, the good thing about going on first is that we can relax and watch the rest of the acts now."

"Sounds like a plan. I think Rufus has saved us some seats with my mates Diego and Hunter. You're welcome to join us."

"Sounds great. Lead the way, Judd."

Judd and Andrew Baker settled down in their seats once they'd found their way to where Diego and Hunter were seated. Fortunately, a beer was waiting for both of them courtesy of Diego and his shovel-like hands. The beer was a bit warm by now and hosted in plastic glasses, a necessary evil for concert venues, but nevertheless the beers were appreciated by the personnel of Sham!

After Durham Durham came Keanu 'the King' Kennedy, an Elvis impersonator who again could never quite match the greatest performer of all time but who gave it a damn good try just as Andrew Baker had done being George Michael. Judd (and others) still found the presence of an Elvis tribute act a little out of place for an eighty's festival, and Keanu was still a teenager, therefore much of his act was of the young Elvis from the late fifties. Nevertheless, his moves were pretty electric and the crowd were more than sufficiently entertained. Keanu's greasy quiff danced almost as much as he did as he gyrated impressively across the stage floor.

There had at least been a distinct eighties' flavour with a cameo appearance by the Pot Shot Boys as they joined the 'King' on stage for a rendition of 'Always On My Mind', a song which both artists had covered. The collaborative performance went down a storm with the crowd.

Culture Pub were next, complete with a female Boy George, partly dispelling the rationale that Rufus and Judd had considered regarding a female Andrew Ridgeley stepping in to temporarily replace George Falmer.

Then followed Aladdin Seine, a French David Bowie impersonator who strictly kept to the superstar's eighties period with songs such as 'Let's Dance' and 'China Girl'. His attire included a trendy blue suit which hung loosely on the slender frame of the would be 'White Duke'.

The evening went very well indeed and a Michael Jackson tribute act who called himself 'Thriller Man' added to the fun.

Then suddenly, as the pretending Jacko danced his way through 'Billie Jean', a cloud of smoke began to appear behind the stage and quickly masked the view of the famous Liver building.

The music was forced to stop and Rufus of all people appeared on stage to announce the bad news. "I'm very, very sorry but due to an unexpected incident the festival will have to cease performing, I understand this is very disappointing news."

And so sadly the festival was over and everyone needed to be evacuated away from the docklands area.

Incident marshalls in hi-vis vests were soon visible and providing instructions so that people could be moved to safety. As Rufus continued to speak over the sound of small pockets of crowd hysteria, bright scary flames could now be seen lapping at the sky. Then hardly anyone was listening to Rufus at all as the sound of fire engine sirens soon kicked in.

The show was over.

The much-anticipated female acts of Ciccone (Madonna), Wild Kim (Kim Wilde) and Banana-Drama (Bananarama) had never even had a chance to grace the stage. The same fate had been dealt to several other tribute artists.

"Shit man," said Diego. "I wanted to see Feel Fascination the Human League tribute."

Judd looked at his friend. "The only thing you'll be

feeling my friend is extremely hot if we don't get out of here soon."

CHAPTER 4
CRUEL SUMMER

It appeared that the evacuation procedures were a success and everyone was out of harm's way. The assembly of people at the evacuation point had a surreal feel to it with the sprinkling of eighties popstars dotted here, there and everywhere.

The collective mood was somewhere between apprehensive and sombre, with everyone hoping that this was only a temporary situation and at some point, they'd be allowed to return to the venue. It had been a very enjoyable event up until now. However, the odds didn't look good as thick smoke could still be seen swirling around the famous Liver Birds perched on top of the Royal Liver Building and up into the Merseyside sky.

The acoustics of the docks that had not so long ago amplified the familiar musical arrangements of the best music of the 1980s were now replaced with the sound of sirens from the emergency services.

Judd didn't expect the show to continue and when Rufus appeared with a policeman either side of him the immediate pocket of the crowd swarmed around him keen to learn what was going on.

Judd quickly found himself becoming the spokesman for the anxious gathering.

"So what's the score, Rufus?"

Rufus had a bleak look on his face. "I'm afraid the portacabins that were being used as changing rooms for the acts have somehow caught fire."

Judd anticipated what the answer would be but he went ahead and asked the question everyone wanted him too anyway. "Can the event continue?"

One of the policemen stepped forward to answer instead of Rufus. "I'm sorry, sir, but there will be no more entertainment tonight. The area is cordoned off and the stage has been deemed structurally unsafe."

Judd became conscious of the crowd's overriding universal groans of disappointment. "What happened?" he asked.

"We don't know yet, sir," answered the other policeman in an even stronger liverpudlian accent than his colleague. "The fire brigade is looking into it. It may have been an accident, but we can't rule out anything malicious either considering that we have also received a bomb threat at the docks."

"Really? Could that have been a hoax?" asked Andrew Baker.

"That's always a possibility but it's too early to say yet. Clearly something has occurred though."

Rufus spoke next. "So, I'm afraid the hotel and the other dockland bars and restaurants are also out of bounds at the moment."

Ciccone the Madonna tribute act stepped forward, complete with cone-shaped bra. "Our change of clothes was in that portacabin so are you saying that they have gone up in smoke?"

"It looks that way," Rufus answered with sincere regret for the situation. Judd's heart sank for his friend, he knew that Rufus had put on a wonderful show and due to what seemed no fault of his own it had ended pretty disastrously.

"If the hotel is also cordoned off then we are all stuck in our stage gear," said Andrew.

Rufus just nodded looking down at the floor.

"I haven't even got my phone with me," said Madonna.

"I have" said, Girl George. Luckily, I have pockets in this jacket but they don't include my money. I left that back in the changing room, foolishly thinking it would be safe." Girl George's statement was typical of how twenty-first century society viewed the necessity of a mobile phone! Judd wondered what would she have done if it had rang whilst she was performing on stage. The irony being that he had forgotten himself that he had tucked his own phone into his boot.

Judd sensed the air of disappointment all round and took control of the situation with an idea that could somehow salvage the evening. "Officer, is the rest of Liverpool open? Is it only the docklands area that is out of bounds?"

"Yes, that's right."

"So Mathew Street is open for example?"

"Yes."

By now, the tribute acts had naturally separated from the majority of audience members. When Judd addressed the crowd, it defaulted to addressing them. "OK, listen up everyone, I've got an idea. We were all having a good time before this happened right?"

Judd could see that no one disagreed.

"Well, we can still have a night to remember for all the right reasons. This is Liverpool for fuck's sake, if you can't have a good time in Liverpool, you can't have a good time anywhere. Now to avoid confusion I think it makes sense that we refer to you by the act you are representing. That includes you too, Andrew. From now on you're George."

"OK," said George.

"Right then, we are all going to go on one almighty pub

crawl and we are going to have the time of our lives. Madge are you up for it?"

"Sounds like a plan," answered Madonna recognising the often-used affectionate nickname of Madge. "But I have no pockets on this little outfit in case you hadn't noticed. No pockets equals no money."

Judd looked Madonna up and down taking notice of the basque she was wearing. "I can see what you mean." He couldn't help but temporarily fixate on the sight of the cone shaped breasts that had been made famous during Madonna's Blond Ambition tour. At least she was wearing nude-coloured leggings underneath to protect her dignity and warmth. "And no mobile phone upon your person either, you say. It'll be OK, we will work something out with the insurance, hey Rufus?"

Rufus shrugged and then nodded.

"Rufus, do you have a credit card with you?" followed up Judd.

Rufus nodded again nervously, sensing where this was going.

"There you have it then. George, you're up for it right?"

"Sure, why not?" answered Andrew Baker.

"Bananarama?"

The Keren lookalike answered for the female trio with a hearty nod and winning smile.

"Prince?"

"Sure."

"How about you Bowie?"

"Yes."

"Jacko?"

"Yep, count me in."

Judd's optimism was clearly infectious.

"Boy George, err Girl George, no Boy George was right. I think. How about you?"

"Count me in too."

"Elvis."

"Uh-huh."

"Like it, I saw what you did there, Elvis. Freddie?"

The Freddie Mercury act sang an improvised operatic version of "Y-ee-sss."

"Duran Duran?"

"Of course," said Simon Le Bon.

This surreal experience went on for a little while longer as Tony Hadley and the Kemp brothers of Spandau Ballet also agreed to tag along. Sadly however, Bryan Ferry, Kylie, Tina Turner, The Pet Shop Boys and most disappointingly for Judd, Kim Wilde, all declined the offer.

Although in truth, now that Judd had the benefit of seeing Wild Kim up close, he noticed that she did not seem to possess anywhere near the same facial attributes as the real thing. This sparked an inner struggle with himself as he didn't want to be so shallow, but this was supposed to be the representation of Kim Wilde, the woman responsible for many a teenage crush back in the day. Including Judd of course. It was simply too difficult not to make the obvious comparison.

"OK then, great. We have a bonafide pub crawl posse. My name is Judd, by the way. Despite what I said for you lot please don't call me Andrew. This is Andrew," pointing to Andrew Baker aka George Michael instantly causing a sea of confused faces. "Never mind, he's George from now on and I'm Judd. And these are my friends Hunter and Diego. Rufus you already know. OK then, everyone follow me for the night that we will never forget."

CHAPTER 5
SWEET DREAMS (ARE MADE OF THIS)

Judd led the entourage of eighties pop star look-alikes through the Liverpool One area amidst second-takes, puzzlement, jeers and terms of endearment alike. It was no different as they marched up Mathew Street past The Grapes pub, Liverpool Beatles Museum and Cilla Black statue to eventually arrive at The Cavern Club. Judd had already decided that this could be the only place to successfully begin to rekindle the night.

One of the doormen first looked Judd up and down and then cast his eye along the surreal queue that formed behind him. In particular the sight of a moustached Freddie Mercury in a white vest, Prince in a purple suit and frilly white shirt, Michael Jackson in the red leather jacket from his Thriller video and of course Madonna in her cone-shaped bra were not lost on him. "Fancy dress is it mate?"

"Something like that," replied Judd as he waited patiently in his CHOOSE LIFE emblazoned T-shirt. "It's a long story."

The doorman decided not to enquire any further. "OK,

come 'ed."

In spite of the obvious eighties vibe that had engulfed him today, The Cavern Club epitomised what Liverpool was all about to Judd. And actually, many others the world over. Although there are other venues that could stake a claim, this is the place which is most often attributed to the birth of the Beatles, and certainly the platform for their explosion onto the music scene as far as live performances were concerned.

After Rufus had stepped forward to pay the entrance fee for everyone on his credit card, Judd continued to lead the group into The Cavern Club. The authenticity of the venue became more apparent with every step of the descending and winding stairway. Although Judd had visited The Cavern before, the feeling of hairs standing on the back of his neck never seemed to diminish on entering. The historic venue would always generate a sense of a magic for those that accessed it.

The thud of heavy bass vibrating through the concrete stairs and brick walls eventually gave way to a more recognisable tune as the underground room opened out to a bobbing crowd of all nationalities clearly enjoying themselves.

A beaming Judd Stone looked beyond the sea of heads to the small stage with the multi-coloured patchwork backdrop of band names. Upon that famous stage were a female quartet, complete with a powerful lead singer, performing a half-decent rendition of 'Paperback Writer' beneath the famous arched ceiling.

Ok, Judd knew that it wasn't the exact same original venue today as the one that once stood a couple of doors down Mathew Street, but the current stage is positioned in the very same place as it always had been in the 1960s and the arches and jagged brickwork were typical of Mathew Street basements of the time. It's fair to say that a leap of faith wasn't required for Judd to immerse himself into the authentic vibes.

After what seemed an age, made more bearable by the entertainment, Rufus surfaced from the bar and ensured everyone received a drink in the customary plastic glasses. Diego helped move things along more quickly by handing out the drinks with his huge hands.

Getting lost in the music, Judd tried to picture how similar this experience would have been in the sixties. He closed his eyes momentarily and tried to imagine the stench of carbolic laced disinfectant which he had read about from various testimonies. His concentration was broken when Rufus spoke to him.

"What a disastrous night."

"I don't think so mate, I'm having a fab time and I think everyone else is too." Judd took a look around and the stars of the eighties were mingling well with one another: laughing, drinking, dancing and generally having a good time. "It's impossible not to have good time in The Cavern, Rufus."

"I know, it is great here, but my eighties festival has literally gone up in flames."

"I know mate. It must be frustrating for you but just try and enjoy yourself. You did well, Rufus. The show while it lasted was really great, you should be proud of yourself and now we simply find ourselves on an earlier than expected celebration party with the main stars of the show. Look on it as an even more successful night than you anticipated. The post-show get-togethers always make the best memories, I remember some of Phoenix's – man, they were wild."

"I'll try, but it's easier said than done. I mean after attending Shania Twain's post tour celebration party in Vegas I'm not sure this is quite on a par."

Judd suspected this was one of Rufus's legendary bullshits but in the circumstances he wasn't going to call his friend out on it. Instead, he began to elaborate on his own real-life encounters in Las Vegas when he was bodyguard to pop star Phoenix Easter, a privilege he was also paid handsomely for. This inadvertently silenced Rufus on the topic.

Then the focus quickly shifted from two of the world's finest female artists to another one.

"Hey, that's our Madge on the stage, isn't it?" said Judd.

"I think you missed the announcement," said Diego.

"What announcement?" asked Judd.

"The band are inviting people up from the audience to do a star turn. I bet nobody anticipated a bonafide Madonna tribute act appearing tonight at The Cavern, did they?"

"Complete with cone-shaped bra too. I should get a commission fee of some kind," stated Rufus who seemed a little disgruntled.

"Oh come on, Rufus, you cannot be serious. Just forget about business for once in your life and enjoy yourself."

"Diego is right," offered Hunter.

"Yes he is," confirmed Judd.

Everyone clapped and danced as Ciccone expertly sang her heart out to the words of "Like A Virgin". Even Rufus began to crack a smile as she approached the final chorus.

Ciccone finished the song to an appreciation of wolf whistles and raucous applause. After taking a bow, Judd, wasn't prepared for what came next. Before she surrendered the microphone, Ciccone, had something that she wanted to say. "Thanks everyone, what an amazing crowd you are. I want to tell you something. It looked as if tonight was going to end up pretty grim following the abandonment of the eighties music festival down on the docks, but luckily one man decided to save the day. Now, he has already performed tonight as one half of Wham! and he makes a pretty decent Andrew Ridgeley let me tell you, but on the way here he told me how much of a Beatles fan he is, so I'd now like to invite onto the stage, Mr Judd Stone, to sing his favourite Beatles song."

"And what is that?" asked the bass player of the band.

Madonna thought for a moment. "Shoot, I don't actually know. You'll have to ask him when he gets up here. Anyway, give it up Cavern Club for the one and only Judd Stone."

Judd was no great singer but he could hold a tune if it wasn't too challenging. In spite of his initial shock at what Madge had led him into, the confidence from his docks performance as Andrew Ridgeley, coupled with the opportunity to now grace the very same stage as his musical heroes, meant nothing was going to stop him now.

As Judd made his way through the friendly audience, people slapped him on the back in good cheer and well wishes. He passed through the arches and eventually onto the stage, approaching it from the east wing. Elevated now above the crowd, Judd, faced the audience and was pleasantly amazed at the rousing applause that he was receiving. Wow, what a welcome.

"So Judd what is your favourite Beatles song?" asked the bass player.

"I'm not sure that I can answer that, it's like trying to choose your favourite child. However, I think I could manage a half-decent stab at "Eight Days a Week.""

The female lead singer of the group, who had now stepped aside to assist the rotating guests invited on to the stage, spoke next to introduce Judd. "OK, Ladies and Gentlemen, please give a warm welcome to Judd Stone performing "Eight Days a Week"".

The familiar guitar riff kicked in to open the track from the *Beatles For Sale* album and before long Judd surreally found himself singing out the lyrics to the song.

He was pleasantly surprised to see how much the crowd were loving it, joining in with the singing and dancing away. Hand clapping was a plenty.

But before he finished the song a scuffle broke out towards the back of The Cavern. As he approached the final chorus, he could see Prince and Michael Jackson being escorted up the concrete stairs by the bouncers.

The night had just become even more surreal.

CHAPTER 6
JUST CAN'T GET ENOUGH

"So what the hell happened?" said Judd now back on the cobbles of Mathew Street following his star turn.

Rufus was standing close by, who had felt obliged to follow the feuding pop star lookalikes when they got thrown out of The Cavern. Several others had also followed, including Diego and Hunter.

"Jacko and Prince decided that the best way to settle their musical differences was via a bar room brawl. Too much to drink I guess," said Diego.

"But I was having a whale of a time in there," said Judd. "In fact, we all were. I don't see why we needed to follow them out."

"It just seemed like the right thing to do," offered Rufus.

"And where are they now?" asked Judd.

"They just got driven away in a police car," said Hunter.

The feeling of surrealness had just raised another level.

"It's a shame," offered Madonna. "We could have given that Cavern crowd a brilliant night to remember in there, we could have all taken a turn at singing a number."

"That's true enough," said Freddie Mercury.

"Never mind, there's plenty of other pubs around here," said Judd. "Let's carry on and get pissed if we can't sing anymore."

"Sounds good to me," offered Tony Hadley.

"So who do we have?" asked Judd. "Who's still with us?"

"I'm game for a few more beers," said Hadley again.

"Us too," said the Kemp Brothers in unison.

"And me of course," said George Michael.

"Where are Bananarama?" asked Judd.

"They never followed us out," said Hunter.

"Yeah, the last time I saw Bananarama they had copped off with some blokes," said Diego.

"No doubt the Fun Boy Three," joked Judd.

"That Keren one had her tongue right down some fella's throat," said Hunter.

"Lucky bastard," said Gary Kemp.

"We fancy a curry, instead" said John Taylor of Duran Duran.

"Pussies," said Tony Hadley.

"Fuck you," said Simon le Bon.

"Elvis, you up for a few more beers?" asked Judd.

"Uh – huh."

"I wish you'd stop doing that."

"Freddie?"

"Yes, why not?"

"Girl George?"

"Yep."

"Excellent. So that just leaves you Bowie and of course you Madge."

"Oui," said Bowie, one of the few words the Frenchman had actually spoken all night, while Madonna nodded and smiled.

"OK let's go, but first of all, Diego, will you get a picture of me by the Lennon statue?"

"Sure thing."

"Can we come too?" asked a female voice.

Judd hadn't noticed the two ladies tucked in just behind Hunter and Elvis.

"You sound local," said Judd.

"We are, so that means we can show you all the best places to go."

Hunter spoke next. "They're a good laugh, me and young Elvis here have been dancing and messing about with them in The Cavern."

"Well, you're very welcome to lead the way then ladies," said Judd. "Tell me, has my friend Hunter here even managed to ascertain your names?"

"No he hasn't," said the younger of the two ladies. The one with long blonde hair.

"He isn't much of a gentleman but don't judge us all by his standards. I'm Judd, pleased to meet you," Judd shook the hands of the two ladies starting with the blonde and then moving onto the darker-haired lady. The latter was a good few years older than the blonde and Judd suspected that the black hair dye was no doubt disguising a cluster of grey strands. Nevertheless, she was very attractive, they both were. Yet something about them also suggested that they'd be fully capable of standing toe to toe with anyone who dared to cross them. It was the dark-haired elder lady who reciprocated the introductions.

"I'm Tatiana and this is Isla. Pleased to meet you Judd and Hunter." The false eyelashes fluttered as she addressed each man in turn.

"OK then, Tatiana, take us to our destination but I need to have a quick snap with John over there."

"That's not a problem as long as Isla and me can get in the pics with you."

"Deal."

As wonderful as Mathew Street was with its vibrant holiday resort ambiance, Tatiana took the gathering of friends and tribute acts on a short walk to a row of pubs in nearby Dale Street. These pubs were a little less lively, a little less noisy, but a whole lot more traditional and equally as enjoyable.

The uncommon mix of personnel within the group only served to keep conversation and frivolities fresh and agreeable. Judd found great delight in the fact that these Dale Street pubs offered the finest real ales, yet the ladies of the group indulged sufficiently in the 2-4-1 cocktails on offer.

However, it soon became time for everyone to take part in necking down a round of shots, courtesy yet again of Rufus' credit card.

Judd led the coordinated activity. "3-2-1-go!...same again Rufus, line them up."

"It just so happens that I have second and third trays ready and waiting," replied Rufus – now more comfortable in the knowledge that his three friends had promised to equally settle the credit card bill once it arrived.

The bar maid followed Rufus to the gathering of tables and placed the trays of shots down for the activity to be repeated.

"That'll put hairs on your chest," said Judd as he customarily slammed down the shot glass after necking its contents.

"I hope not," said Tatiana. "I don't want hairy tits."

"I don't want you to either," said Hunter. "I hope to catch a glimpse of them later."

"You cheeky bastard," laughed Tatiana as she playfully slapped him. "What kind of a girl do you take me for?"

"One that likes a good time," replied Hunter leaning closer towards her.

"Fair enough," said Tatiana.

The second and third round of shots went down just as quickly as the first.

"I feel like dancing," said Tatiana.

"Me too," said Isla.

"Listen boys, there's a new club opened in town. Me and Isla have the night off from working there but I think we should go, what d'ya reckon?"

"Are you lap dancers?" asked Hunter, his eyes lighting up.

"No, we're barmaids you eejit."

"So you want to go to your place of work on your night off?" asked Judd.

"That's how good a place it is," answered Isla. "And my uncle owns it so there's no need for us to pay an entry fee."

"Sounds like a no-brainer," said Hunter. "The night is young."

"Unlike you," quipped Judd, keen to pour water on Hunter's ever-inflating ego.

"Right then come 'ed," said Tatiana.

And so the pub crawl across Liverpool had finally found one last venue to end the night on a high. And *a high* was just what Hunter had in mind.

Everyone was undoubtedly having fun. Judd and Diego were leaning on the mirrored pillar looking out across the dancefloor, watching the party of tribute acts dancing in complete character even after all of the alcohol that had been consumed. The club was split into separate rooms, each one having its own distinct theme, so naturally the eighties room had won the choice.

Judd smiled as he noticed the club attendees being given an added bonus to their evening's entertainment, being able to dance and mingle amongst the likes of George Michael, Madonna, members of Spandau Ballet, David Bowie, Boy George and Freddie Mercury. Rufus was really letting his hair down as he effervescently and randomly popped up between the dancefloor occupants, alcohol doing nothing to improve his unorthodox technique of cutting shapes. In fact had there even been a technique?

"I can't make out if Rufus reminds me of a penguin stepping on hot coals or a huge lump of jelly. Sometimes he is as rigid as a board and then other times it's as if he has no bones in his body," shouted Judd above the noise.

"He certainly looks a plank, but he is enjoying himself I guess," answered Diego. "No doubt he is telling anyone who will listen that he learnt his moves personally from John Travolta or Paula Abdul."

Judd laughed. "Yeah, I've noticed that his bullshit hasn't diminished over the years. He's harmless enough but a bullshitter none the less."

"Sometimes his bullshits are very entertaining. I'm sure he convinces himself that they are actually true. I see Hunter's ego hasn't diminished over the years either. It's about time he stopped chasing skirt like he was still a teenager."

"Yeah, you're not wrong there, Diego. He can still be an annoying arsehole at times. Mind you, that Tatiana seems to fancy him to be fair. Although she probably doesn't realise that the only person Hunter is capable of loving is Hunter. How's the wife and kids anyhow Diego? Not really had time to ask you properly?"

"All good thanks pal, and now Judd Stone is a dad too. Never thought I'd see the day to be honest."

"Yeah, it's great mate. I love Billie to bits. I just wish I hadn't fucked things up so spectacularly with Brooke."

"Judd, you know I love you right so don't take this the wrong way, but you've always somehow managed to press the self-destruct button on yourself. Sometimes I want to shake some sense into you."

"I know mate, I can be my own worst enemy sometimes. I get it."

"At least you have Billie, hey? Make sure you never let her down."

"I won't mate, I really won't. Billie is my world. I'd literally kill for her and I'd literally die for her. No questions asked. Anyway, fancy another?"

"Yeah, cheers."

Hunter and Elvis were indeed getting on famously with Tatiana and Isla respectively.

Elvis was doing all of his trademark moves while Isla engaged in the more contemporary style of dancing such as twerking. To be honest, together they made a handsome couple.

Hunter and Tatiana were bumping and grinding as suggestively as they could get away with in a public space, which led Tatiana to eventually suggest the inevitable.

"Let's go outside."

"That's a song by that fella," said Hunter pointing to George Michael.

"Huh?"

"Outside. It's a George Michael number."

"Oh yeah," smiled Tatiana. "Anyway, I mean it."

"Are they coming too?" asked Hunter looking at Elvis and Isla.

"The more the merrier. Come on we know a way out the back."

Hunter didn't need asking again and he allowed himself to be led rapidly by the hand across the dancefloor. Isla shrugged at Elvis and then she did the same as her friend. She grabbed the king of rock and roll by the hand and led him outside.

"Where the hell are they going?" asked Judd as he returned with two bottles of cider. Like most clubs, decent real ale was off the menu.

Diego just shrugged.

Once outside the two couples found themselves in a typical Liverpool alley amongst a couple of large industrial bins, one for all kinds of rubbish and one for recycling the countless empty bottles from the club. A large rat became captured in the beam of the streetlight, scurried past, but then soon retreated out of sight.

"What a truly romantic setting," joked Elvis, but he was soon silenced once Isla's tongue entered his mouth.

"Before we get jiggy with it why don't we really get this party started," said Hunter.

"Well what do you have in mind?" asked Tatiana.

Hunter smiled and reached into his pocket. "I think I should introduce my friend Charlie to the party."

"Hell, yes," said Tatiana.

Isla looked concerned. "Tatiana, I'm not sure about this. My Uncle Richie doesn't allow drugs in his club."

"Relax, Isla. We are outside the club now," said Tatiana.

"I'm not sure Isla's uncle would see it like that," said Elvis. "Hunter this ain't a good idea."

"On the contrary Elvis. This is a great idea," said Hunter. "Isla have you ever had sex while high on cocaine? You'll find Elvis's hips here even more electric thank you could ever have imagined."

"You're being very presumptuous," said Isla folding her arms partly as a body-language defence mechanism and partly to cut out the night's chill.

"Knock it off, Hunter," said Elvis.

"Isla, chill babe. It'll be fun," said Tatiana before turning to Hunter. "Come on then big boy show me what you got."

Elvis and Isla became mere spectators as Hunter used the lid of the closest industrial bin to host the white coloured contents of his small plastic bag. Like the stereotypical big time Charlie that he was, Hunter used his credit card to form the powder into lines and then rolled a twenty pound note which could enable the snorting of the product. He promptly handed the twenty pound note to Tatiana, who was totally bought into the whole experience.

"Ladies first," grinned Hunter.

Tatiana pushed her dark hair behind her ears to keep it out of harm's way. Next she took the rolled up note, placed it in her left nostril and snorted a line of coke. The drug tantalisingly connected with her senses and she momentarily shook her head as she felt an instant buzz, before repeating the process in her right nostril sniffing up her second line in milliseconds.

She looked at Hunter through watery eyes and dilated pupils. She smiled and he smiled back.

But then her mouth quickly turned from hosting a smile to hosting a foaming of saliva, it was as if she had just snorted a line of washing powder rather than cocaine.

Suddenly, totally withdrawn from everything around her, Tatiana seemed to hang in mid-air for what seemed an age but in truth was only seconds. The froth from her mouth continued to flow before dropping to the ground and shaking violently for another few seconds.

Then she moved no more.

Isla screamed.

"Fucking hell dude, what have you done?" said Elvis.

Hunter dropped to his knees and cradled Tatiana's head. "Tatiana, wake up, wake up." But her head just flopped about as her neck seemed to lose control. Her eyes still expressed dilated pupils but now they were glazed over as she stared at nothing in particular. In desperation he slapped her face hoping for a reaction.

But there was nothing

Hunter put his ear to Tatiana's mouth, hoping to detect a sign of breathing.

Nothing.

He turned to Isla and Elvis

"I think she's dead."

CHAPTER 7
UNDER PRESSURE

On seeing a hysterical Isla enter the club, Judd, knew something was very wrong. This was further validated when doormen could be seen dragging Elvis and Hunter up some stairs. Judd sensed that they weren't about to discuss the back catalogue of Elvis's hits.

"Come on Diego, I think there's some kind of trouble going on."

Judd and Diego collected a bemused Rufus on the way and made their way up the same stairs. George Michael to his credit decided to follow as well.

The three friends and the musical icon gained some ground on the commotion ahead, but the door where everyone had passed through was still slammed shut before they managed to reach it.

"What in the name of Colonel Tom Parker is going on?" asked Rufus.

"I really don't know," answered Judd. "But we need to find out."

"Do we?" Rufus had never been the most courageous of men.

"Hunter is in there."

"And no doubt whatever trouble he is in he was asking for it."

"Rufus has a point," said Diego.

Judd looked incredulously at his huge friend. "Hunter may be a first-class prick but he is still our first-class prick."

"OK, Rufus. Judd has a point too," said Diego. "What happened to the Fab Four, hey?"

"OK, OK. I guess I feel a certain amount of responsibility for young Elvis anyway."

Judd led the creeping to the door and put his ear to it whilst Diego, Rufus and George Michael waited on in anticipation. No sooner had Judd began to listen when the door was suddenly opened by a man almost as huge as Diego. The giant grinned a toothy grin through his dark whiskers before pointing to a CCTV camera positioned above the door. Judd felt a little foolish.

A voice could be heard from within. "Come in Gentlemen and join the party."

The four men entered and the giant closed the door behind them before assuming a guarding position to block any attempt of exit. Not that Judd had any intention of doing that unless it was with a safe and secure Hunter and Elvis.

Straight ahead sat a man behind a desk who had provided the voice of the invitation. He reminded Judd of the English actor Simon Shepherd but his stare was a hundred-fold deathlier and his whole persona suggested danger, a role that would be unusual for Shepherd to ever play.

He was flanked either side by men who resembled bears rather than humans, and Judd had quickly evaluated them to provide muscle on a wider scale than just managing the door of a nightclub. He made the same assumption for the beast who was guarding the door behind them.

Isla seemed to have slightly calmed herself but Judd sensed that she was still clearly distraught, whilst Hunter and Elvis were still each being gripped by the scruff of their neck.

"Look, there's clearly been some sort of misunderstanding here," began Judd. "Whatever our friends have done they are very sorry and we will happily leave your club."

The scary version of Simon Shepherd nonchalantly leaned back in his chair before answering Judd very calmly in his Liverpudlian accent. "I'm afraid that won't be possible, lad. You see a simple apology just won't even scratch the surface to make amends of just how fucking annoyed I am right now."

"I'm sure we can sort this out," said Rufus.

"Correction, I can sort it out," said Simon Shepherd.

"So what have they done that's so *fucking annoying*?" said Judd, typically growing a little impatient.

Simon Shepherd narrowed his eyes. "You need to make sure that you don't add to my annoyance with that tone, lad."

"He's sorry," said Rufus. Judd shot Rufus a look for portraying such weakness and deciding to speak for him.

Simon Shepherd leaned forward in his chair. "These two morons have caused me a lot of trouble tonight. Tell me, what kind of an operation do you think I'm running here?"

"A night club," answered Rufus. "And may I say, a very nice one too. This is one of the finest nightclubs I've ever had the pleasure of entering."

"Not a bad answer my friend, and you have provided an answer with a great deal of accuracy. So we can all agree that this establishment is by no means a dead girl storage facility?"

Judd frowned. "Of course not, what makes you say that?" Even he was a little apprehensive as to what the forthcoming reply was going to be.

"I say it because I have a dead girl in the vicinity of my club. And not just any dead girl either. She was one of my finest barmaids and she was a friend of my niece here. So, you see these two acquaintances of yours have not only killed a girl in close proximity to my club, they have compromised my workforce capacity whilst, and this is the most serious part by the way, shattering my niece's heart into little pieces. So what do you have to say about that?"

Judd was astounded at what he was hearing. How could this have happened? "Are you sure?" he feebly asked.

The nightclub owner raised his voice. "Yes I'm fucking sure, or are you calling my niece here a liar to top everything else?"

"Not at all," said Judd.

"And if you were even a little bit doubting the word of my niece you already know that I have CCTV all around this place, don't you?"

"Yeah, of course. OK, so what happened?" asked Judd.

"Why doesn't Elvis here tell us. He was there at the scene of the crime after all?" said Simon Shepherd.

Elvis couldn't speak.

"Come on Elvis, you were never known for being shy, were you? And you know what lad, if you're looking for trouble you've come to the right place." The bears and beasts in the room all sniggered at their boss's wit.

Elvis still couldn't speak and instead looked down at the floor.

"Break his leg, he won't be shaking it anytime soon," came the astonishing order from Simon Shepherd and with that one of the doormen stepped forward, pulled out a hammer and raised it to smash it into Elvis's kneecap.

"Wait, please. I'm sure we can sort this, just tell me what has happened, this isn't making much sense at the moment," said Judd.

"Hold back the hammer just for a moment, Charlie, lad." Simon Shepherd then addressed Hunter pointing a finger at him. "You. Do you find the name of the man that's going to end your life a little ironic?"

"Charlie?" answered Hunter.

"Yes, Charlie," Shepherd had by now switched to full on angry mode and he slammed his hand on the table making everyone in the room jump. "I don't have girls killed on my premises and I don't have drugs dealt or consumed on it either, so pretty boy, I'm sure that you fully comprehend why you have really pissed me off."

"Drugs?" asked Judd, beginning to understand what was unfolding here.

"Yes Einstein, drugs," Judd swore he could see actual venom spraying from Shepherd's mouth. "This piece of shit has come into my club, upset my niece and killed my barmaid by supplying her with drugs – cocaine no less – Charlie. He's a cheeky fucking bastard and both him and Elvis Presley here are going to fucking pay."

"Why not just call the police?" asked Rufus.

"Thanks a lot, Rufus," said Hunter, this prompted a slap round the back of his head from one of the hardmen for daring to speak out of turn.

"I do not need the police sniffing around here asking questions about drugs and dead girls, even if these two fuckwits are responsible," said Shepherd getting more psychotic by the second. He turned to one of his beasts. "Razor, is the Undertaker on his way?"

"He is Boss."

"The Undertaker?" asked Judd.

For the first time the club boss revealed an insight into his more sinister ways of taking care of business. "In my line of work I need somebody to get rid of the odd body or two, so poor Tatiana can be taken away to avoid those unneeded questions and then Elvis and Hunter here can also benefit from his services and if you're not careful you and all your fucking friends here will be joining them."

It was confirmed to Judd what he had already suspected. This guy was a gangster. He also fully understood what was happening here but he also knew that he couldn't let any of it happen. He looked at Diego and a telepathic connection seemed to unfold.

Judd moved swiftly towards the heavy holding the hammer and knocked him out with a single punch whilst Diego put one massive hand around the neck of the beast that was holding Hunter and used his other one to squeeze the life out of his groin.

George Michael felt obligated to wade in and struck the bouncer holding Elvis, however the thug hardly flinched.

The gangster's crew hadn't expected the audacity of this attack and were taken by surprise, Simon Shepherd opened the drawer of his desk and reached inside.

But then proceedings were surprisingly halted when the heavy guarding the door fell to the floor.

"Stop right there or I'll put a bullet in you."

Simon Shepherd pulled his hand away from the drawer and placed them in the air where they could be seen.

"Tilda?" said Judd astonished to see the sister of his best friend standing there pointing a gun at the gangster. In all the commotion she had escaped being spotted on the CCTV. It seemed that she had also used the butt of the gun to attack the guardsman from behind and knock him unconscious.

"Tilda, is it? So now I know who you are but do you know who I am?"

"Of course I do. Don't most people in Liverpool? You're Richie Mercer, you own this club and most of the city. In other words you're a nasty little gangster."

"Yet knowing all that you still choose to point a gun at me, Tilda?"

"When you've spent most of your life in captivity and had both your husband and brother killed by people even more evil than you could ever dream to be, then one tends to be less caring about such particulars. In any case you do not pull a gun on George Michael and Andrew Ridgeley."

Mercer didn't quite understand the reference to Wham! but wasn't in the mood for clarification at this stage.

"You're making a big mistake, Tilda."

"Like I care." Tilda moved forward keeping the gun pointed at Mercer and then quickly changed tack to grab Isla and held the gun to her blonde head.

Mercer's eyes widened. "You really are on a death wish, lady."

"Back in your box, Mercer. Now I guess that Jaguar outside with the number plate RM LPL 1 belongs to you? So this is how things are going to play out. You're going to give us the keys to your motor and we're going to slip away quietly and you're going to let us do it because we are taking your lovely niece here with us as insurance. She won't be hurt if you just let us do what we want. Now give the keys to Judd, and while you're at it we will have the keys that locks the door to your office too. Your sleeping bear here really should have locked the door you know."

Judd stepped forward.

"So your name is Judd. You've made quite an impression on me, lad."

"Just do what the lady says and hand me the keys."

Mercer gave a wry smile and complied. "You know that I will catch up with you, don't you? People who cross me don't ever get away with it no matter what head start they may have. And if I find one hair out of place on my niece's head and just one scratch on my car, I'll be holding you personally responsible, Judd."

"You're confusing me with somebody who gives a shit, mate," said Judd. "Although I have no intentions of your niece coming to harm. If at all possible." Then Judd's eyes strayed to something hanging on the wall behind Mercer.

"It's a nice guitar isn't it, Judd? It once belonged to Tony Iommi," said the gangster. "And your shitty eyes are not worthy of laying sight upon it."

"You're a Black Sabbath fan?"

"Yes, I am. This city is Beatles mad but my musical poison is Sabbath. On hearing your accent it would seem that they are from your neck of the woods."

"Totally. And closer than you think. I grew up in Aston, Birmingham. Ozzy Osbourne grew up just around the corner from me in Lodge Road. He and the other members of Sabbath were a good deal older than me, but I knew of them and can tell you all about them another time."

"Then I'll look even more forward to eventually catching up with you, Judd. But I suspect that you're being economical with the truth somewhat, you're at least two to three decades younger than the band members."

"Bullshitting is more my friend's department," said Judd nodding towards Rufus, who looked a little hurt. "I said I know of them, not knew them personally. I do however know relatives of them very well indeed, but more importantly I know other things about the band. Things that would make even your spine shiver Mr Liverpool Gangster."

"Really? I'm intrigued."

"In the wake of Black Sabbath's success, and much of what was owed to it was a sixteenth century book presented to Geezer Butler by Ozzy Osborne. It was written in Latin and gave an insight into the occult and witchcraft. Geezer read it and the next day he saw a black figure at the foot of his bed. This inspired their music and the rest is history. If you're half the die hard fan you claim to be you most likely knew that little story already, but what you don't know and what I do know, is that I met the person, the very dark and scary person who initially gave the book to Ozzy. So perhaps this person also taught me a thing or two about witchcraft aye?"

For the first time Judd could sense a glimmer of discomfort in the eyes of Richie Mercer. Could Mercer be one of these guys who could confidently be a menace to society but feared anything to do with the unknown?

Trying to save face, Richie Mercer, attempted to laugh it off. "Bollocks."

"Perhaps it's for me to know and you to find out, Mr

Mercer?"

"Are you threatening me, Judd?"

"No, not at all. I'm just having a conversation that perhaps is due to be continued."

"Oh, you can bet your life on it, Judd. You know what, I'm beginning to like you, lad. You've got balls. I could do a lot with a man like you, but we will have to take a rain check on that for now."

"Goodbye Mr Mercer."

"Until we meet again, Judd."

Tilda spoke next. "Come on Judd, we will lock the door on the way out and keep Mr Mercer and his gang of reprobates locked in."

"Like caged animals?" sneered Mercer.

"If the cap fits," answered Tilda.

CHAPTER 8
BEAT IT

Tilda kept the gun buried into the small of Isla's back so not to draw attention to the escape from the club. Judd was just ahead of the two newly acquainted ladies and they were swiftly followed by a bunching of Rufus, Diego, Hunter, Elvis and George Michael.

From the dancefloor, Madonna, noticed the swift exit of her friends and could read the unrest on their faces amidst the flashing lights and laser beams. She signalled to Girl George, David Bowie and Freddie Mercury. Once they were in earshot she still needed to raise her voice for them to hear her over the loud music. "We need to leave; I think something has happened. I think there may be some kind of trouble with the others."

The three tribute acts were willing to support the cause along with Madonna and promptly followed the entourage that lay just ahead to see what was happening.

The members of Spandau Ballet got left behind oblivious to what was going on, as they had since met up with some local girls, mirroring the earlier fortunes of Bananarama in The Cavern.

"What's going on?" asked Madonna once they were all outside.

"There's no time to explain," answered Judd.

"But we have to get out of here," interjected Rufus.

Judd looked at the key fob in his hand, pressed the button and the locks of the waiting Jaguar popped open in unison with the flashing of the car's lighting system. He looked around and quickly realised there were now too many of them to fit inside the car. "Madge, go back inside the club, this doesn't concern you. Nor you pair."

Bowie spoke next in his French accent. "If you are in trouble then we are all in this together."

"Mercer said he had CCTV; he will know by now they are with us. It's safer if we stick together," said Rufus.

"And how are twelve of us going to fit into this car?" said Judd.

"Look, we don't have much time. We need to move quickly," said Tilda still holding the gun in Isla's back.

Judd looked up the street and his eyes locked on a potential solution.

"Tilda, you're sober right?"

"Yes."

"Diego, as you are twice the size of any of us, I'm guessing that you're in a fitter state to drive than the rest of us are. With your huge frame, you always need a ton of booze to even remotely begin to fuck you up."

"None taken. Anyway, it's funny how this experience has had a sobering effect on me, Judd. What's it matter anyhow, there's still only one car?"

"Not necessarily, big man. Tilda, you drive the Jag. Give me the gun and we will take Isla with us. I'm more comfortable with the danger being with me anyway, she will be the priority for Mercer and his cronies. I'm sure you'll want to be near George even in these circumstances so you take him as well as Bowie and Freddie. Oh, and take Hunter too."

"No way," said Hunter.

Judd shot Hunter a stern look. "Listen you conceited prick. I can't bear to look at you at the moment, so you'd better go with Tilda or I swear I'll fucking kill you myself where you stand."

"And what about the rest of you, Judd?" asked Tilda.

"We're going in that," Judd pointed up the road where a Rolls Royce limousine decorated like a Romany Gypsy caravan was situated. "We can get seven of us in that with a squeeze, as long as Diego drives."

"And where are we all going?" asked Tilda.

"I haven't decided that bit yet, just get behind the wheel of Mercer's Jag and stick close to that chrome bumper."

CHAPTER 9
DRIVING IN MY CAR

The Rolls Royce was an exact replica of John Lennon's 1960's psychedelic decorated Phantom V model. The eye-catching vehicle, complete with bright yellow body paint and flowery images, usually served as an innovative method for glorified taxi driver Arthur Gibbs-White to chauffeur eager Fab Four enthusiasts around the sites of Beatles Liverpool. However, at this moment in time the purpose of the Rolls Royce had transitioned to becoming a very unlikely getaway car.

Fortunately for this evening's unexpected occupants, Arthur, who had undeservedly been tossed out of the driver's seat of his own car by Diego who swiftly traded places with him, had installed an engine that was more in tune with the demands of twenty-first century traffic speed.

Ten minutes or so into the getaway, the mini convoy of the psychedelic Rolls Royce and the black Jaguar continued to zoom along Liverpool's roads, but it hadn't escaped the occupants of either car that a third vehicle was now also in hot pursuit.

"It looks like Mercer has managed to find a car to chase us, Judd," said Diego.

"Looks that way," answered Judd.

"What did you expect?" shouted Isla from the back seat. My uncle is the most feared gangster in Liverpool. He will hunt you down and kill you all for daring to kidnap me."

Nobody chose to answer the gangster's niece but this was by no means a reflection that the precarious situation was lost on anyone.

"We're approaching the M62 now, Judd. I take it we plan to head back towards Birmingham?"

"Yes mate, follow the M62 and then onto the M6 South. Despite what the pretty lady says in the back, if anyone wants to chase us all the way to our home turf it won't be us who ends up second best when we all eventually meet up."

Suddenly, Diego and Judd were blinded by bright lights coming towards them.

"What the fuck?" announced Judd, as the inside of the Rolls Royce lit up.

"What's going on?" asked Diego.

"This is a motorway for Christ's sake," said Rufus who was sharing the rear passenger seats with the others. "It's supposed to be one way traffic."

Judd's eyes adjusted enough to recognise what was happening. "That may be so, but the reality is we have a number of cars heading straight for us," declared Judd. "There's at least one in each of the three fucking lanes. We have no way out."

Isla sneered. "I told you not to fuck with my uncle. Even after locking him up, he's managed to reach out to his connections to get to you. You take on my uncle you take on an army."

"That's what you think sweetheart," said Judd spotting an opportunity present itself. "Diego, pull off here, there's a slip road ahead. Take a sharp left turn. Now."

"OK, hold tight."

Diego turned the steering wheel sharply to his left causing the Rolls Royce's tyres to screech and the vast body frame of the car to swing away from the motorway. Luckily Tilda read the situation well and was forced to do the same in the Jaguar. The occupants of both fleeing cars found themselves giving way to the force of gravity such was the ferocity of the sudden movement. "I'm sorry," said Rufus who inadvertently squashed Isla. She responded with an icy stare.

"I have no idea where I'm heading to now," declared Diego.

"Don't worry about it, just keep going," replied Judd. "Rufus, is Tilda still with us?"

Rufus took a look out of the back window of the Rolls Royce. "Yes she is, but so too now are a stream of other cars whom I assume are connected to Isla's uncle. How on earth is this ever going to end well?"

"It won't for you," said Isla.

"You're really starting to get on my tits," said Madonna surprising everyone, but it had the desired effect to silence Isla's snide comments.

The car chase continued and soon the cars were forced to travel in single file as they hit the narrower rural roads of north-west England.

"That's the second time you've tried that you bastard," said Tilda as she looked into her rear-view mirror at the Audi A3 after it had just connected with the rear bumper of Tilda's adopted Jaguar. "You'll need to do better than that to rattle me," she said, holding her nerve and driving admirably well at high speed. The driver of the Audi became impatient. He spotted a widening in the road, manouvered to the right, increased the pressure on the accelerator pedal and decided to try and overtake both of the two leading cars in a bid to bring the chase to a halt.

Once the Audi had passed Tilda's Jag, it soon found itself side by side with the psychedelic Rolls Royce. Now able to peer into the opposing car, it was ascertained that only the front two seats of the Audi A3 were occupied.

"So who is the ugly bastard in the passenger seat, Isla?" asked Judd.

"I don't know all of my uncle's contacts, but clearly he has many and that *ugly bastard* will be only too happy to get his hands on you."

"Well, it's a pity for him then that that's not going to happen," said Diego as he suddenly manouvered the car into the side of the Audi A3. The superior weight of the Rolls Royce forced the pursuing car to come off the road and come to an abrupt end into a cluster of trees.

"One down, and about three more to go," said Judd as he noticed Isla turn away deflatingly whilst her kidnappers gained a slight upper hand.

A second Audi A3 tried the same manouvere and was soon speeding alongside the Jag. The driver realised that trying to overtake both cars was probably a bit too ambitious, considering what had just happened to his colleague.

"Shit, he has a gun," said Hunter, as another 'ugly bastard' in a passenger seat pointed it straight at Tilda.

It was Diego who saved the day once again, although he hadn't known anything about the gun being pulled. Fortunately, just as the goon was about to pull the trigger, Diego, swiftly dragged the Rolls Royce onto a road that forked from his left. It was a single traffic road and once Tilda had gratefully followed, the Audi A3 had actually missed the acute turn and continued straight ahead. This resulted in a more even car chase as the single file convoy now consisted of the psychedelic Rolls Royce, the black Jaguar and just two remaining pursuing vehicles.

"I hope this colourful tank isn't too wide for this road," said Judd.

"Only time will tell," answered Diego. "I'm just putting my foot down and hoping for the best."

"And now its pissing down with rain," said Rufus. "So

please be careful, Diego."

Rufus wasn't wrong. Diego was finding it increasingly more difficult to see clearly as he naturally drove faster than he was legally allowed to along the country lanes. Diego's vision was becoming further impaired as the windscreen wipers struggled to beat off the driving rain as it hit the glass.

At least the chasing pack were in a similar position but it wasn't the rain that caused the primary issue for them, instead it was the accompanying wind of the storm that quickly consumed the car chase.

A falling branch just clipped the rear chrome bumper of the Rolls Royce but it was therefore destined to fall into the path of the Jaguar and Tilda had no chance of avoiding it. The front nearside tyre burst instantly and the car almost turned over but she just about managed to stay upright. Nevertheless, it came to an abrupt stop, as did the chasing car behind it as it heavily shunted the Jaguar from the rear.

A complete silver birch tree followed the fallen branch and completely blocked the road separating the entourage of cars from the Rolls Royce ahead. Diego brought the car to a stop realising that Tilda's Jaguar was in trouble behind him.

"I can't see them," said Judd. "The foliage of the fallen tree is too dense."

"Do you think they've made it?" said Rufus. "That thing could have done some serious damage."

"Who's got a phone?" asked Judd, forgetting again that he did so himself in his boot.

"Only those who weren't performing, remember," replied Madonna. "Except Girl George."

"Shit of course." Girl George began to fumble in her jacket but Judd grew impatient. "Diego, give me your phone," said Judd. "Quickly."

Diego reached into his inside jacket pocket and passed the phone to his friend. Judd's first instinct was to phone

Tilda but of course Diego had no reason to have her number saved to his contacts. Dynamically reassessing his options, Judd, hit the dial button to call Hunter.

"Come on, come on, pick up." The phone was answered after three rings but a silence followed which prompted Judd to speak first.

"Hunter, are you all OK?" Judd activated the phone's loudspeaker so that everyone could hear. "Hunter, speak to me."

"Hunter is fine, but I can't promise that he will remain that way when we take him back to the boss."

Judd hit the mute button. "They've got them." He unmuted again.

"Listen, was anyone injured in the crash?"

"Miraculously no, but as I said I can't promise that your friends will remain so lucky in the long run. We already have the woman, the prick you call Hunter and the George Michael looking dude on transit back to Liverpool. My boss can't wait to ask them what they thought they were playing at pulling their little stunts in his office, and once my colleagues get beyond that tree you'll be heading for the same punishment."

"Don't you dare fucking hurt them."

"You're in no position to try and negotiate this situation, lad."

"What about the other two? The ones dressed like Freddie Mercury and David Bowie. Are they dead?"

"Nah, they're OK. We have just left them two clowns sitting in the back of the car, they're surplus to requirements. I think Freddie may have pissed his pants though, he looked a little put out with it all. And my boss is going to be a little put out by the repairs that will need doing to his Jaguar. Now that's enough chat for now, you're beginning to bore me. I have this number so my boss will be in touch when he has decided what he wants to do about you and your friends, that is unless my colleagues don't get to you first. That tree won't be laying across that road forever." The phone went dead.

Suddenly Diego put his foot down and the wheels spun on the saturated surface.

"What are you doing?" screamed Judd.

"You heard him. There are cars behind us full of gangsters. Probably with guns as well and they are after our blood. I'm getting us out of here."

"But what about the others?"

Rufus interjected. "Look, we can't get past that tree for now and if we do there will be Mercer's goons waiting for us on the other side. We know that Bowie and Mercury are safe and the other three are on their way back to Mercer."

"And what do you think he plans to do with them, huh? Welcome them back into his office and make them a cocoa to get over the shock?" Judd was exasperated. "We need to turn this car around and get back to Liverpool."

"Listen Judd, I don't like the fact Tilda, Hunter and George are heading back to Mercer any more than you do, but this storm is getting fiercer by the second," said Diego. "If we head back to Liverpool I need to try and find an alternative route due to that tree blocking the road and looking at this weather we may not even make it."

"Diego is right," said Rufus. "We need to try and find shelter for the night, take stock and hope we can do something in the morning when the storm has hopefully blown over."

Judd looked at Madonna. "What do you think?"

"I don't think we have a lot of choice but to agree with your two friends."

"Elvis?"

"It makes sense, man."

Judd just slumped back resignedly in the seat of the car.

Isla then offered a surprising interjection. "Look, think about it, Judd. My uncle knows that you still have me so that's mutual leverage for the position of your three friends. He will want me home safe and sound so while you have me I think your friends will be safe, even in the custody of my uncle."

"That makes sense," said Girl George. "And this storm really is a bastard."

Judd looked ahead and he could see that the visibility through the windscreen was by now beyond dangerous.

"OK, OK," said Judd. "You need to bring this magical mystery tour to an end soon then, Diego. Pull over somewhere safe when you can."

Suddenly another branch broke from a tree and fell onto the road. By some amazing stroke of good fortune, when the alert Diego swerved the car to avoid the obstacle he was able to enter a road that presented itself on the left. After about two miles more of dim light, torrential rain and even narrower road, Rufus, spotted a small beacon of hope as lightning flashed all around them.

"Look there's a building of some sort on that small hill to the right of us."

"I can't see it?" said Judd.

"The lightning revealed it, I saw it too," said Madonna. Right on cue another streak of lightning momentarily lit up the sky and this time everyone caught a glimpse of the establishment.

"There are no lights on, it may be a barn or perhaps no one is home. It's too difficult to tell but I guess it's a shelter for the night," said Judd. "Do we all agree?"

Everyone agreed.

CHAPTER 10
HOUSE OF FUN

Judd was first to reach the door. "It's locked but I can tell that it doesn't have much holding it firm. Stand back and I'll put some welly behind it."

"Please do, Judd, and hurry. This weather's terrible out here. It's making my mascara run," said Madonna.

"Mine too," said Girl George.

"With all due respect, ladies, I think we have more important things to worry about than your make-up being compromised," said Rufus. "Although, I do recall Liza Minelli saying the same thing to me once during one of her visits to the UK."

Rufus's remarks fell on indifferent ears as the door burst open courtesy of Judd's meaty shoulder. "We're in."

Diego entered after Judd, just in case there were any surprises waiting, and was then swiftly followed by the others as they escaped the torrential rain.

"Is there a light?" asked Madonna, pleased to be out of the storm but a little unnerved by the surrounding darkness.

"I've just tried the switch," answered Judd. "But either

the bulb has gone or the electric is cut off."

"Here, I'll use the torch on my mobile phone," offered Girl George.

"Good thinking," said Judd, as visibility instantly became clearer courtesy of the torch. "That's worked a treat."

"Yeah it has, but I can't get any signal," said Girl George.

"And maybe it would have been better leaving our eyes ignorant," said Rufus. "Just look at this place."

The torch light on the phone surprisingly projected a much more powerful beam than imagined, however it still cast an eerie arc as it struggled to flood into every corner and parameter of the room.

"Fuck me when was the last time anyone lived here?" said Diego.

"It's like we've gone back in time," observed Madonna.

Neither Diego or Madonna were mistaken. There was no evidence afoot of living in the twenty-first century, and not much more of even the twentieth century.

There didn't appear to be a television present in the building, however, there was some sort of old turntable perched precariously on top of a homemade bookshelf. It was the type of record player that had speakers built within its frame.

The bookshelf was crudely put together with bits of unmatching wood and its shelves hosted album sleeves as well as books.

Cobwebs clung onto almost every available opportunity in the room, creating a multitude of silky coverings. Also, a number of wicker baskets were dotted here and there, each with a random cloth of yesteryear covering any contents that may be within.

A rag rug covered a section of the quarry tiled floor, neither of which seemed to have benefitted from any cleaning agents in a while.

A couple of the walls were absent of plaster, exposing

the natural stonework of long ago, and none of them were decorated. Except that was for one of those dark and eerie portraits of someone from centuries before, where the eyes followed you no matter which way you turned. A beveled mirror also hung above the open fireplace. Over the passage of time, the reflective glass of the mirror had fell victim to desilvering as a number of dark spots were in situ.

Rufus noticed there to be a small number of candle holders scattered around the place and proceeded to light the only two that were housing any candles, albeit they had already been partly used. The drip-by-drip gathering of the once melted wax could have provided the illusion of eerie shapes to the most dormant of imaginations. Furthermore, the protruding stone of the walls seemed to conjure up what seemed to be twisted faces amid the flickering flames.

At least the light from the candles was enough for Girl George to save the battery on her mobile phone and she put it away.

There weren't many windows in view and an even smaller amount of curtains to cover them, just more random pieces of cloth haphazardly positioned over the odd pane. The wind howled through a broken corner of one window and Judd collected a lonesome cloth from the floor before stuffing it into the jagged hole in an attempt to try and plug the force of the elements.

"This place sure gives me the creeps," said Madonna.

"At least it's dry," said Rufus. "But I can't find myself disagreeing with you, Madonna."

"I wonder what's through that door?" asked Madonna, looking at the only doorway out of the room other than the one that they had used to gain entry from the outside.

"I would have thought that it leads to something like a kitchen or a bathroom," answered Judd. "Or both."

"You reckon this place has running water and a bog?" asked Diego.

"There's only one way to be certain," answered Judd

and with that he ventured through the doorless opening into the darkness.

"Be careful, Judd," said an increasingly anxious Madonna.

To her relief, Judd, soon returned.

"Well there is certainly electricity in this shithole, so it must be a bust bulb that prevented the light from working. I opened the fridge and it is definitely working. It's even colder than what this place feels like."

"What was in it?" asked Diego. "I'm a little peckish to be honest."

"You are kidding?" asked Elvis. "You wouldn't seriously eat anything from this cesspit, would you?"

Diego just shrugged.

"It was practically empty expect for a dead rabbit and half a pint of milk. Signs that this place is actually being used in spite of its appearance," said Judd.

"And a bog?" asked Diego.

"There is, although it ain't the cleanest mate."

"No shit, Sherlock."

"Yes shit. That's kind of my point."

"Fuck it, I badly need a slash." Diego walked past Judd and the bathroom was so close everyone could awkwardly hear Diego's pee hit the dirty water of the toilet.

"Can you see enough not to piss on your feet?" shouted Judd.

"Just about," replied Diego

The sound of water against water was interrupted again when Madonna spoke. "A dead rabbit, that's gross."

"I guess whoever lives here lives off the land," said Judd.

"Or they sacrifice animals. Madonna's right, this place is too creepy," said Girl George

"It isn't the most homely, I'll give you that," said Judd. But don't let your imaginations run away with you."

"I reckon this could be the home of a Satanist?" said Girl George again,

"What?" said Rufus, a little anxiously.

"A Devil Worshipper, you know, a Satanist."

"I know what one is, but a dead rabbit in a fridge doesn't necessarily mean that. Does it?"

"Maybe, maybe not…" said Girl George looking back towards the now closed door where they had entered through. In doing so everyone else spotted it too, including Diego who had now reentered the room. His jaw nearly hit the floor. "Oh shit," he said.

Girl George continued. "…But that pentagram on the back of the door could definitely mean that something evil is occurring in this house."

CHAPTER 11
CARELESS WHISPER

"Oh my God, she's right," said Isla. "Not only have you kidnapped me you've brought me to the Den of Satan."

"You're getting a little ahead of yourself," said Judd. "We haven't exactly kidnapped you, we are just kind of borrowing you for a while. And as for that shape on the door it's just a five pointed star. It's probably been drawn on there for a kid or something."

"Judd, I know you're not that naïve," said Girl George. "That thing is the sign of the occult."

Judd didn't answer, deep down he knew that this place was weird and the pentagram only served to underline that in all honesty. But this was also the only available place of shelter whilst the storm raged all around them. He just wanted to play things down to try and allay their fears and get them through the night ahead.

But Girl George wasn't letting go. "I'm telling you, if this place is being used by someone it's by a member of the Church of Satan."

"I think Girl George may be right," said Rufus. "I remember the time when I thought I'd met the girl of my dreams but it all turned a little pear shaped when she told me that she wanted to drink my blood. That same girl wore a pentagram around her neck."

"Really," said Judd in a more than sarcastic tone. He figured that this was another one of Rufus's endless bullshits.

"We need to get some sleep," said Diego.

"I ain't fucking sleeping in here, no way," said Madonna.

"Me neither," said Isla.

"Look it's fine," said Judd. "I tell you what, so that you all feel safe, Me, Diego, Rufus and Elvis will take a shift each at staying awake by the door. We still have a gun too, remember. You ladies go to sleep, then in the morning when the storm has passed, we can get out of this Godforsaken place. OK?"

"I dunno, I'm still not sure I'm ready to sleep," said Girl George. "Let's see what vinyls we have in the bookcase. We may as well listen to some music to take our mind off things if we're having to stay put."

"OK, that's not a bad idea to be fair," agreed Judd.

"Well, you guys can all do what you want but I'm gonna sit me down in this old chair and have some kip," said Diego. "It's been an emotional evening."

Even in the dimness of the candlelight, clouds of dust could be seen filling the air as Diego's huge frame collapsed into the armchair. It caused the big man to cough a little before closing his eyes.

"Come on," said Judd. "I'll have a look through the records with you."

Judd and Girl George knelt next to one another so that they could reach the records on the bottom shelf.

"I wonder if these are alphabetised?" asked Girl George pulling out the first album on offer.

"Well it's possible as you've just pulled out a Black Sabbath album, I doubt there's gonna be an Abba album amongst that little lot."

"To be honest, I don't really fancy listening to Black Sabbath in the circumstances," said Girl George putting the album back and then randomly reaching for another one from the centre of the pack. "Here you go, this'll do. The Beatle's White Album."

"One of my faves, though clearly the collection is not in alphabetical order after all then," said Judd. "I tell you what, if any of The Beatles albums were going to make this collection on tonight of all nights I guess it would have to be The White Album."

"Why is that?" asked Girl George.

"Well, it was enough to inspire the likes of Charles Manson to order his crazy followers to take the lives of people up in the Hollywood Hills, albeit he totally misconstrued the meanings of the songs, of course."

"Nice! Anyway, shall we play it?"

"Do you like the Beatles?"

"Do you?"

Judd smiled. "You don't know me very well do you Girl George? Yes, I love them. Probably to the point of obsession. Look, can I call you something other than Girl George, it seems a bit weird. What's your real name?"

"It's Paris."

"Really? Wow, that's a cool name actually."

"Thanks. My mom told my dad that she was expecting me when they were at the top of the Eiffel Tower during a city break. So I guess it made sense."

"Do you mind if we don't actually listen to The Beatles?" interjected Isla. "Growing up in Liverpool I've kind of heard them a lot. Also overhearing what Judd's just said about the Manson murders, I kind of think it'd be good to give that particular album a miss in the circumstances. This place is super creepy."

"Sure," said Paris. "If that's how you feel, I'll keep looking." After passing by a couple more albums she came across a book sandwiched between the album sleeves.

"What's this?" she said. "Paradife Loft? "What the Hell

does that mean?"

"It looks like old English text. I think it's meant to read Paradise Lost," offered Judd.

"Oh, I see. Well that would make sense, about the text that is, because this book is definitely old. It looks like it should be in a museum rather than randomly placed within a record collection."

"I have to agree with you but I'm wondering if it really is randomly placed."

"What do you mean?" asked Paris.

"Well, next to where that old book was placed, there seems to be something else there that also isn't a record either."

Paris returned to the bookshelf and pulled out what appeared to be a varnished piece of wood, however it only appeared that way until Paris turned it over to reveal the alphabet depicted in black font within the shape of two arcs placed one above the other. The first arc displayed the sequence of letters from A to M and the second the sequence from N to Z.

Then, underneath the letters sat a straight, horizontal line of the first natural numbers in sequence: 1,2,3,4,5,6,7,8,9 before finally finishing on a 0.

Then, even further underneath the numbers sat the simple word 'Goodbye'.

In the first uppermost corner on the left hand side the word 'yes' was scribed, whilst the opposite uppermost corner on the right hand side of the board was displayed the word 'No.

When Paris had turned the board over, it had caused a tear-dropped shaped carving of wood to drop and swing from a piece of ancient string which married it to the board for safekeeping. Judd knew straight away that this tear-drop shaped wood, which also housed a small glass window, was known as a planchette. He also knew exactly what they had stumbled across. "It's a Ouija Board," he remarked.

Paris instantly dropped the Ouija board as if handling it was burning hot to the touch. Still on her knees, the board hadn't had far to fall, saving it from damage.

"As if this place didn't freak me out enough," said Isla. "Now we have found a fucking Ouija board to boot."

By now the commotion had also caught the attention of the others. "Let's do it," said Elvis. "It could be fun."

"It could also be dangerous," said Madonna.

"What's the worst that could happen?"

"Do you really want me to answer that?"

"These things don't really work anyhow?" said Elvis. "We'd just be passing the time away."

"The hell they don't," said Rufus. "I remember when I did one of these with the members of The Doors and we contacted Jim. He made it crystal clear that Mr Mojo was Risin'."

"Bullshit, Rufus," said Judd, clearly annoyed at his friend's inconsiderate timing to divulge yet another one of his lies. "You've never even met The Doors."

"Yes I have, when I was promoting a show in L.A."

Judd just rolled his eyes, he didn't have the inclination to delve any further.

"OK, well let's do it and then we can see if this thing really does work. I still don't think it will, but if it does, I feel safe enough with Judd and Diego being here," said Elvis. "Even though Diego is flat out over there."

"I have to say, I think his snoring is the most scary thing about tonight," said Judd.

"Fuck it. I'm up for it," said Paris, collecting the board once again from where she had dropped it.

Judd looked at Madonna to see what her next reaction would be.

"OK, OK. Let's do it," she conceded.

When Judd looked at Isla for collective confirmation she just shrugged and then nodded.

Curiosity can be a powerful draw.

"OK, it's settled then. Let's set it up. Oh, and Isla,

while you're with us please just think of yourself as one of the gang. This isn't a kidnap, not really," said Judd.

"Judd's right, Isla. I've got no axe to grind with you," said Madonna.

Isla managed a smile. "OK, I guess you guys aren't as scary as this place anyhow."

"We'll have to do it on the floor," said Paris.

"I thought you'd never ask," joked Judd.

"In your dreams," she answered as she moved a few steps on her knees and placed the board in a part of the floor that would allow everyone to form a circle around it.

Slightly hesitant, the group took their places. Paris faced the board head on with Isla and Judd flanking either side of her. The remainder of the circle hunched together so that everyone could grab a decent view of the Ouija board. It was Paris who opted to place her hands on the planchette, ready to enable whatever was about to happen.

"Ready?" she asked.

"Ready," nodded Judd, followed by Elvis and then one by one everyone took a turn in confirming that they were committed to the ritual.

Suddenly, a loud bang occurred before they even began.

"What the -" said Madonna.

"It's OK, it's just thunder and lightning," said Judd.

Everyone settled again.

"OK, I'm going to begin," said Paris. "Is anybody there?"

"How original," said Elvis.

"Shut the fuck up or we won't do this," said Paris.

"OK, OK. I'm sorry."

Paris took a second to prepare herself one more. "Is anybody there?" The lightning cracked again but this time the congregation didn't even flinch as they were prepared for it.

"Is anybody there?" asked Paris a third time.

A noise was heard but it was not quite as loud as the

lightning.

"That's just Diego farting," said Rufus.

"How gross," said Madonna.

"Is anybody there?" said Paris for a fourth time.

Nothing happened either worldly or unworldly.

Paris repeated the words for a fifth time and finally the planchette began to move upwards. "I swear I'm not doing anything," said Paris, slightly taken aback and wide-eyed.

"It's OK," said Judd. "Just let the planchette guide you."

The small glass window of the planchette rested over the word 'Yes'.

"'Yes', it's saying 'yes', someone is there!" said Elvis.

"Shush," said Madonna.

Paris took a deep breath. "Did you die in this house?" The planchette darted across to the word 'No."

"I don't know what to ask next," said Paris, still a little freaked out that some unknown energy was guiding her movements.

"What year is it?" asked Madonna.

The planchette made a slight scraping noise as it guided Paris's fingers in the order of 1-6-1-2.

"The year is 1612?" asked Paris. The planchette shot north to the word 'Yes."

"The year of the witch trials," said Judd.

"Huh?" asked Madonna.

"The Pendle Witch Trials. Could be a coincidence. We aren't exactly near Pendle."

"Not that far away either really though," stated Rufus. "Pendle's in Lancashire, right?"

The planchette gave the answer to Rufus's question. 'Yes.'

"Are you a witch?" asked Elvis clumsily.

The planchette shot to 'No.'

"None of them were," said Judd. "The whole thing is now widely accepted as a catastrophic miscarriage of justice. Ten people were hung for trumped up witchcraft charges."

"Maybe there was no smoke without fire," said Rufus.

"You could be right, Rufus," said Madonna. "It all sounds very creepy."

"Were you one of the people hung?" asked Paris to the spirit.

The planchette moved to the word 'No.'

"It doesn't appear that this spirit is connected to the Pendle Witch Trials," stated Paris.

"Mmm. Maybe not, but there still could be a connection yet," said Judd. "Ask for the spirit's name."

"What is your name?" asked Paris.

The planchette moved slowly beneath Paris's fingers as it spelled out its answer. 'O-L-D.'

"Old!" said Elvis. "That's not a name. they must be just telling us they died when they were old, perhaps?"

"That would figure," said Madonna.

"No, I expected that," said Judd. The others looked confused. "May I take over the questioning a minute, Paris."

Paris nodded.

"Is Elizabeth the name that you were given at birth?" asked Judd.

The planchette guided Paris to the word 'Yes.'

"I think we have Old Demdike here with us," said Judd. "She was said to be the original witch of Pendle and many of those that were hung were related to her. She died awaiting trial hence why she answered that she hadn't been hung when Paris asked her."

Next a dog's bark suddenly appeared, but it was no more than a single woof.

"There are no dogs around here are there?" enquired Paris.

Judd continued to assess what was going on with this particular spirit. "Old Demdike was convicted in part because of the evidence brought against her by her niece Jennet who was considered to be a key witness. Jennet was nine years old and she said that she had witnessed Old Demdike take the form of a brown dog."

The candles flickered on and off.

"I'm sorry," said Judd to the spirit. "I understand that this can't be easy for you to relive with us."

"They believed the evidence of a nine-year-old girl?" asked Madonna.

"I guess Jennet gave them what they wanted to hear," said Judd.

The candles flickered again, almost losing their flame entirely, before the planchette shot to the word 'Goodbye.'

"Well that was short lived," said Paris.

"I guess Old Demdike didn't want to chat after all," said Elvis.

"I read once that it takes a lot of energy and effort for a spirit to communicate with the living. Perhaps Old Demdike just lost contact," said Isla.

"Maybe she felt offended," offered Judd. "I referred to her as a dog, albeit I was only relaying the story regarding her niece and conviction as I know it."

"But we definitely heard a bark," said Isla, now feeling much more comfortable in the group. At least herself and the others were all tangibly alive so it currently made sense to begin to bond with them.

"Maybe a spirit of a totally random dog came through. Animals pass over too, right?" asked Madonna.

"I guess they do," said Rufus. "Maybe Jennet was correct after all and she had seen the old lady turn into a dog."

"Or maybe imitating a dog was easier than speaking?" said Judd. "We've seen words pointed out on the Ouija board but we haven't heard any. A single woof is maybe an easier way to make an audible connection."

"Considering what you told us though Judd, it is weird that the sound we heard was a dog's bark," offered Elvis.

"Shall I try again?" asked Paris.

"Yes, but I'm not sure we will contact anyone quite so

prominent in history again," said Judd.

"Is anybody there?" asked Paris. The candlelight flickered again. It seemed a door to the afterlife had been well and truly opened.

"What is your name?"

Paris's fingers were guided to a sequence of letters: 'J-O-S-H-U-A.'

"Hi Joshua," a child's laughter echoed around the room.

"Something different to a dog's bark," said Elvis stating the obvious.

"Are you a little boy?" continued Paris.

The planchette moved to its answer: "Yes".

"You were very young to die, Joshua. What happened?"

The planchette set off again slowly guiding Paris's fingers over a collection of letters. 'C-R-A-N-K.'

"Crank?" asked Paris, a little confused.

"Must be a crank that killed him?" offered Elvis. "You know a nutter, like."

"Or perhaps a crank was the weapon that was used," said Isla.

"Are you OK now, Joshua?" asked Paris, keen to move away from any macabre details for Joshua's sake.

The planchette moved again and spelt out two further words. 'W-I-T-H F-R-I-E-N-D-S.'

"I wonder if he is telling us that he is now with friends or is it instead a question for us?" said Judd.

"How many friends are you with?" asked Paris.

The planchette moved to the number '3'.

"All kids?" asked Rufus.

Not for the first time today, the small glass window revealed the single word 'Yes'.

"Boy, that's rough," said Elvis.

"What happened to you all?" asked Rufus.

'M-E L-U-C-K-Y.'

"Lucky, but you died a child?" said Paris. Confused at

the answer provided.

The exact sequence of letters was repeated again: 'M-E L-U-C-K-Y.,

"He seems pretty adamant," said Rufus.

"What about your three friends? What happened to them?" asked Paris.

A single word was spelt out: 'A-T-E.'

"What the fuck?" said Elvis. "Ate? Is he saying his mates were eaten?"

The candle flickered and the planchette moved to "Goodbye".

"He's gone," said Paris. "Poor little kid."

"Poor little kids by the sound of it," said Elvis.

Everyone took a moment to reflect on the seeming tragedy of lives being lost so young.

"Keep going," said Madonna.

"You've changed your tune," said Elvis.

"It's really interesting now we are doing it," said Madonna. "It is still a bit scary though."

Paris composed herself. "Is anybody there?" asked Paris.

Nothing happened.

"Perhaps we have gone as far as we can?" said Judd.

"Keep the faith, Judd," said Rufus. "Go on Paris, try again."

"Is anybody there?"

The planchette kicked into life and moved the glass window over three different letters: 'E-V-A.'

"Eva, is that your name?" asked Paris.

The planchette jumped up to the word "Yes."

"Is this your house?" asked Judd.

The planchette guided Paris to depict a small circle before returning to the affirmative word of 'Yes.'

'Did you die here?" asked Paris.

Again Paris was guided to form a small circle before reconnecting with the word 'Yes.'

"Were you murdered?" asked Elvis.

Same again. 'Yes'.

"Who by?"

The planchette moved towards a new set of letters: 'E-V-I-L.'

"I think we should stop," said Madonna. "This is getting too weird now."

"Bloody hell, Madge. Make your mind up," said Elvis.

Then the planchette continued independent of any questions being asked of it. 'B-E C-A-R-E-F-U-L.'

"Well that confirms it," said Madonna.

"OK, perhaps Madonna's right," said Judd. "It may be best to leave things be."

The planchette moved to the word "Goodbye".

"There, even Eva agrees," said Madonna.

Paris removed her fingers from the planchette whilst everyone relaxed their posture reflecting on what had just happened.

"Well, I have to admit that I am a sceptic no more," said Elvis.

"That was something else," said Rufus.

"I guess we should pack this thing away," said Paris. "What did Eva mean by be careful? Do you reckon whoever killed her is the owner of this house?"

"Could be, I mean she spelt out the word Evil and that pentagram on the door still gives me the willies....and that's not an invitation to crack a sick joke, Elvis."

"I wasn't going to, Madge."

"It is possible that the owner of this house is Eva's killer," said Rufus. "We may have fell lucky tonight that the storm has kept the owner away."

"Right, I'm definitely putting this away." As Paris reached forward to collect the Ouija Board, she fell backwards startled when the planchette began to move all by itself. Everyone looked on spellbound.

'S-I-M-O-N-E.'

"Who's Simone?" asked Madonna.

"It could be one of two people or both?" said Isla.

"How do you mean?" asked Judd.

"Simone was the name of my cousin and her daughter."

"And they're both dead?"

"My cousin definitely is, she took her own life."

"I'm so sorry to hear that, Isla. Wait, so your cousin, Simone, she was Richie's daughter?" asked Judd.

"Yes, she was and the other Simone is, or was, his granddaughter. She's missing presumed dead, but her body has never been found. We still hope that we can find her alive and well someday."

"For all Richie's faults I really feel for him with this one," said Judd genuinely. "And of course, for you too, Isla."

"Hey guys, the planchette is moving again," said Rufus.

The next six letters that were spelt out were the most unexpected yet.

'H-U-N-T-E-R.'

CHAPTER 12
LEAVE IN SILENCE

"I should chop off your hand and send it to your uncle," said Judd.

"So much for your sympathy," spat Isla.

"That was before I found out he'd killed my friend."

"Wait, we don't know if Hunter is dead for sure," intervened Rufus.

"Oh really," said Judd. "He just came through on a fucking Ouija board."

"Only his name did," replied Rufus. "We don't know for sure it was him, now please calm down, Judd. Remember, Mercer still has Tilda and George Michael."

"Well little Miss Gangster here had better hope they're still alive." Judd, feeling frustrated, kicked the Ouija Board in temper. Paris hastily collected it and finally placed it back in the bookcase hoping it was out of harm's way. She randomly pulled out a record in the hope that playing music would inject a more amenable atmosphere.

"Hey, let's put some music on instead, to lighten the mood. What do we have here?" she said eyeing up the record sleeve. "It's a band I don't recognise."

"I bet it's an old blues song that attracts demons or curses or something. You know like what happens in the movies? A scary old blues song is the catalyst for a lot of scary shit," said Elvis.

"I'm not sure playing a record could make anything any worse tonight," said Paris, inwardly annoyed at Elvis's failure to embrace her attempt to enable a change of mood.

Judd on the other hand calmed himself enough to assist Paris with her quest and pressed the button to fire the record player into life. As the button surged electricity through its ancient wiring, the speakers projected a deep boom signaling that power was present in the device. Paris took the record out of the sleeve, blew a gathering of dust from its surface and carefully placed the black circular vinyl onto the turntable. Next, she lifted the arm of the needle and placed it onto the beginning of the record, which now saw the in-built speakers give way to a loud crackling sound as it connected with the initial grooves. Eventually the music kicked in. Paris began to dance. "Hey, Judd, this sounds right up your street. It's a Merseybeat type of record isn't it?" Paris's assessment wasn't wrong, the track possessed jangling guitars underpinned by a driving drum beat.

"Well, we aren't far from Liverpool. It's a familiar sound all right, yet I don't recognise this song at all. Who's the band?"

Paris managed to remember the name of the band. "Castiel and the Creatures of the Night."

"That's typical of the Merseybeat era," said Judd. "Bands often took a lead name followed by the group name. Gerry and the Pacemakers, Rory Storm and the Hurricanes, Johnny and the Moondogs etcetera etcetera. Most had been inspired by Buddy Holly and the Crickets."

"Creatures of the Night though," said Isla. "Sounds a bit creepy. And what language is that, French?"

"I think it's Latin, which seems a bit weird I have to

say," said Judd, who still hadn't joined Paris to dance. "And that chord that falls on every fourth bar sounds a bit off too, neither element are typical of the genre."

"Definitely weird," said Paris as she continued to dance alone.

"Probably why we've never heard of them," said Elvis. "Castiel and the Creatures of the Night obviously never took off. Shit name, weird chord changes and singing in Latin! Hardly the ingredients of the Rock and Roll Hall of Fame, is it?"

"You know the more I hear that chord it sounds like the tritone."

"Speak English, Judd," said Paris. "It's bad enough listening to this song in Latin."

"Sorry, the tritone is also known as the Devil's interval."

"Well that figures," said Isla.

"Too right," agreed Madonna.

"The thing is it wasn't really used in popular music until Tony Iommi introduced it into Black Sabbath's music much later than the Merseybeat era. He played a triad with a flatted fifth to deliberately make a sound that resonated evil."

"It certainly sounds evil to me," said Madonna. "Can we turn it off please, I really don't like it."

"You'll have no quarrel from me," said Judd.

"It looks like it is coming to an end now anyway," said Paris as she finally stopped dancing herself.

"Again, typical of the time," said Judd. "Songs didn't last much more than a couple of minutes back then."

The song ended on a single chord, which naturally was the tritone once again.

But in actual fact, it hadn't ended.

After a few seconds of crackles, a new voice projected from the grooves of the record through the speakers. This voice seemed more chilling and darker than the singer had done. It appeared to be repeating a single phrase over and over again.

"That doesn't sound like the same singer," said Isla.

"Agreed," said Judd.

"And is that still Latin?" asked Isla.

"I'm not sure, it sounds a bit more nonsensical to me," said Judd. "Sometimes playing the end of a record backwards reveals a hidden message. Lots of Heavy Metal bands have done it over the years to inject a satanic or scary phrase, I wonder if this is the case here?"

"Well I don't want to find out," said Paris, and with those words she took the arm of the record player and raised the needle from the record, instantly muting the ominous loop of voice. Once she placed the arm back on its cradle the turntable stopped altogether after a few decelerating spins. Paris quickly followed up by hitting the off button causing the deep boom sound to generate once again through the speakers.

This was then followed by unsettling noises of a more natural kind as thunder rolled and the rain struck even heavier than before against the windowpanes.

"It's not letting up out there," said Rufus. "So what now?"

"I vote that you guys and girls join Diego over there in the land of the nod. I'll stay awake just in case," said Judd.

"Incase, what?" asked Rufus.

"Just in case, that's all."

"Sounds like a good idea," said Isla.

"I'm still not sure I can sleep, I'm going to read this old book *Paradise Lost* instead," said Paris. "I can use the torch light on my phone so not to disturb anyone."

"OK, but can we all sleep close together?" asked a spooked Madonna.

"I thought you'd never ask," said Elvis.

"You're not funny greaseball," retorted Madonna.

"So, most of us are either gonna have to sleep on the floor or go where none of us have been yet," said Isla.

"Where's that?" asked Rufus.

"Upstairs."

CHAPTER 13
BLACK VELVET

"Wow, you live here?" said Kadence adjusting her mass of jet-black hair. Some of her black lipstick had smudged across her left cheek and had also found its way onto Yasmin's face and neck. Kadence was a goth, not usually Yasmin's type it had to be said, but the two girls had hit it off straight away after meeting less than a mile away in the bars of Birmingham's Gay Quarter, often referred to as Gay Village, earlier in the evening.

Black was certainly Kadence's go-to colour. As well as the black make-up, her gigantic black boots finished climbing up her legs just below the knee and she was squeezed into a black crushed velvet coat-tailed jacket. Although she wouldn't be in any of it for long if Yasmin got her way.

"Kinda, well not really. Just sometimes. It's my boss's place," answered Yasmin.

"And he lets you have a key? Must be some boss to let you have the run of this place."

"To be fair he is a good bloke, although I wouldn't tell him that too often. I like to keep him on his toes."

Judd lived and worked in Birmingham's iconic Rotunda building, a cylindrical high-rise building that formed a vital part of Birmingham's skyline. The vibe was considerably different inside the building than when Kadence had been stood outside it watching the satanic street preacher hours earlier. Little did she know back then that she would be stepping inside it tonight with a girl who she fancied like mad.

Yasmin was Judd's acerbic yet loyal Personal Assistant. She was also the sister of one of his best friends, Sab Mistry, whom he had once served on the Force with before eventually establishing himself as a Private Investigator. Personality wise, Yasmin and Sab were not alike at all, but Judd loved them both dearly and was glad they were both in his life.

Suddenly, a dog appeared across the floor and began to excitedly jump up and down Yasmin demanding instant fuss.

"And who is this gorgeous little fella?" asked Kadence.

"This is Mr. Mustard. I call him Muzzy for short, and he's the reason I get to stay here. I look after him when my boss is away," In the next breath, Yasmin changed her voice to one of coochie-coo baby talk as she fussed the dog. "And Muzzy and me are the best of friends, aren't we Muzzy? Yes we are." Muzzy responded affectionately.

"Ahh, he's lovely," acknowledged Kadence. "But I'm afraid Mr. Mustard here is going to have to play second fiddle tonight as I want you all to myself for a few hours."

"Oooh, promises, promises. So how did I end up being the luckiest girl in the whole of Birmingham tonight?"

"Only Birmingham?"

"Don't push it," laughed Yasmin.

"I knew you'd be good for me. Let's just say that I have a sixth sense."

"A sixth sense, aye? Interesting, tell me more."

"Maybe later. I have other plans right now."

Yasmin smiled and then the two girls began to kiss

passionately as Muzzy retreated back to his bed, armed with the knowledge that he'd have to wait patiently in line for any further attention to come his way.

CHAPTER 14
THE STORY OF THE BLUES

Judd hadn't exactly looked around upstairs, partly on account of him struggling to find a light and partly out of concern from the ladies who had begged him to come back after he had briefly reached the top of the staircase. Judd was never shy on displaying courage but he complied with the request to return as he was keen not to fuel the anxiety of his new friends. He hadn't really seen anything due to the darkness but he was equally confident enough to declare upstairs as safe. He also figured that if anyone was going to show they would have done so by now. Nevertheless, none of the others had fancied taking the stairs so the room or rooms above them remained unexplored. No one wanted to discover what lay in wait up there. It had been the kind of night that possessed all the necessary ingredients to feed the imagination. It seemed easier for everyone to settle down the best they could in the one room.

Diego was still snoring away in the chair that his huge frame had completely engulfed. Even the commotion surrounding the Ouija board and playing of music had failed to stir him.

Madonna and Isla had opted to share the room's only sofa and were sleeping top and tail. By now the cones on Madonna's chest had crumpled and almost flattened. Elvis had grabbed the other available chair and Rufus was lying on the floor, albeit upon a couple of blankets that provided a limited amount of comfort that he had found stuffed in one of the wicker baskets.

"So what's the book like?" asked Judd, sitting with his back against the door and the pentagram above his head.

"With all the old English that's in its pages, it's almost as difficult to understand as that creepy Merseybeat song," answered Paris. She was sitting opposite Judd with her back against the side of the sofa where the other girls were sleeping peacefully. "This book also seems a bit weird and creepy. Par for the course with this place I guess."

"How do you mean? Regarding the book that is not this place, that's a given."

"Well the content for a start. This guy Milton who wrote it must have been totally Team Satan. Not that I've read every page, there must be thousands of lines to this poem."

"It's a poem, huh? I didn't realise that."

"Yeah, I think so. Although it seems to be split into books, a bit like the Bible in that respect I guess."

"I don't think the Bible was Team Satan."

Paris managed a smile. "No of course not, but this *Paradise Lost* still has Adam and Eve featured in it."

"That's interesting. Perhaps if you were to read it to the end Satan eventually comes unstuck?"

"Maybe, but according to the version of events in this book, he is a pretty formidable ruler now he's in Hell it would seem. To be honest, I think he is being portrayed as a hero and I bet whoever owns this house sees Satan as a hero too. Who do you think lives here Judd?"

"Some weird fucker that's for sure. But don't worry, we'll be out of here in the morning. We just need to wait for this storm to pass."

"What are you going to do about your friend and the George Michael guy?"

Judd ran his fingers through his hair, a familiar characteristic when he had something to think about. "I haven't figured it out yet, but while I have Isla, I have some leverage."

"Would you really hurt her if you felt that you needed too, you know because of her uncle's actions?"

"What do you think?"

"I hope you wouldn't."

Judd took a turn to smile. "Like I said earlier, you don't know me that well. Between you and me, I wouldn't. I could never willingly hurt someone of the female species."

"Not willingly?"

"Not at all if I can help it. Never physically anyhow, that much I can say. But I'm only human and I've made mistakes in other ways. So, yes, I have hurt women I'm ashamed to say and sometimes in quite dramatic style."

"I knew that you were a heartbreaker the moment I set eyes on you, Judd Stone," smiled Paris.

Judd laughed. "I'm not sure if that's a compliment or not. I won't ask. I noticed when referring to Mercer's captives you said friend, rather than friends. I assume you meant Tilda and not Hunter?"

"Sorry, it's just Isla's uncle seems a bit of a gangster and then the whole Ouija board thing. I'm not holding out much hope for Hunter."

"It's OK, don't apologise. You may be right yet but until I have concrete evidence, and no I don't think the Ouija board is concrete evidence by the way now I've had time to reflect on things, I need to assume that he's OK."

"You know what? I've had enough of this book," said Paris, firmly closing the cover shut. "And I'm a bit cold, can I come over and sit by you"

"Sure," said Judd. Paris shuffled over using her butt to manouvere the short distance and buried her head into

Judd's chest as he put his arm around her. He noticed the pleasant smell of her hair, something between exotic fruit and vanilla and was thankful that she had lost her stage hat earlier in the evening. The thunder rolled again before he spoke. "Warmer?"

"Yes, thanks Judd. And I feel much safer to be honest with you. Anyway, tell me about some of these women you've hurt."

"You may never speak to me again. And I quite like the vibe of you feeling safer with me, I wouldn't want to spoil that now, would I?"

"I won't judge, I promise. Believe me, I'm no angel either, Judd. I'd just like to get to know you a little better and I can tell underneath all of your bravado and smouldering good looks there's a damn fine heart in there, somewhere."

"Flattery will get you everywhere. OK, I'll tell you some stuff. To be honest it would help me to talk about my latest fuck ups. I think it may be a bit therapeutic you know."

"It's definitely not healthy to bottle things up, Judd. I'm a good listener too."

"You know what, Paris? You're wise beyond your years. If I had my wallet I could show you a picture of the most special lady in my life."

"What's her name?"

"Billie. She's my little girl. My daughter. I'd literally die for her."

"Nice name, as in Billie Holliday?"

"Yeah, that's right, but in actual fact she was kind of named after a good friend of mine who died, William."

"I get it. How did he die?"

"He was shot."

Paris pulled her chest away and looked at Judd with shock on her face. "That's awful."

"I know. His wife got killed too in the same shooting. I also got shot in the attack but obviously I was a lot luckier."

"Did they catch who did it?"

"Erm, let's just say that justice was served. My wife also got shot in the same attack. She survived too and that's where my most recent fuck up really begins."

Paris nestled back into Judd's chest. "Go on."

"You're sure that you will definitely speak to me again?"

"I promise."

"OK, here it comes… No I can't. I can't even find the words to admit what I did. It was unforgiveable."

"Please Judd. It's OK, honest. Just say it."

"OK, you asked, remember. While my wife Brooke lay in a coma in hospital I screwed another woman."

"Just once?"

"No a few times."

"That is pretty terrible, Judd. But I'm still not judging. I know you're a good guy deep down."

"Thanks for the vote of support, Paris. I can't say that I have felt much like a good guy ever since I did that too her though. Long story short, she found out. She quite rightly dumped me and now she and my little girl live with a whole different guy."

"That must be tough."

"It is, but no less than I deserve."

"Do you still love your wife?"

"I do. I mean, I really do, you know. I'd get back with her in a heartbeat but the reality is she hates my guts. If it wasn't for me seeing Billie, she'd happily never have anything to do with me ever again."

"I'm truly sorry, Judd."

"Hey, you've got nothing to be sorry about. The whole crazy mess is down to me and there's not a day goes by that I don't regret what I've done to her."

"But you're there for your little girl?"

"Always."

"Well that's more than my dad ever did for me. You

need to stop beating yourself up, Judd."

"Maybe I will one day, although I can't see it being any time soon."

"I think I'm finally ready to go to sleep now, Judd, do you mind if I stay close to you though? I feel much safer being with you."

Judd found himself planting a gentle, brotherly kiss on Paris's aromatic head. "Go for it, Paris. Sweet dreams."

CHAPTER 15
WAKE ME UP BEFORE YOU GO-GO

Kadence woke needing a pee. She took care not to wake Yasmin and she sat on the side of the bed to gather some energy before attempting to stand up.

She fumbled for the switch of the bedside lamp and smiled as she looked back at Yasmin who was sleeping like a baby, the dim light catching the peaceful expression on her face. Kadence's smile was also inspired by the recollection of the reason why her energy levels were so low. In spite of meeting only a few hours earlier she and Yasmin had felt few inhibitions in exploring one another's bodies.

Sure, the alcohol had helped loosen up any bashfulness but Kadence felt a very natural connection with Yasmin and the chemistry between them had been able to flow with ease.

In all the throes of passion, Kadence now realised that the curtains hadn't been closed on the bedroom window. However. she figured that the high position of the room was more than enough to protect the modesty of the two lovers from any unwanted voyeurism.

Kadence's eyes were drawn to the driving rain hitting the glass of the Rotunda building. As the water ran down the windowpane, she could make out the odd flash of lightning through the blurred watery images that were heavily concealing the Birmingham skyline.

Commanded by her impatient bladder, Kadence, finally stood up and wearily made her way towards the bathroom. She passed Mr. Mustard on the way, who, unlike Yasmin stirred and raised his head, but after a very feeble woof he soon lowered it again. He knew that Kadence presented no danger.

She opened the bathroom door, pulled on the cord which turned on the light, and sat down on the cold toilet seat to conduct her business.

Once her bladder was emptied, she stood up, flushed the chain and took the short amount of steps to the wash basin. She turned on the hot water tap and then squeezed a small amount of liquid soap into the palm of her hand, massaged it with both hands under the running water to form a lather and then once done turned off the tap.

Kadence looked in the mirror that was positioned above the sink, ruffled her black hair slightly and smiled again finding her own image comical as she realised that she hadn't taken her excessive make up off before going to bed.

After drying her hands on the nearby hand towel, she noticed a watch that had been left on a glass shelf amidst the partly-used toothpaste tube and razor. It looked a nice timepiece and she figured that it must belong to Yasmin's boss as he owned the apartment that she currently found herself to be in.

Kadence picked up the watch, with no other intention but to have a closer look at its beauty, when she instantly felt a burning sensation flare up in the pit of her stomach coupled with a deep intuition of fear. Flashes of incoherent images began to dominate her mind. This included bright lights, then flipping to contrasting darkness peppered with intermittent gunshots.

Images of evil little people followed, appearing something akin to elves or gnomes laughing hysterically.

Then Kadence felt an unnerving tightening around her neck and began to find it difficult to breathe.

Despite the sensation of choking, Kadence found an ability to scream and before long both Yasmin and Mr. Mustard were by her side.

"Kadence, what the hell is wrong?"

"I'm sorry, Yasmin. It…it's this watch," said Kadence, hastily placing it back on the glass shelf where she had first found it.

"It's just a watch, Kadence," said Yasmin confused, but she could clearly see that Kadence was disturbed by something. "Fuck me, you really do look terrified."

"I told you that I have a sixth sense, didn't I?"

"I thought you were joking."

"No, I wasn't. My grandmother has always described it as a gift but when I get feelings like this, I find it more of a curse."

"You're not making a lot of sense, Kadence."

"The watch, does it belong to your boss?"

"Yes, it's Judd's as far as I know."

"Then I'm sorry to tell you this, Yasmin, but I think he's in real danger."

CHAPTER 16
TO CUT A LONG STORY SHORT

As Judd's phone rang and woke him up he instantly panicked, realising that instead of keeping guard as he'd promised, he had instead dropped off to sleep. He also felt a little foolish as he had clearly had his phone in his possession all along, totally forgetting that he'd tucked it inside his boot before going on stage.

The phone continued to ring as he quickly looked around to assess the welfare of his companions. Judd was relieved to find that everyone was OK and still sleeping soundly just as he had left them.

Still allowing the phone to ring out, people began to stir with the noise. Even Diego who had been sleeping like the proverbial log and who had so far slept through both a Ouija board and music!

Paris slowly released her head from the comfort of Judd's chest. "You'd better answer that," she said.

"But how the fuck is it ringing? We have no signal here, remember?"

"Shit, you're right. More weird stuff in this Godforsaken place."

Judd finally pulled the mobile phone from his boot. "Of course, I can still be called over the social media network independent of a regular phone signal. Am I using cellular data or wi-fi perhaps? Who cares?" He recognised the name and profile picture of who was calling and accepted the call… "Yasmin, Hi. Do you know what time it is?"

"Judd are you alright?"

"Yes of course I am. Are you? Is Mr. Mustard OK?"

"Yeah, yeah we're all good."

"Then why the call at this hour?"

"Are you sure you're OK? Nothing has happened to you?"

"Well it's been an eventful night with some pretty hairy scrapes, but yeah, generally I'm OK. Yasmin, what's this all about?"

"This is gonna sound a bit weird but stay with me. I have, erm, a friend here with me, by the way I hope you don't mind…"

"Friend, huh? Right. I get it. I don't mind as long as you change the bed sheets after."

"Don't be so crude…anyway this friend, Kadence her name is, she picked up one of your watches and she kind of freaked out. She has a kind of a gift."

"What kind of a gift? Like psychic stuff you mean?"

"Yeah, exactly that. Look, I think it'll be easier if I put her on loudspeaker."

"Hi Kadence, I'm Judd."

"Judd, you're in great danger."

"Wow, nice to meet you too."

"Sorry, it brings me no pleasure to tell you such a thing."

"And you know this from handling my watch?"

"Yes, it's a gift. Not the watch, although it may have been for you."

"I knew what you meant. I once knew someone who had a similar talent, Kadence." Judd's heart sank as the image of Crystal Chamberlain entered his mind. She had been the wife of his best friend William Chamberlain and she had possessed psychic abilities. Both Crystal and William had been cruelly gunned down in the incident he had told Paris about earlier in the evening. "So what did you see, Kadence, you know when you touched my watch?"

"It's not just what I saw it's what I felt too. Look, I'm not a liar but I can't always explain what happens to me. It just happens."

"It's OK, just tell me Kadence. I mean you could save my life, right?" Judd was trying his best to make Kadence feel comfortable whilst demonstrating that he fully got this kind of thing.

"Well, it started with a burning sensation in my stomach, but that can be a common thing for me when I undergo these types of experiences. This seemed much stronger than usual, like I was literally on fire. Then I got the usual flashes of bright lights and contrasting darkness but I heard gunshots, Judd, and that concerns me."

"I have been shot in the past, Kadence. Do your visions ever pick up on past occurrences?"

"Mmm, I'm not sure. I guess they could do."

"Then there's no need to worry, Kadence. I'm sure that's what you've picked up on. Thanks for caring though."

"I'm not so sure, Judd. I still get the feeling that you are in danger. I received these images of evil little people laughing hysterically. Then I got a sensation of being strangled, I could hardly breathe."

"That's interesting, but I don't think it was me who connected you to the sensation of being strangled. Listen, it sounds like you're pretty open minded about the occult and things, right Kadence?"

"Very."

"OK, I'm going to put you on loudspeaker now our end," by now everyone was awake and taking an interest in the phone call as they gathered around Judd and Paris. "To be honest with you it has been a weird night altogether. We were daft enough earlier to do a Ouija board to kill some time. You may have somehow connected with me from handling my watch, but you may have picked up on whatever vibe is going on here, or all of the above.

"Through the Ouija board I think we were potentially contacted by one of the so called Pendle witches. Old Demdike to be exact. Now apart from her, the other guilty witches were all hung so that may explain your feeling of strangulation?"

"I'm aware of the story of the Pendle witches. I just hope that it isn't you who is going to be asphyxiated at some point, Judd."

"I'm sure that Yasmin can testify to you that I can handle myself pretty well, Kadence. There's no need to worry about me. I think I'm capable of sorting out any little people too, especially with my friend Diego being here with me. He's the size of a house."

"How many of you are there in total and where are you?"

"There are seven of us, and we are in a shitty little cottage somewhere north of Liverpool."

Kadence thought for a moment. "Crank," she said speaking her thoughts aloud.

"Who, me or you?"

"Sorry, no I reckon you could be near to a place called Crank. It's a small village in Merseyside with a big story. It could explain the little guys in my vision at least."

"Well funny you should mention that. The word Crank came through earlier on the Ouija board as well. I've never heard of the place. But perhaps I was wrong about Pendle? Geography was never my strongest subject, but apart from being up north I'm pretty sure that we haven't got as far as Lancashire when we drove away from Liverpool city centre."

"I can't explain the Pendle connection, just yet," said

Kadence. "But Crank seems a good starting point."

"Carry on, Kadence, we're all ears." As Judd invited Kadence to reveal her knowledge on this mysterious Merseyside village a crash of thunder and streak of lightning ceased the moment as if that too was signaling for Kadence to proceed.

"OK, can you all hear me OK?"

Judd looked around and the huddle became more intense as the phone became the focal point.

"Yeah, Kadence. We're all good."

"OK, there are quite a few legends associated with Crank but the tale I'm about to tell you dates back to the eighteenth century. I'm guessing near to where your cottage lies is Crank Caverns."

"Paris interjected. "Hey, remember The Merseybeat record? The Cavern? Crank Caverns? Perhaps there's a connection?"

"Maybe?" said Judd. "You could be onto something there, Paris."

"Any way, carry on please, Kadence," said Paris.

Kadence did just that. "These caverns in Crank are vast, dark and mysterious and it is unlikely that humans have ever reached the entirety of their pits.

"Anyway, one day so many years ago, four boys decided to venture into the caverns just for a bit of fun spurred on by tales of people going missing in the area. And in actual fact three of the four were never seen again."

"And the fourth?" asked Madonna.

"He escaped. Just. But this poor kid would have been haunted by the experience for as long as he lived according to the tale he told following his escape. But his revelations had to wait as he was in shock for days."

"What happened?" asked Paris.

"When the boy eventually spoke, he told how he witnessed small bearded men savagely kill his three friends and he literally ran for his life as they then closed in on him too. He told how he stumbled across old bones as he fled the scene but managed to find a small chink of light that led to an opening at the surface. As he scrambled through it one of the bearded creatures grabbed at his ankle and yanked him backwards. Sensing that he was literally fighting for his life, the young lad found a final surge of energy and his persistence paid off as he successfully managed to climb out of the cavern."

"Shit, that's so scary. Poor Kid," said Madonna.

"Was his name Joshua by any chance?" asked Paris.

"I'm not sure," answered Kadence.

"A boy called Joshua reached out to us during the Ouija board and spelt out the word Crank. I think he took his own life," said Judd.

"Who could blame the poor kid if it was him that contacted you," said Kadence. "It sounds like it fits though, doesn't it? Anyway, there's even more to this chilling story."

"What happened next?" asked Madonna, echoing everyone's thoughts as they hung onto every word of Kadence's incredible tale.

"There had been tales of other folk going missing in the area but it was the boy's revelations which led to the caverns becoming a place of interest. After hearing the boy's tale, two heavily armed soldiers ventured into the caverns to investigate and their torches, or oil lamps perhaps, revealed not only human bones but also bones with tissue still upon them, complete with bite marks and hanging flesh as if it had definitely been ripped by something or someone eating it."

"Could it have not simply been animals, in terms of the meat and bones or whatever was eating them?" asked Judd.

"No, the method of biting was very particular. By all accounts it definitely pointed towards human cannibalism taking place. The soldiers also reported how they got this eerie sense of being watched. They could hear laughter in the shadows and the speaking of a language that they didn't recognise. But every time they tried to try and catch who was making the sounds, the light revealed nothing. Freaked out by all of this, even the two soldiers retreated from the cavern very smartish like."

Just as the lighting had struck to signal Kadence to begin her story it crashed again as she finished.

"Well, thanks for scaring the shit out of us, Kadence," said Paris.

"That was such an awesome story," said Elvis, as another roll of thunder appeared.

"It sounds like the storm isn't easing where you are," said Yasmin over the loudspeaker. "Please take care, Judd."

"Now I know for sure that it's a weird night," answered Judd.

"Because of the scary story?" asked Paris.

"No, Yasmin showing that she cares about me."

"Very funny. It's all a bit too freaky, for me," said Yasmin.

"You can say that again," said Madonna.

"Go and get some sleep, Yasmin. You too Kadence. We are all fine here, we'll be leaving in the morning once this storm passes," said Judd.

"Will you phone us if there is any hint of trouble," said Yasmin.

"I promise," said Judd.

"OK, bye for now," said Yasmin. "And please do stay safe."

"Bye, nice speaking with you. Kind of," said Kadence.

"Likewise," said Judd.

Paris frowned and silently mouthed the word 'Nice!' as she and Madonna just looked at one another whilst another flash of lightning, accompanied by a crash of thunder, momentarily shook and lit up the room.

CHAPTER 17
SHE'S OUT OF MY LIFE

Slightly earlier that evening, Richie Mercer had obviously been enjoying himself as he watched his three prisoners tremble with fear. Sitting side by side on un-cushioned chairs, each one had their hands tied behind their back.

"So are any of you cheeky fuckers ready to tell me where your scummy mates have taken my niece?"

"I honestly wish we knew," said George Michael.

"It's true," said Tilda. "We have no idea."

"Well, you'd better come up with a viable answer pretty soon because my patience is running very thin indeed," spat the gangster. "I'm going to have to start removing fingers from each and every one of you until I get some co-operation."

"You're an animal," said Tilda.

"Well that's rich coming from the lady who pulled a gun on me. Wait, a lady wouldn't do such a thing would she, but a tramp would? A tramp who's clearly got a death wish too."

"I've never claimed to be a lady," retorted Tilda. "But you're not even human."

"You need to watch your mouth."

"The truth is, Mr. Mercer, because you were chasing us we just sped away to nowhere in particular," said George Michael. "Where the others have finally ended up, we really can't say."

"Why should I believe you? You may be stupid enough to try and play me. While I don't know where my niece is, you've probably figured out that you also have a chance of staying alive. But that's OK, I'll let this storm pass before I track them down and when I find them, I won't be very happy if you haven't provided me with any kind of assistance."

"You can chop off every single finger from us if it pleases you but we can't tell you what we don't know," said an unwavering Tilda.

Mercer went quiet for a few seconds. His eyes were cold but the reality of the situation was beginning to find its way through the cogs of his brain. "Perhaps it's in your best interests to take my mind off things for a while. I tell you what, to try and sustain my ever-decreasing patience and to pass the time away, you could sing me a song, George."

"What?" Such a request was the last thing that George had expected in the circumstances.

"You heard me, lad. Sing me a song. Keep me entertained while I figure all this out, unless you want me to find my own entertainment, like slicing one of your pinkies off for example… Or worse."

"What do you want me to sing?"

"Now let me see. Ha ha, I have the very song considering your predicament. Sing me the song 'Freedom'. Very fitting, don't you think, as you no doubt want yours?"

"The Wham! version or the George Michael solo version, which was technically known as 'Freedom 90'?"

"Both. And I want to hear every single word."

Keen to comply but concerned that the obvious

pressure would blur his ability to remember all the words of the two songs, George opted for a chronological approach. He had barely begun to sing the opening line of Wham!'s 'Freedom' when Hunter's phone started to ring.

"How very rude to interrupt proceedings," said Mercer. He reached into Hunter's pocket and pulled out the ringing phone.

"Castiel, what sort of a fucking name is that?" said Mercer as he watched the caller's name pulsate on the screen.

"He is someone who's boots you are not worthy of licking."

Mercer gave Hunter a sharp backhander across his face for his insolence. Blood trickled from Hunter's mouth. Mercer answered the phone and waited.

"Hunter?" said a voice at the end of the line.

"He's a little *tied up* at the moment, Castiel."

"Who is this?"

"Someone who you don't want to piss off, Castiel, and you already have because your timing is shit. I was being very pleasantly serenaded, so do one." And with that, Mercer killed the phone.

"You shouldn't have done that," said Hunter. "Not to him."

Mercer punched Hunter again, almost causing him to lose consciousness. "Are you forgetting who I am, you stupid prick? You'd better start showing me some fucking respect and I haven't forgotten that you killed my niece's friend either. You are treading on very, very thin ice.

"Now let me have a little look on your phone whilst I have it… A text here from a chap called Efan claiming 'It's done.' So what's done?"

Hunter was still fighting to stay awake and couldn't readily provide an answer.

"Forget it. Your texts are boring anyway. Let's look in your gallery instead," Mercer orchestrated a few movements on Hunter's phone as he continued to entertain himself before a look came on his face that was somewhere between disbelief and rage. "You absolutely sick fuck."

Hunter's head was still positioned on its side following the force of Mercer's punch, but his gradual return to lucidity found his line of sight connect with a photograph on the wall. Due to the pride-of-place Tony Iommi guitar and other artwork, the photograph had not been too obvious to notice before, but now it was all that Hunter could look at. It was a photograph taken somewhere exotic and sunny of a pretty young blonde woman holding a child, and the child was the image of her. Hunter began to snigger.

Whilst Hunter sniggered, Mercer's facial expression grew increasingly angry. He was still swiping through the photos on Hunter's phone and he clearly didn't like what he was seeing.

"Most of these are kids, what's wrong with you?" exclaimed Mercer.

Hunter eventually moved his head to face Mercer once again. Incredibly, he looked smugger than smug over something. "Yeah, and that was your kid and grandkid in that photo, I assume? Doesn't life throw up some funny little coincidences every now and again?"

"What do you know about them, you piece of filth?"

"I know that you ain't seen at least one of them for quite a while now."

Mercer punched Hunter so hard a tooth shot across the floor. Next, the gangster grabbed Hunter by the collar and shook him ferociously. "Where is my granddaughter? Where is she?"

Incredibly, Hunter just laughed through the blood bubbling from his mouth.

Mercer was so incensed that he pulled out a knife and, without hesitation, cut off Hunter's right index finger. Callously, he then tossed it aside as Hunter screamed in agony.

"Where is she, where? You'd better fucking tell me."

Hunter then felt two more punches to his face, causing another tooth to spill onto the floor.

For all Hunter's bravado, he inevitably buckled under the ferocious assault. However, he could hardly find the wherewithal or energy to speak… "OK, OK. Crank." His voice was barely a whisper.

Mercer struck him again. "Speak up, you piece of shit."

"Crank. Crank Caverns."

Mercer took his knife and shoved it upwards under Hunter's jaw, piercing the anterior triangle of his neck. Looking into his victim's mouth, Mercer saw the blade sticking vertically through the tongue and hard palate. Pleased with his work, Mercer took an age to withdraw the knife and with it released a waterfall of blood all over his victim.

Mercer leant forward and whispered menacingly into Hunter's ear. "You're still alive, ain't ya, soft lad. That's OK, for now. I want you to die slowly. And there's no doubt whatsoever that you are going to die."

Mercer wiped the blade of his knife on Hunter's jeans before placing it back in its sheath, which was strapped under his jacket. He then turned his attention to the other two people in the line who were inwardly praying that they weren't going to suffer the same fate.

Tilda and George had immeasurable shock on their faces.

"I guess I need to give my friend The Undertaker another call. I'm keeping him very busy lately. But before I do, George, will you please finish singing your songs to me. After 4 shall we? 1-2-3-4."

CHAPTER 18
TRUE COLOURS

Even earlier in the day, before the storm gripped Great Britain, Father Cullis returned to his church pleased with his day's work.

He was wise enough to not even dare to claim any type of victory. Nonetheless, he was content that a significant seed had been planted in the battle against the underworld of Satanists. An underworld that he knew was rapidly growing beneath the radar.

Many modern-day priests realised they had to think differently to their predecessors, but actually bluffing by presenting oneself as a Satanist, with a little reverse psychology thrown in, was very inventive and probably unprecedented.

Concerned about the tracking of the Bull Ring Shopping Centre's CCTV systems, Father Cullis had refrained from getting changed in the shopping centre toilets.

In contrast to the bustling city centre, his church was nestled within a quiet suburb of Birmingham where movement of people was often minimal. Father Cullis still had the presence of mind to look around for prying eyes before he passed through the iron gates of the church that were covered by a small arched roof.

Father Cullis was disguised so well that even his most devoted parishioners might not have recognised him, nevertheless, confident that he was alone, he walked up the graveled pathway with tombstones of differing proportions flanking either side of him. Never off duty, he noticed that the grass was getting a little too long. He made a mental note to reach out to the local gardener to come and tidy things up a bit.

In no time at all, Father Cullis reached the ancient wooden door of the church and placed the key inside the lock. The door was always locked when he was away from the premises to prevent any acts of vandalism or theft – an unfortunate sign of the times. The door creaked as it opened. He stepped inside, closing the door behind him. This time, he left it unlocked: which was a little lazy of him, but there weren't too many hours ahead until the next church service so he had seen little point in locking it again. He'd also left it unlocked before without issue when he'd been in and around the vicinity.

As he strolled along the tiled floor, Father Cullis breathed in the agreeable fragrance of Frankincense which remarkably still lingered from the last service that he had delivered. He took it as sign that his earlier unorthodox actions had been approved by God.

He walked down the aisle towards the altar, as he had done hundreds of times before, and for the first time in a while, his stale eyes found the large stained-glass window and the sunlight casting its kaleidoscope of colours across the church. He took it as a second message of God's approval.

This priest also moved in mysterious ways.

Making his way into the vestry, he opened the cupboard door that held his more familiar attire. With a sigh of relief, he removed the long black wig, which had been hot and sticky. Once it escaped the clutches of the hairpiece, Father Cullis fluffed his natural grey-peppered hair to try and relieve the flatness of his locks.

Next came off the dark glasses and his deep-blue-coloured eyes needed to adjust to the change in light. Removing his black 'I heart Satan' T shirt, he allowed himself a wry smile as he folded it away and reached for his cassock. He lifted the sacred garment from its hanger, slipped it over his head, and completed his look by positioning the obligatory clerical collar.

Only now, in God's house, dressed according to his station, Father Cullis could relax. He moved away from the vestry and entered his nearby office. He sat down on the leather-bound chair and opened up the lid of his laptop before firing it into life via the power button.

After a few seconds a random screensaver of a mountain range appeared and Father Cullis was invited to input his password. After doing so, he scanned the machine for his email account and waited for his emails to load.

However, he ignored the messages awaiting him. Instead, he went into his drafts folder and found the email that he had created earlier, purposefully choosing to come back and proof-read it once and for all before hitting send. And that time was nigh.

He read through the draft in his head.

Dear Mr. Stone,

My name is Father Cullis and I am writing to you as I understand that you are a very credible private detective, but more importantly, I also understand that you are a man with a very open mind who has experienced things that many other private detectives would not have the capacity to even begin to comprehend.

I don't kid myself that you are a religious man but I do believe that if a priest is taking the time to write to you about a subject that for many may seem outlandish, I have every confidence that you will take me seriously. Please read on…

Father Cullis noticed a couple of typos as he read through the remainder of the email, validating his decision to allow time to pass before finally sending it to PI Judd Stone. Wholesale changes weren't necessary, though, and apart from the odd rephrasing, the email soon found its way through the ether to Judd Stone's inbox.

Pleased with himself, Father Cullis went to close the lid on his laptop, but in doing so, he just about caught sight of a figure in the reflection of the screen.

As he turned, he felt a heavy object glance the side of his head. He was instantly dazed, but in the split second that he moved after seeing the reflection, he undoubtedly saved his own life.

Father Cullis realised that there had been a need to defend himself and he struck out at his attacker, connecting very well on the man's chin, causing him to stumble.

Despite the priest's best efforts, the object came down hard again towards his head. In split-second desperation, he put forward an arm and felt excruciating pain surge through it as he blocked the ferocious blow.

Amongst the commotion, Father Cullis managed to get a closer look at his attacker, but he had no idea who he was. There was no time to dwell on his identity as punches flourished. In spite of the disadvantage of the weapon, Father Cullis began to gain considerable advantage over the intruder.

A well-aimed kick saw the weapon fall from the attacker's hand. It had been a golden candlestick collected on the way to the priest's office.

The attacker sensed that the odds were now very much against him. He ran for the door, but only after he had pulled a knife from his pocket and left it embedded in the priest's stomach.

He ran through the churchyard and into his car, that was parked less than twenty feet away from the gates.

As he sat in the driver's seat, he couldn't believe what he then saw through the windscreen.

In spite of his injury, Father Cullis was running straight at the car, his cassock flapping aimlessly like the cape of a demented superhero. The knife was still sticking out of his stomach.

The criminal hastily turned the key to start the engine of the car. Revving the accelerator, he decided that he only had one option. He drove straight at the oncoming priest. Father Cullis ended up mounting the bonnet, rolling up and over the windscreen and roof, before finishing up on the road at the rear of the car.

Father Cullis was most likely dead, but the attacker had made that mistake just moments earlier with an incorrect assumption following the stabbing, so to make sure, the car was reversed over the priest's body and then forwards again before making a getaway.

Once it was safe to do so, Efan pulled over and reached for his phone. His hands were still shaking as he punched in a single text message destined to reach a series of like-minded people. It consisted of just two words: 'It's done.'

CHAPTER 19
LIFELINE

"I think I may have worked this out," announced Kadence.

"Really?" answered Yasmin sitting forward attentively on the sofa. Kadence was sitting on the floor amongst a plethora of maps and papers which fortunately, Judd, a natural hoarder, had readily available within his apartment.

"Or worked something out, at least."

"I'm all ears."

Despite the hour, Kadence, was wide awake and she spoke with an associated level of animation. "Take a look at this map. This is where Crank is and therefore roughly where Judd and the others are right now," said Kadence pointing to a spot on the map which she had already marked with an X.

"OK," answered Yasmin, as yet none the wiser.

"Well, it was also the area where the legendary cannibalism occurred. You know in the caverns of Crank, where we think Joshua had that dreadful experience but lived to tell the tale, unlike his not-so-lucky friends."

"This I already knew, Babe."

"I know, I know, I'm just providing context for now. Bear with me. Watch. If I take this ruler and draw a diagonal line through Crank and then slightly upwards towards the north-west it cuts through Pendle Hill."

"The place where those witches were put on trial?"

"Exactly. Although alleged witches is probably a more accurate description, to be fair. And remember the trials led to hangings, hangings that perhaps should never have happened. Such activity can manifest an energy."

"OK, but anyone could draw a line from Crank to Pendle Hill quite easily. It doesn't really prove anything, Kadence."

"That's true, but it got me thinking. I became intrigued to understand if I were to continue the line where it might take me. Look, if I continue the line southwards it takes me into Liverpool."

"So?"

"Liverpool must have a rich history of murders and unorthodox deaths; the line could easily pass through any such location. There could be a connection where it passes through."

"Judd and the others were in Liverpool earlier. Knowing Judd as I do, an unorthodox death could well have happened not too long ago in Liverpool," Yasmin suddenly realised that in truth she didn't know Kadence that well and such a comment could appear quite alarming.

Fortunately, Kadence took it in her stride. "I did wonder what made them end up in Crank. I'd really love to talk to Judd again in case I'm onto something or not."

"What if you go back and continue the line towards the north-east, where does that take you?"

Kadence took her pen and ruler and continued the line in the direction that Yasmin had suggested. "Unremarkably it takes me to the north-east of England, kind of Hartlepool and Durham way. I'm not aware of any notorious deaths around there but I don't claim to know everything."

"It is entirely possible that there have been murders or the like that way though."

"I know, but I am a little disappointed to be honest, because just a little bit further south and the line would have hit Whitby which would have been very interesting."

Yasmin managed a smile. "Just because you're a Goth you can't assume that vampires are real, you know?"

"Never say never," replied Kadence only half joking. "I'd have to research the north-eastern area to know for sure but nothing I know springs to mind."

"What if you go south-west, you know even further beyond Liverpool. Into Wales I guess?"

"OK, here goes," Kadence continued to draw the line. "Yep, kind of Barmouth, Tywyn way."

"Ooh, nice. My sister, Sab, and me had some fab holidays there as kids."

"Me too! I love Barmouth, but again I'm not aware of any meaningful murders or anything obviously untoward happening there. But then again, I should have pointed out by now that it is less likely about the villages, towns and cities and more about the buildings."

Yasmin looked confused. "What do you mean?"

"Well, my theory is ley lines."

"Ley lines?"

"Yeah. Ley lines are lines that we don't regularly see on a map and we can't consciously see them even if we were walking along them. But they do exist and are made up of electromagnetic energy. If you follow such lines they quite often connect churches with one another and other sacred places of worship. This often includes ancient pathways and historic landmarks too. For example, both Stonehenge and the pyramids are said to sit on ley lines. These theories have been around since about the 1920's, or rather the concept was discovered then by those generations, because the actual construction of ley lines have clearly been happening for centuries upon centuries upon millennia."

"Wow, that's pretty mind blowing. I'm beginning to

fancy you for your brain as well as your looks."

"Glad to hear it," smiled Kadence.

"Do you think this is really what's happening here? Ley lines?"

"Well if we can connect say the house that Judd and the others are in near Crank, or Crank caverns themselves perhaps, with say Malkin Tower then I think this would explain what came through on the Ouija board. I'd really like to speak with Judd again in case he can throw any light on anything else along the ley line."

"Like in North Wales and the North East of England?"

"Exactly."

"I'm going to call him now," said Yasmin… "Damn, the line's engaged."

"Keep trying."

"I will. By the way what is Malkin Tower?"

"It was the home of Elizabeth Southerns."

"Who?"

"Elizabeth Southerns, also known as Old Demdike. She came through on the Ouija board to Judd and the others. Malkin Tower was also the home of her granddaughter, Alizon Devize. She too was said to be a witch along with her grandmother and Alizon was one of those who was ultimately hanged. Malkin Tower was an instrumental building in the case of the Pendle Witch Trials."

"Why so?"

"It was alleged to have been a witches coven."

CHAPTER 20
CALL ME

Just as Judd had given up hope of the call ever being answered Brooke's voice appeared. "Hello."

"Oh, Hi Brooke, how are you?"

"Judd, do you know what time it is?"

"Yes, sorry Brooke, I'm kind of having an emotional night and I just wanted to see if you and Billie were OK."

"Of course we are OK. Or I *was*, because you have now woken me up you selfish idiot. An emotional night for you aye? Well why should I care? Everything's always about you isn't it Judd Stone."

"I'm sorry Brooke, but both you and Billie are the most important things in my life. I just wanted to know that you are both OK. Can you give Billie a kiss for me please?"

"I'm not waking her up just to satisfy your insecurities Judd. Now please go away. I'll call you in the morning, OK? That's the best I'm willing to offer."

"Then that's fine, Brooke. I'm sorry I called but it's only because I care. Sweet dreams."

"Whatever. Good night." As Brooke placed the hand set back onto its cradle she turned over in bed and was surprised to discover that there was a vacancy where Efan should have been sleeping.

Just as Brooke had hung up on him, Judd's phone fired quickly into life again and he answered it after a single ring. The name and image that lit up the screen were familiar. "Yasmin, Hi."

"Hi Judd."

"Is Mr. Mustard OK?"

"Yeah, he's fine, fast asleep in fact. Unlike me, Kadence and you it would seem."

"I'm not sure I can sleep again tonight to be honest. I dozed off a little earlier but it wasn't for long. Why are you calling?"

"As it turns out, Kadence, is not only the most sexiest woman on the planet but she also has the brains of Einstein."

"Sounds like she's a keeper, Yasmin."

"Well, you never know. I could do worse, I guess," Yasmin winked at her new girlfriend which inspired Kadence to blow her a kiss. "Listen, Judd. She's tried to make sense of your Ouija board experience, you know, all the stuff that you told us about earlier. Did you tell us everything by the way?"

"Yes, I think so. Well, the highlights anyway."

"Go over it again, please. One more time and this time don't leave anything out."

"OK, I'll try. Well, we did a Ouija board and it spelled out a few numbers, words and names. We had the numbers 1-6-1-2 spelt out which I took to be a year, 1612, which I know was the year of the Pendle witch trials."

"OK, that's worth knowing, go on."

"We got the word OLD spelt out, I took this to be Old Demdike who was again connected to the witch trials, although why she would come through while we are here in Merseyside I can't explain."

"This is precisely something that Kadence may be able

to shed light on, but carry on for now."

"OK, we had another couple of names come through, you know spelt out on the board: Eva and Joshua. Joshua it seems was the young lad who was involved in the Crank Caverns legend and Eva it seems was killed in this very house. The name Simone came through, but we can explain that one, then do you know what Yas? The name Hunter came through. I fear that Hunter may be dead."

"I hope not Judd, but if he is dead he would have been killed in Liverpool, right?" Yasmin and Kadence's eyes connected.

"I guess so. That looks most likely," answered Judd, not quite sure where Yasmin was going with all this.

"Who is Simone?"

"I think that name came through to a girl we have with us called Isla. The name was significant to Isla."

"OK, interesting. Did anything come through naming places or buildings in Wales or the north-east of England."

"Not that I'm aware of. "

"Are you sure?"

"Yes, nothing significant I'm sure about Wales," Judd ran his fingers through his hair and his eyes looked left as he searched his memory. "Nor the north-east of England as far as I can recall either. Why do you ask?"

Isla had overheard both her's and Simone's name mentioned. Taking a more vested interest in the telephone conversation, she approached Judd. "Judd, may I speak with your friend?"

Judd had mellowed a little towards, Isla. He knew he shouldn't blame her if Hunter was dead. "Sure, I'll place it on loudspeaker. Yasmin, I have Isla listening in now."

"Hey, Isla. My phone is on speaker too so Kadence can hear us."

"Hey," said Kadence.

"Hey. Listen, you may want to know that when Judd fell asleep, Elvis and me decided to do another Ouija board."

"You crafty pair of bastards," said Judd.

"Did anything come through?" asked Yasmin.

"It did, and it was a bit scary to be honest so we didn't do it for long. Even Elvis got scared and he thinks he is the hardest man on the planet."

"The hardest man on the planet is sitting right next to you, Isla."

"My Uncle Richie may dispute that."

"Let's hope there's never a need to find out one way or the other. So tell me, what happened? Why was it so scary?"

"At first it was OK, but it was very sad. We didn't get a name but we got four letters spelt out. "B-A-B-Y."

"Baby?"

"Yes, baby. If it was a dead baby that came through it is very sad. I had a family member go missing as a very young girl, she's presumed dead now I guess, and the name Simone as you know came through earlier. That was her name, the girl's, but it was also my cousin's name. My cousin killed herself. Simone was her little girl. I wondered if it could have been her, but she was a little older than a baby."

"I'm very sorry to hear this, Isla. It all sounds really sad. Did anything else come through?"

"There was then a name that came through: Jones, but that name means nothing to me."

"Jones, that's primarily a Welsh name, right?" Yasmin looked at Kadence as she spoke. Kadence nodded and took to the search engine on her own phone as she attentively listened to the conversation unfold. "Anything else?" asked Yasmin.

"Arran."

"Aaron?"

"A-R-R-A-N. Arran."

"Oh right, I'm not familiar with that spelling."

"It's not a name, it's a river I think."

"It is, shouted Kadence. "And guess where? Wales."

"Really?" said Yasmin and Isla in unison.

"Did you get a date with this one?" asked Kadence.

"Yeah," said Isla, "A year I think. 1876."

Kadence placed down her phone and followed the line on the map that she had drawn, representing her suspected Ley line, going into Wales. "Dolgellau Police Station."

"Huh," said Yasmin.

"The line leads us to the Old Dolgellau Police Station. It's not too far away from Barmouth in North Wales. Listen to this that I've found on the web...*the most notorious person ever to be held in the Old Police Station of Dolgellau was a Cadwaladr Jones who was arrested after claiming to find dismembered body parts of Sarah Hughes along the riverbanks of the river Arran, near Dolgellau. Jones knew his victim through the domestic service she provided at his father's house. The murder was extremely gruesome and was even more tragic when the surgeon who examined her body discovered that she had been pregnant.*"

"Pregnant? Oh my word, that could possibly explain why the word 'baby' came through to you, Isla," said Yasmin.

"Yes, I guess it could. There wouldn't necessarily be a name given to an unborn child, so the word baby was provided through the Ouija board and Cadwaladr Jones may have simply been revealing, probably bragging, who the killer had been and an additional life that he had taken. What a bastard."

"Well that bastard hung for it in 1877," said Kadence. "It was Dolgellau's first execution since a murder that had occurred in 1812 when a maid had been murdered."

"OK, this is all tying in with what Kadence is exploring here," said Yasmin. "She has laid down a map and plotted a ley line using a ruler and pen. So far it has pinpointed locations for the Crank legends, Malkin Tower associated with the Pendle Witches trials and now the Old Police Station in Dolgellau. They are all in line with one another. She also thinks Liverpool could be on the same ley line."

"My friend was killed earlier by Hunter outside my

uncle's club," said Isla,

"Killed by Hunter?" Yasmin was beyond shocked.

"Accidentally I guess, not that that makes it any easier," replied Isla. "He provided her with some dodgy coke."

"So that's why Judd and you lot are where you are. You were run out of town?"

"Yes, that's true for your friend, Judd, and the others, but I wasn't ran out of town. Judd, has kidnapped me to hold me as ransom for my uncle." Isla's tone was becoming increasingly hostile.

Yasmin stopped short of apologising for her boss's behaviour, although she was disturbed by the revelation. She figured Judd had his reasons for his actions. "This sounds complicated but I take it Hunter isn't with you?"

"No, my uncle has him." Yasmin closed her eyes and felt the pieces of the jigsaw fall into place. She didn't speak her thoughts aloud, but this confirmed to her that Hunter must be dead. She stayed on topic but still managed to guide the conversation away from the more confrontational elements. "So anyway, regarding this ley line theory, did anything come through on the Ouija board for the area by the River Tyne or anything in the north-east?"

"No, quite the opposite, actually," said Isla.

"What do you mean?"

"Well, I am aware of ley lines and how they connect buildings via their electromagnetic energy."

"You sound as clever as Kadence is Isla."

"I doubt it. Anyway, your theory doesn't really add up because we got three clear words and a date: R-I-P-P-E-R, ripper, and the name Jack. J-A-C-K."

"Jack the Ripper," blurted out Judd. "And you're telling us this now. That's pretty amazing if Jack the Ripper came through to you. What was the date?"

"1888," replied Isla.

"That links in," said Judd. "But Jack's murders took place in Whitechapel, London. They can't fit into the ley line you speak of Yasmin."

"Damn, that's true," said Yasmin. "I really thought Kadence was on to something."

"Maybe I still am," said Kadence. "Listen to this, courtesy of my search engine and a few key words that I entered: *Jane Beadmore's body had been disfigured almost beyond recognition. In the days following his arrest it became apparent that Waddell had become obsessed with the killings in Whitechapel of Jack the Ripper and had vowed that he would also commit a crime that would attract horrific details*."

"Blimey, they never did catch Jack the Ripper and there are theories that suggests that he came from Liverpool," said Judd.

"That is true, but if this is our Jack, or merely a copycat, he wasn't from Liverpool or London as it happens," said Kadence. "Waddell was hanged at Durham Gaol in the North East of England after brutally ripping his victim apart at Ouston Waggonway. Well, this clinches it for me. Your Ouija board is conjuring up victims of deaths that should never have occurred all along this ley line. However, just be mindful that with a Ouija board there's always the risk of trapping the odd evil spirit or two along the way."

"Thanks for the information, Kadence," said Judd. "It's amazing stuff and I'm really grateful that you've taken the time to make some sense of all of this for us. Especially at this hour!"

"It's a pleasure," said Kadence. "However, I now think it's time that I devote some attention to my new girlfriend. I think she's feeling a little neglected."

Yasmin playfully flicked Kadence the middle finger.

"Fair enough. Really though, I mean it. Thanks for all your help," said Judd. "Bye for now."

"Bye."

As Isla passed the phone back to Judd he could see that Yasmin had cleared at the other end and the call had finished. However, his phone wasn't done yet and it rang straight away. He was surprised to discover that it was Brooke.

"Hey Brooke, thanks for getting back to me. I guess you had a change of heart, huh. Did you give my little princess a kiss from her daddy?"

Brooke's tone was frantic. "Judd, Billie is missing. And so is Efan. What are we going to do?"

CHAPTER 21
YOU CAN SLEEP WHILE I DRIVE

Efan looked in his rear-view mirror and cast an eye over the small child sleeping soundly in her car seat. It was a scene that had played out many times before with Efan driving Billie around the local streets in a bid to send her off to sleep. Billie, along with her strong determination, often had other ideas though. She repeatedly liked to fight bedtime. Ironic then that she should be sleeping soundly at this particular moment in time unaware of what Efan had planned for her. Incidentally, Efan took the child's strong will as a direct genetic reminder of her biological father - and he hated her for it.

Yet all Brooke ever saw was this superhero boyfriend doing marvelous things such as sending her princess off to sleep.

It could take time but ultimately it never failed, the soporific effect of the tyres rolling over the road. Except on this occasion it hadn't needed much effort at all, Billie had already been out for the count when Efan had lifted her from her cot only minutes earlier.

"That's it Honey, you stay asleep and it'll all soon be

over." Efan said this with an evil smile that he always kept well hidden from Brooke. "I've waited a long time for what's in store for you."

Efan also interpreted Billie's strong will as a sign that she could well be the chosen one.

He and his acquaintances understood the second coming was amongst them and this time it was a girl. As such the second coming needed to be stopped with no chances taken.

The current state of the world made Efan and the others who shared his views believe that their prophecy was indeed coming true. They had come about this belief and prophecy through studying the ingredients of history and current affairs, astrological charts and practices of witchcraft. Even the Bible had got a look in.

Man had turned upon man. Woman upon woman. Man upon Woman and Woman upon Man. Love Thy Neighbour – what a joke! Society was more selfish now than it had ever been. Blood was being shed at will. Wars were in situ, knife and gun crime were at an all-time high in any given city, and unprecedented catastrophes such as earthquakes were now also more common than ever before.

It was obvious to them that Satan was winning the battle.

But equally, that meant that everything pointed to the need for a reaction from Heaven. And the most logical reaction would naturally be the second coming of God in the form of Human.

Yes. The conditions for the second coming to claw back a more stable existence for God's creation and his associated flock was now.

They knew that the child had already been born. They knew it to be a girl and that she was in England.

They also knew then that any females that met the correct criteria had to be killed.

It was the only way to be sure that they could prevent

the balance of good from being restored. It was a mammoth task for the disciples of Satan to undertake, but they had their angels of death positioned everywhere. Blended within all walks of life, undetected, going about their Master's work.

There had been an alarming amount of tragic "accidents" in recent times concerning infant girls. Children had drowned – such a shame how an innocent trip to feed the ducks could lead to tragedy. Others had been hit by cars – a similar fate to Father Cullis.

And there had even been baby girls who had never got to see life outside of a hospital ward, courtesy of those loyal servants of Satan working in maternity hospitals.

But the plan had now evolved to becoming a mass slaughter. A celebration and offering to Satan. Disciples were to bring female children to the Church of Satan. And this Church was being hosted in the caverns of Crank. It would be a festival of death. The brainchild of Castiel.

In all honesty Efan had his doubts, not many, but some. Not that he would dare air his opinions to Castiel and the others. Questioning the masterplan would result in certain death for him let alone the infant girls.

Anyway, doubts or not, he was being paid handsomely for bringing Billie to the party and he needed the money. Efan had found himself to be in serious financial debt to some of the most ruthless gangsters in Britain, as well as through more legitimate methods.

His car business was in jeopardy as was the nice house he and Brooke shared. Brooke didn't have a clue of course, and soon this kid sitting in the back would become his meal ticket to fixing all of his problems and having Brooke all to himself. He never liked the idea of a little brat spawned by Judd Stone getting under their feet anyway.

Yes, for Efan Carruthers, life was about to get good.

Efan looked again into his rear-view mirror. Perfect, Billie was still fast asleep. He noticed a pair of headlights in the distance which rapidly got closer to the rear of the car.

Efan became more unnerved when the lights started flashing behind him. He put his eyes forward with the intent to put his foot down on the open road. Except it wasn't open.

Luckily he had moved his eyes forward in just enough time to slam his brakes on and try and avoid crashing into the car that was blocking the road.

He closed his eyes desperately hoping that metal wouldn't strike metal. He opened them again when he realised he had been successful in stopping without incident.

"Shit," he said to himself as he thought about the man-shaped dent left at the front of the car by Father Cullis. "The police must be onto me."

The car behind still had its headlights on full beam and this distorted the image that stepped out of the vehicle. A few steps later, the figure emerged out of the stream of light and appeared at the passenger door. When the door wouldn't open due to the car's inbuilt automatic locking facility, glass soon shattered everywhere as the butt of a gun enabled access. In actual fact, Efan, was so scared he would have willingly pressed the release button which would have avoided such extreme action. Surely this wasn't normal procedure for police business was it?

"Hello Efan," came the raspy Birmingham accent through the broken glass. Efan now realised at once that it wasn't the police who had caught up with him on this chilly night, but instead it was much worse.

It was Ray Talia, the psychopathic gangster who Efan owed money too. The smashing of the glass had been a typical impatient action of the vicious man. Owing money to a man like Ray Talia was the biggest mistake of Efan's life. So far.

"And where are you going at this time of night, Efan? You weren't leaving town to try and get away from me now were you? Were you hoping to run away from your little debt?"

"On the contrary Ray. I'm going to get some money for you and then we can be all square."

"Really, so what are you planning to do? Work a nightshift somewhere? I'm not sure a single night's work would generate enough money for what you owe me, boy."

"I can't really tell you what I have planned, Ray, but please just trust me. Give me a day or two and I swear I'll have your money."

"Yeah, yeah Efan, I've heard it all before. Tick tock, tick tock, tick tock. The thing is your time is up."

"Please Ray, I'm not lying. I can get you the money."

Talia took a glance at the back seat and spotted the sleeping baby. Amazingly the sound of broken glass hadn't woken Billie. "Well, what have we got here?"

Talia stuck his arm through the smashed window, reached for the latch of the rear car door, opened it and bent over Billie. Before unbuckling Billie's car seat he pointed his gun at Efan as a warning not to intervene. He lifted the sleeping child into his arms and moved back to the open window to speak to Efan.

"OK Efan, this is your final warning. You have just forty-eight hours to get me my money or the kid gets it."

"You don't understand, I need the child to get the money."

Talia became incensed. "What have you got planned? If you're a fucking nonce I'll kill you right here and right now you lousy piece of shit."

"No, no it's nothing like that. I promise you, Ray."

"Well in that case the kid is coming with me and you have forty seven hours and fifty nine minutes to get me my money. No money, no kid. Simple enough for you?"

Efan nodded.

"And then I'll decide if there will be no Efan either, but right now I'd say the odds don't look good for you."

CHAPTER 22
MONEY FOR NOTHING

"Judd. Judd! Hello. Are you still there? Can you hear me?" asked an extremely anxious Brooke.

Almost one hundred miles away, Judd Stone, despairingly looked down at his mobile phone realising that the battery had just died at the most devastating time possible. Only moments earlier he had come to learn that his daughter was missing.

Worse still, he had no idea what to do about it.

"Has anyone got a signal on their phone?"

The universal reply was 'no' as his friends checked the small amount of phones that were present in the group.

"Fuck. Has anyone got a charger?"

The response was exactly the same.

"Looks like this storm has now even compromised any network for the socials too," said Rufus.

"Shit."

"What's wrong, Judd?" asked Paris sympathetically.

"My daughter is missing. I need to get out of here and find her."

"You can't Judd, this storm is still much too fierce,"

said Diego.

Judd knew that Diego's words were true, Merseyside was still in the eye of the storm that was only beginning to inch further south.

"I've got to do something."

"Do you have any idea where she could be?" asked Madonna.

"No, none at all, but I do know that Brooke's dickhead of a boyfriend is also missing."

"Well perhaps he has just taken her somewhere?" said Rufus. "There may be a very innocent explanation."

"Where the fuck would he be taking her in the middle of the night without telling Brooke?" snapped Judd. "I've never trusted that slimy fucker."

"It's weird that they are both missing," added Diego.

"I don't give a shit about Efan, but I want my daughter back and now I haven't even got a phone that fucking works. I'm just stuck here paralysed in this fucking shithole."

"Judd, you need to calm down, mate. I can't begin to understand how you are feeling but losing your head won't solve anything."

Judd put his head in his hands knowing that Diego was speaking sense once again. "I just feel so fucking useless, Diego."

"You owe Ray Talia money! Are you insane, Efan? Ray Talia is Birmingham's most dangerous gangster," said Brooke.

"I needed the money and I had no other choice or nowhere else to go. The business has been suffering lately."

"No matter how bad things get you don't borrow money from someone like Ray Talia, because when you owe him money he does things like kidnap children. If Billie is hurt in any way, I swear I'll kill you Efan. How could you be so stupid?"

"Relax, Brooke. Talia is a psychopath but he is old school. He wouldn't harm a child; he is just holding her until I get him the money."

"I wish I could share your confidence, Efan. Ray Talia is not my idea of a satisfactory childminder for my kid. If Judd was here…"

"There you go again. Judd, Judd, Judd."

"He is Billie's father whether you like it or not," said Brooke.

"I'm that little girl's dad and you know it."

"I know that she is being held captive by a crazed gangster because of to you. Not exactly Dad of the year criteria is it? And anyway, what were you doing driving about in the middle of the night with her? I really panicked when you were both missing."

"She woke up so I took her for a drive to try and get her back off to sleep."

"Funny, I didn't hear her wake."

"Well I did. Perhaps you're not the great mom that you like to think you are." With those words Brooke struck Efan hard across the face causing his head to jolt to the side. As he brought his head back Brooke saw a change in Efan's eyes that she didn't recognise.

"Right, let's cut to the chase. If you want to see your brat again I need money."

"A brat now is she? What happened to you being Superdad?"

"Your violence just got me angry that's all."

"Or did it trigger you to express how you really feel about Billie?"

"Money. Now."

"What are you talking about?"

"I know that Stone sends you money every month and you squirrel it away in an account for Billie."

"That money is for when she goes to university or needs it for something in the future. It's her money not mine."

"It's in your name as her parent so you can easily get it for me. She doesn't need a nest egg just yet does she? In fact, if things had gone to plan, she wouldn't be needing one at all. But I on the other hand need that money and I need it now. I'm getting very impatient with you, Brooke."

"You really don't care about Billie, do you? My God my eyes have been opened tonight. And what do you mean she wouldn't need the money at all if things had gone to plan? I don't know you at all do I Efan? Are you actually capable of hurting my little girl?"

An inane grin spread across Efan's face. "You really don't know the half of it, my dear."

"What were you doing with Billie. Where were you taking her?"

"It really doesn't matter now does it, as Talia has her? Ironically, she's probably safer with him than me right now. Of course, at first I fancied you, who wouldn't? And the brat was part of the package, I knew that, but then when I realised that her birth dates aligned with the birth of the second coming my position became very advantageous indeed, and I realised that it was *He* who had led me to you. It must have been his will. I had waited so long and so patiently for everything to be realised and then Talia stepped in to ruin everything."

"You're fucking insane. Second coming? What are you talking about? Billie's just a little girl and you think God sent you to me?"

Efan laughed like a hyena. "Not God. Satan."

Brooke took a step back. "Efan, you're scaring me now. Billie really is just a normal little girl."

"Maybe, maybe not. Just shut up and get me the money so I can pay off Talia then you can get your brat back from him. Just see it as using her money to get her back. Simple really."

"You're a monster. How am I supposed to get the money at this time of night?"

"Don't act so dumb. I know you do online banking.

Simply move it into my account and while you're at it you can empty that other account that I also know you have. I may not be able to fulfil my obligation to Satan but at least I will have enough money to get away and make a fresh start."

"What are you talking about? We have a joint account, you know that."

"Which I have already depleted, thank you very much, but I know that you have another account and a few ISAs in your name. You always were a secretive little bitch."

"How do you know?"

"I made it my business to know. Where I was taking Billie and to who I was taking her to would have got me my money, but now things have changed. So now that your precious little daughter has let me down it's up to you now Brooke to help me out."

"Were you going to sell her or something?"

"Something like that. Use your imagination. If she was potentially the second coming of God in Human form, what would I, a confessed Satan worshipper, possibly have had in mind for her?"

"You're evil as well as insane. You're worse than Talia. Much worse. To think I've been sharing a bed with you. And how do I know once she is returned that you won't take her to wherever you were taking her to all over again?"

"I guess you will just have to trust me. Now for the last time get me my money," Efan's demand was accompanied by him grabbing hold of Brooke and shaking her. She desperately attempted to fight back with punches, scratches and kicks to good effect, but ultimately Efan was too strong for her and she fell over in the scuffle.

As she fell she hit her head on the corner of the table and instantly lost consciousness.

A deflated Efan felt like he still wouldn't be getting hold of any money in the near future.

Brooke looked dead as blood trickled from her temple.

"Thanks for agreeing to come with me, Diego," said Judd as he steered the psychedelic Rolls Royce down the M6 Motorway in the direction of Birmingham.

"What are friends for, mate? Once I knew you were determined to head out into the storm, regardless of how dangerous it could be, I couldn't let you go alone. Besides, we need to find that beautiful little girl of yours."

"You're a good mate, Diego. We seem to have left the worst of the rain behind us. We should be with Brooke in about half an hour and then I can try and ascertain where Billie might be."

"We'll find her, Buddy. Keep the faith."

"I've got to believe that she'll be OK, Diego. I couldn't survive without her."

With Brooke out of action, Efan, still desperate to get some money, took to ransacking the house. If that deceitful bitch could keep accounts from him who's to say that there isn't any real hard cash stored away somewhere within these four walls.

He had played the part of being the man of Brooke's dreams to perfection, yet he knew that she had never fully trusted him when it came to finances. Although she had fell in love with him and could never have imagined the reality of Efan's intentions, Efan sensed that Brooke would always look out for two people ahead of him, and that would be herself and Billie.

And having that tosser, Judd, hanging around like a bad smell was something he had never been comfortable with either.

Efan frantically pulled up carpets and split open sofas and mattresses looking for money. He smashed vases on the floor instead of simply looking inside them. He was like a man possessed, desperate to find any trace of hidden cash.

As things evolved, Efan somehow found the presence

of mind to decide that he wasn't going to pay Talia even if he were to find any cash. He didn't care about Billie and now Brooke was dead he would definitely use the money to get away and make a brand new start.

He also realised that he could yet be traced to the killing of that stupid priest, Cullis, so getting as far away as possible made perfect sense.

A new start in a new country, that's what was needed.

Efan had also failed to get Billie to Crank, therefore if Billie was the child of the second coming, unless Talia did harm her by default, she remained alive and that wouldn't please Castiel either.

Yet despite all of his frantic efforts, Efan, hadn't even found a single penny. Perhaps his desperation had clouded his senses. Who keeps money in the house these days anyway?

Perhaps he should try to access her accounts instead by cracking her passwords. They should be easy enough to decipher, Brooke would use something simple connected to her favourite people or things, like Billie1 perhaps.

Or maybe even Stone1. His paranoia was increasing by the second.

Efan scanned the room looking for Brooke's laptop computer and as he did so he spotted the aquarium, quickly evaluating that it may just have a double purpose. He rushed over to the fish tank and wheeled it to one side. The wall had a natural raw brick design absent of any plaster and decoration. He looked at the wall and realised that his hunch seemed correct, the tank had been shielding a section of bricks that were not cemented. Efan swiftly removed two of them and straight away he could see the main bulk of a brown paper bag that had previously been concealed.

Efan hastily discarded the other surrounding loose bricks and grabbed the bag which was bulging sweetly at its sides.

Looking inside his eyes lit up. Bingo! It was indeed full

of cash. He estimated that the money ran into thousands of pounds. He also fathomed that although there was a princely sum at hand, it still wasn't enough to pay Ray Talia what he owed him anyway. However, there was certainly enough to get him out of the country and make his fresh start.

Clearly, Satan must be looking after him.

Then suddenly he heard a groaning sound from across the room. Brooke was moving.

She was alive.

Efan kept the bag of money secure in his right hand and picked up one of the bricks with his left.

Subconsciously, he thought he noticed light stream across the room, but it didn't really register as he was so intent on making his way towards Brooke.

He lent over her and could see that she still wasn't fully awake. Her eyes were yet to open, but she was groaning and stirring. Full consciousness couldn't be far away.

"I'm sorry Brooke, but I can't leave any loose ends here," and with those words he raised the brick above his head, ready to drive it down onto the face of the woman he had claimed to love, in a bid to callously finish her off.

And that was when he felt the breath rush out of him as a strong and unexpected force smashed into his side.

Efan only realised what was happening when he looked into the eyes that hovered above him. They belonged to Judd Stone and Efan felt the weight of his archenemy pinning him to the floor.

Then he felt excruciating pain as Judd punched him again and again.

CHAPTER 23
HANDS OFF...SHE'S MINE

"Good morning, Ray. Long time no see."

"Well, look who it is. Judd Stone. My sister is currently sunning herself on a Spanish beach, she fancied a little holiday so here I am running things all by myself. No rest for the wicked aye?"

"I haven't come to see Gia. It's very much you I've come to see and you had better hope that you can help me."

Gia Talia was an on-and-off old flame of Judd's. A captivatingly attractive and dangerous woman who got the lion's share of both beauty and brains compared to her psychopathic brother.

"I'm not sure I like your tone, Stone." One of Talia's heavies stepped forward as he spoke, but Talia raised a hand to halt the intervention.

"And I'm not sure that I like the fact that you've taken my kid."

Talia looked confused. "What are you talking about?"

"You have my daughter Billie, and if there's a single hair harmed on her head, Talia, I don't give a shit who you are I'll fucking kill you. I'll happily lose my life but know this, I'll take you down with me, and I promise you it will be the end of your days."

"Judd, you need to calm down. I can see you're considerably upset and for that I'm willing to allow your comments to pass. But not for much longer I won't, so bear that in mind. Now listen, I don't have your kid."

"Did you or did you not stop a car in the middle of the night and take the child from it?"

"Yes, but that kid isn't yours, it belongs to some lowlife called Efan who owes me money."

"Efan is Brooke's live in lover, or rather was. It was his car that was taking Billie my daughter for a drive."

The penny seemed to dropped for Ray Talia. "Well fuck me sideways. I had no idea. Why didn't the little shit say anything? Judd, I would never have taken her knowing that she was your kid."

"And if Gia was here still running things, I doubt the mistake would have been made in the first place. The bottom line is you have taken my child in order to hold another guy to ransom. Now I'm telling you that you need to give her back to me."

"And what about my money? This Efan character still owes me big time."

"Holding *my* kid isn't going to get it you."

Talia turned to another one of his heavies. "Go and get the kid." Within a couple of minutes Billie was reunited with her father looking none the worse for her ordeal.

"I may be a dangerous man, Judd, but I'm disappointed that you could even think that I could hurt a kid. We old school gangsters have certain codes of conduct when it comes to certain things, she was only a bargaining tool to squeeze out what Efan owed me. She's been well looked after, I can assure you."

"Are you expecting me to say thank you?"

"My sister would never forgive me for this if she knew. For some reason she's always had a soft spot for you,

Stone. I don't think she needs to know about our little misunderstanding, do you? Look, how can I make it up to you, Judd?"

Judd thought for a few seconds as he kissed the head of his precious daughter who was now safely in his arms. "There are a couple of things you can do actually?"

"A couple of things? Really. You're pushing it now, Stone. But go on."

"Follow me to the car, Ray."

Diego and one of Talia's heavies shot each other a telling look as he and Talia stepped towards Judd. This was still a tense situation that was yet to play out.

Judd held his daughter close as he led the way out of Talia's property to the car. The same car that Efan had been driving when it ran over Father Cullis hours earlier.

Judd figured that it would be a swifter and more inconspicuous ride than the psychedelic Rolls Royce. When he opened the boot the need for being inconspicuous was plainly evident.

"Is that Efan?" asked Talia. "His face looks like piece of meat. I can hardly recognise him."

"It's him all right."

"Is he dead?" asked Talia.

"As a dodo," answered Judd. "My first favour is I'd like you to get rid of this stinking corpse for me. I presume that you have many tried and tested ways in your line of business."

"You presume correctly. But wait a second. If he's dead, which I no doubt believe that he deserves to be, then he has nevertheless died owing me money. So what now?"

"There's some legal wrangling to be done, but again I presume that you and Gia can sort it out considering the kinds of people you have on your payroll and in your back pockets." Judd reached into his pocket and dangled a pair of keys in front of Talia. "Here."

"What are these for?"

"The keys to Efan's car dealer business. Well to the

Birmingham branch anyway. There will be keys for other sites across the UK. You and Gia can add car sales to your business enterprises and make more money than this dead piece of shit could ever owe you."

"Isn't Brooke his next of kin?"

"She is, seems he had no family and the cheeky bastard thought he could have mine. I've already discussed it with her. She wants nothing more to do with Efan including his businesses. It's all yours. Considering that you have held my daughter for a good many hours, I'd say that me handing this to you on a plate seems quite a generous offer in the circumstances."

"Fair enough. I accept the proposition, Judd. Now, what's the second favour?"

A mischievous smile crept across Judd's face.

CHAPTER 24
A DIFFERENT CORNER

"So you're a bit of a Wham! fan?" asked Andrew Baker aka George Michael.

"Just a bit," replied Tilda. "As you can tell I'm a woman of a certain age so I was around when it all began. I was smitten from the start."

"I hope my representation of George is good enough for a dedicated fan such as yourself. In truth, I know I can never match him for singing ability but I like to pay my own personal tribute to him. I'm a tribute artist not an impersonator. The real George Michael was an amazing talent."

"You're keeping his music and memory alive, Andrew. That's the important thing, and from what I've seen your tribute is more than adequate. What's more surprising is how Judd managed to pull off a half-decent Andrew Ridgeley."

"Ha ha, yes he did quite well didn't he? He saved my bacon to be honest. I still haven't got the balls to do a solo George act. I need someone on stage with me sharing the pressure."

"I'm hoping Judd can find a way to save your bacon again. Mine too for that matter."

"This Mercer guy does seem a nasty piece of work."

"I won't deny that, but I have *Faith* in Judd that he will think of something. No pun intended."

"Maybe we shouldn't wait for Judd's intervention."

"How do you mean?"

"Well who knows what this dude has really got planned for us even if he does get his niece back. I mean, look what happened to Hunter right before our very eyes. I think we need to try and escape."

"If we do that, he will definitely kill us."

"Only if he catches us."

"I don't know," said Tilda. "I don't fancy our odds against Mercer and his band of merry men. In case you hadn't noticed, I'm not exactly built for running either. Besides he had a much clearer motive to kill Hunter. I say we wait it out."

Suddenly Andrew Baker did an impromptu display of his finest jazz hands. "That's a shame because I've just managed to finally wriggle my way out of these ropes. Now please don't tell me that you don't want me to untie you."

Despite what she had just said, Tilda didn't hesitate. "Well that changes everything. I think staying put now would be a tad foolish in the circumstances. It's a bit surreal that I find myself saying this: Come on, untie me Mr. George Michael."

Richie Mercer was sitting in his office finishing off a whisky. He was comfortable drinking spirits at any time of the day including morning time. He moved the glass and watched the swirling liquid meander in between the ice before taking his final swig.

"Flint, go and check on our two hostages in the basement. Now that the storm seems to be clearing, me and a few of the other boys are gonna head up to Crank. I want you to stay behind and keep an eye on them and things in general. I need to visit that place to see if I can get any idea of what happened to my two princesses. Not to mention that I also need to locate Isla. I'm not going without back up so I've called a few of the boys in."

"Sure thing, boss." Flint made his way down the corridors and stairs to the basement and eventually opened the door.

"Now!" shouted Tilda and before Flint knew what was happening to him, Andrew Baker brought a chair down on his head sending the sizeable thug crashing to the floor. Tilda moved quickly to tie his hands behind his back before he could gain consciousness.

"Ready?" asked George.

"Ready."

Pretty soon they were running out of the same door that Flint had only just entered through.

"What the F…" said an astonished Richie Mercer when he caught sight of two unlikely figures running out of his establishment courtesy of his CCTV camera. "The cheeky bastards have managed to escape. Barney, John, get after them."

"Are we heading to anywhere in particular," asked a breathless Tilda.

"You know Liverpool better than me," answered George. "I'm just running away. It's as simple as that. Trouble is those two goons are gaining ground on us.

"Turn the corner here, they may not notice and therefore carry on straight ahead."

As they turned the corner, a top of a church came into view at the far end of the very straight street that they entered. It was the type of church top that resembled a castle with a single cubic tower complete with battlemented parapet and a pinnacle erected on each of the tower's uppermost corners. The sides of the tower that were in view revealed a clock face on each of them, giving the impression that such a clock must be situated on all four sides of the brown-coloured construction.

George Michael instinctively looked for a street sign and he soon found one nestled high against old red brickwork. It sat between sash windows that were positioned either side of it. The black writing that protruded outwards from the white background of the thick metal sign revealed the street's name as being Bold Street.

Much of the architecture that flanked either side of Bold Street had been impressively crafted out of similar, if not the same, substance as the church. George took this to be sandstone.

"How are we going to get through these crowds and navigate the market stalls?" asked Tilda. "They're going to catch us, I know they are. I don't think I can run anymore."

"Just keep going, Tiida. We must keep going. You can do it."

Just a couple of steps later both Tilda and George felt a strange sensation wash over them. It was as if they had run through an invisible door which somehow was tangible yet not in existence all at the same time. Bright lights appeared for a millisecond and then they found themselves still to be in Bold Street. But suddenly things looked very different.

The crowds of people before them diminished in scale and they clearly became different people wearing different clothes. Most of the women were wearing mini-skirts and sported either beehive hairstyles or cloth hair bands across voluminous hairstyles of dyed blonde hair.

The men were dressed in suits and their hair was predominantly styled as mop tops or with the odd teddy boy quiff.

"There's not a Beatles festival this weekend is there?" asked George.

"Not that I know of. Besides, less than a minute ago

these hordes of Beatles and Brigitte Bardot clones were not present in this street. Please tell me you noticed this too, George?"

"Yeah I noticed it. We are either both going crazy or we are experiencing something very weird together. Real but weird."

Next they heard the sound of a vehicle horn honking behind them, and they quickly moved to the pavement realising that the pedestrianised area which they had previously ran into was now a working road.

Tilda and George looked on in puzzlement as the vehicle that had warned them away with its horn, turned out to be an industrial van of some description. Furthermore, it was clearly decades old in style, yet it looked practically brand new.

The two comrades now realised that the cars driving back and forth along Bold Street were also of the same era, looking very old fashioned in their style.

"What the fuck is happening here, Tilda?"

"I haven't the foggiest, but at least we have lost those pair of goons," answered Tilda.

"Yeah, that's true."

They began to walk along the street, feeling that the need to run was no longer necessary. Something strange had happened but at least they now felt safe.

"Look at the prices of those baby clothes in this shop window," said Tilda.

"You mean this store that wasn't here when we first entered the street?"

"Yes, that's the one. What is going on, George. Have you noticed how everything is labeled in prices of 'd', not in decimal pence or pounds. It's like we have gone back in time."

"Perhaps we have. Do you think we have entered a time slip."

"Do you have any other explanation?"

"Bloody hell. I was going to sing "Freedom" at first

when we seemed to have shook off those two boneheads of Mercer's, but now that song may not be appropriate. I'm concerned that we may be trapped here forever. In another time."

Tilda spotted a chap with a pile of newspapers he seemed to be selling from a kiosk. She strolled over and grabbed a copy of the *Liverpool Echo* and looked at the front page. The date read 30 August 1965.

"Oi, are you gonna buy that?" said the vendor in a strong scouse accent.

"Err, no thank you. Sorry."

Tilda turned to George Michael. "It's 1965, George. We are in 1965!"

George was speechless.

They walked on a bit further. "And now look at this book shop. Look at the sign above it and the style of its font. It looks so akin of the time."

"It certainly does," agreed George.

"In actual fact, this is all quite an amazing experience and we are safe, George. Let us be thankful for that."

George nodded.

Meanwhile back at the beginning of Bold Street, Barney and John looked at one another in confusion.

"Where the fuck did they go?" asked John.

"Fuck knows, Lad. It's as if they have disappeared into thin air."

CHAPTER 25
TWO TRIBES

"This is a pretty impressive convoy, Ray. When I said I'd like some muscle to tackle Richie Mercer, I wasn't expecting you to call in so many troops," said Judd.

"I know of Mercer's reputation. By all accounts he is to Liverpool what I am to Birmingham and if I'm gonna piss in his pool we need to be prepared. To be honest with you I didn't like the sound of him taking hold of the sister of your dear departed friend William. What's he doing picking on women for fuck's sake? It has given me a nice little excuse to have a showdown with Mr. Mercer once and for all. Did you know that he tried to muscle in on the Birmingham club scene not so long ago, the cheeky bastard. He got scared off but I never really felt that we taught him a good enough lesson for trying to claim a stake in Brum."

Judd, Talia, Diego and a fearsome looking driver called Tank led the procession of cars out of Birmingham and into Liverpool. The Aston Martin was now the third car Judd and Diego had travelled in during this very long and eventful night, having left the more awkward Rolls Royce behind. As for Efan's car, it had by now been crushed into a small block of metal, complete with Efan's remains being somewhere intertwined. In doing so it inadvertently meant that the car that had been used to kill Father Cullis would never be traced – but then again neither would Efan.

"OK, we're here," announced Judd.

Mercer was metaphorically caught with his pants down when the army of Birmingham Gangsters, along with Judd and Diego arrived. He was standing in the doorway of his club with no more than a handful of his heavies standing either side of him, which included the returning Barney and John, and a sore-headed Flint.

Not that Mercer was easily scared.

As the first car emptied, Mercer scowled as he immediately recognised Judd and Diego. Then not long after he recognised a third occupant from the car.

"Well, what do we have here? Ray Talia. Birmingham's finest. What brings you here along with these pair of chumps?"

"I believe you have something that belongs to them?"

"Really?"

"Really. A George Michael lookalike, a friend called Hunter and a lady named Tilda. Now, you holding the lady against her will particularly made me feel a little, shall we say, perturbed, Mercer."

"Perturbed?"

"Correct. Perturbed. Holding ladies hostage. Not very nice is it?" The irony seemed to be lost on Talia that he had not long been holding an infant child hostage.

"The thing is, these two chumps have something of mine. My niece. So I agree, holding ladies hostage is not nice at all."

Judd spoke next. "Give me the three people who Ray has just mentioned and I will take you to your niece. I can assure you that Isla is fit and well."

When Mercer hesitated to respond Talia jumped in. "Is there a problem, Mercer? It's an easy enough transaction."

"There is a slight problem as it happens, yes."

"Go on."

"I had to kill the bastard called Hunter."

"Why?" asked Judd, feeling his fists clench.

"Well, in addition to the piece of scum being responsible for the death of my best barmaid and friend of my niece, I then discovered something very unsavoury about him."

"Takes one to know one," quipped Talia.

"Doesn't it just, Talia," batting the insult straight back. "He mocked me about the disappearance of my little grandchild. He knew something about it and I wasn't about to let that go now, was I?"

"Hunter?" said Diego.

"Bullshit," said Judd in disbelief.

"If you're calling me a liar then it's the last words you're ever going to speak," and in that instant Mercer pulled out a gun which resulted in at least a dozen being pulled on him by Talia's entourage.

"Don't be silly, Mercer. My boys will shoot you down right here in your own backyard if you don't behave yourself," said Talia.

"Bring it on," said a defiant Mercer.

"If you fetch me Tilda and George Michael right now, I may look a little more carefully at your extraordinary claim about the dead guy," said Talia.

"Where are they?" asked Judd.

"They're not here?" answered Mercer.

"If they are also dead then you won't need Ray and his boys to gun you down because I'll tear you apart with my own bare hands."

"Relax. They aren't dead, they're just, well missing. But I advise you not to push me unless you really do want to end up like your lowlife pal, Hunter."

"Why should we believe what you are saying is true?" asked Judd.

"Because it is," came a familiar lady's voice.

Judd's eyes widened. "Tilda. You're OK?"

"Where the fuck did you two go?" said Mercer. "At least you've had the good sense to return. You thought better of trying to give me the slip, huh? You realised that I wouldn't be too impressed?"

"Hardly," said Tilda. "George and me had well and truly given you and your two goons the *slip*. More successfully than you could ever imagine, actually. We got as far as St Luke's Church and then I managed to spot Judd in a car heading this way, so we figured the safest thing would be to reconnect with, Judd."

"So, you gave two of my men the slip and knocked another of my hardest men unconscious. Is this true Flint?" asked Mercer.

"They jumped me man," said Flint appearing embarrassed.

"We are talking about a woman and a George Michael lookalike, Flint. Not a couple of heavyweight boxers. Barney and John, I'm not too impressed with you either."

"Your boys not up to much, aye Richie?" Talia's taunting caused a ripple of laughter amongst the Birmingham contingent.

"Keep pushing and you'll find out just how effective my boys can be," the two gangsters stared into one another's eyes. Neither one flinching for even a brief moment. Mercer continued. "So anyway, it looks like you have your two companions back. So now I'd like to see my niece?"

"She's not here but she is safe," said Judd.

"I only have your word for that."

"She's in a house near Crank."

"Near Crank caverns?"

"Yes," said Judd, noticing a fresh sense of attentiveness in Mercer.

"We are just on our way there now. At least we were until you Muppets showed up."

"Really?" said Judd, mellowing his tone even further.

"Your granddaughter was called Simone wasn't she? Isla told me. Isla's a nice kid to be honest with you, she really is being well looked after."

"Yes, that's right. Simone. And your lowlife mate Hunter knew all about her disappearance."

"Judd turned his attention to Tilda. "Are you and George really OK?"

"Yeah, we are fine. We weren't hurt to be fair and I'm afraid Hunter isn't the man you thought he was."

Judd looked to the floor, confused that Hunter could have warranted such decisive action against him by Mercer. But any denial that he harboured regarding his deceased friend was gradually becoming a sense of reality. He placed his eyes on Mercer. "OK, I'll take you to your niece, Richie, and then all this can go away?"

"Oh, you will take me to my niece, you've got that part right. But if you expect me to forget that you cheeky Brummie wankers dared to square up to me on my own turf then you're very sadly mistaken." As Mercer spoke more cars appeared either end of the street. "And here are the rest of my boys who are scheduled to accompany me to Crank. I'm not entirely sure what we are going to find there but I felt that there may be a need to have safety in numbers, especially if I am hunting down a nest of child killers."

Judd's stomach turned as he contemplated that Hunter, a friend whom he had known for decades, could possibly be a child killer.

The car doors opened and more mean looking Liverpudlians appeared. They too drew their guns and a standoff ensued.

Diego stepped in. "Look, we are not your enemy here and you're not ours either. It seems that we all need to head towards Crank for one thing or another."

"Diego's right," said Tilda. "If something sinister is happening up there then we are stronger together."

Judd spoke next. "Hunter was always a bit of a prick,

but him being involved in the disappearance of your granddaughter really fucking angers me to be honest. I'm ashamed that he was ever my friend.

"Look, we certainly have some common ground here, Richie. My own daughter was being taken somewhere earlier, courtesy of another prick called Efan."

"Efan?"

"Yeah, not that he's a problem anymore."

"A guy called Efan was contacting Hunter on his phone."

Judd looked puzzled. "I didn't think they knew one another."

"Efan ain't that common a name now is it? I bet he was going to Crank too, with your daughter. What the fuck goes on up there?"

"There could be a connection, I guess."

"If your kid is OK now, you're one of the lucky ones?"

"Stand your boys down, Ray," said Judd.

"No fucking way, he can stand his down first."

"Not fucking likely, lad," said Mercer. "And leave you lot with your guns pointing at us."

"So, what are your testosterone fuelled gangsters going to do?" interjected Tilda. "Stand here all day pointing guns at each other or worse still simply open fire resulting in multiple deaths? If that happens it will achieve nothing."

"Fair point," said Mercer. "Talia, tell one of your lads to point a gun at my head."

"What?" said Talia.

"You heard me, and Flint, you point your gun at his head. I assume you can manage to do that considering George Michael and a woman knocked you out?"

"Yes boss," said Flint and he did manage to do what he was instructed.

Talia decided to point his own gun straight at Mercer.

"That's OK, that will work. Now you, George Michael over there."

"Err, yeah."

"You use that beautiful voice of yours to count to three and on that count of three everyone on both sides of this coin puts their guns away apart from my friend Ray and Flint here."

"Do it," said Judd.

"OK, One. Two. Three," said George and all guns were lowered except for the two remaining guns.

"So far so good," said Mercer. "Now then my handsome looking troubadour, count to three again and Ray, you lower your gun and Flint will lower his at the same time. If either fails to comply we're simply going to have a blood bath here with Ray or myself being the first to have it spilled and neither of us wants that."

Judd Stone knew what a psychopathic individual Ray Talia could be and he wasn't overly confident that he would keep his side of the bargain here. "Ray, please do as he says. This makes perfect sense."

Talia just smiled, which Judd took to mean a variety of different things and not necessarily something that could end well.

George Michael counted once more. "One. Two. Three." Everyone breathed a sigh of relief as the remaining two guns were lowered in unison.

"Right then, now the handbags have been put away the lead car will be me, thee and him," announced Mercer picking out Talia and then Judd with the nod of his head each time.

"Right then, off to Crank we go," said Talia. "If there's one thing that unites us old school gangsters, Mercer, it's raining down justice on a bunch of fucking nonces."

CHAPTER 26
THE WINNER TAKES IT ALL

The landline telephone in Judd's flat rang out loudly until it was answered. "Hey Yas, is Kadence still with you?"

"Err yeah, hold on." Yasmin passed the phone to Kadence after shaking her awake. It had been an eventful night and there was a need to catch up on sleep even though it was now close to midday. "It's Judd for you." Then Yasmin's head hit the pillow once again.

"Hello, Judd."

"Hey Kadence, I've got you on loudspeaker, I'm in the car with a couple of, err, friends. One of them has kindly allowed me to use their phone."

Incidentally all networks were now back up and running since the storm.

"OK."

"We're on our way to Crank, you see, and I just wondered if your unusual knowledge on certain things may be able to help us."

"OK, I'll try."

"Thanks. For starters, remember when you told us earlier about the legend of the cannibalistic little people up there?"

"Yes."

"Well, is there anything else Crank is notorious for?"

The line went quiet for a few moments as Kadence searched her brain. "Erm, I'm not too sure."

"Think," said Judd. "Please. It could be really important."

"What about child killing?" asked Talia bluntly.

"Well, the legend has it that the little people did kill children, most notably Joshua's friends. But I believe that they would target anyone who entered the caverns, not only children."

"We have joined some dots and we think some sort of paedophile ring may be happening in Crank," said Judd.

"It's always possible, but that could be anywhere really. It's not something that I'd say is exclusive to Crank, if it's a thing there at all. I will say this though: those caves in Crank are very cold and dank and therefore would only appeal to those with a taste for the macabre."

"Like Satanists?" said Mercer.

"Yes, like Satanists. And Satanists I'm afraid can be linked to sacrificing children which would fall in line with your theory. Children are usually sacrificed as an offering to Satan in return for protection and prosperity."

Judd spoke next. "That house we were in near Crank. Where the others still are. There was a pentagram on the door."

"Really? Wow, that's a sure sign of witchcraft."

"And my Isla's still there?" growled Mercer.

"Don't worry, she's safe," said Judd.

"How can you be so sure?"

"Trust me, she's being well looked after," Judd hoped that there was no hesitancy in his answer to the Liverpudlian gangster, knowing he couldn't truthfully be one hundred per cent definite regarding Isla's safety. Keen to move on, he continued speaking with Kadence. "I think even my own daughter was on route to Crank."

"Really? That's terrible. Is she OK now?"

"Yeah, long story short she's home safe and sound."

"I don't think my granddaughter was so fortunate," said Mercer.

The line went quiet for another moment. "Are you still there, Kadence?" enquired Judd.

"Yeah, sorry. Something has just occurred to me. I could be wrong, but you've only mentioned female offspring. You're unaware of boys being taken?"

"Only the ones all those years ago from Joshua's story," answered Judd.

"What month was your daughter born, Judd?"

"June."

"When was your granddaughter born, Mister?"

"February. The name's Richie."

"So she was a Pisces?"

"Err, yeah that's right."

"OK, that figures."

"What's this all about?" asked Judd.

"I think they're hedging their bets. Sadly, if you look worldwide at both female infant mortalities and records of young girls going missing over the past few years, a spike is present for those born in either February or June. What's curious however, is that the deaths of babies have been decreasing in more recent times but the records of young girls, rather than actual babies going missing, have considerably increased."

"Why?"

"It's all to do with the belief that the second coming has occurred. It's a conspiracy theory of course, but certain followers of Satan believe this to be the case. Look at what is happening in the world. 2016 was an awful and unprecedented year regarding the deaths of well-renowned musicians. The Devil often plays a part in stories about music, right?"

"Yeah, that's true actually," said Mercer. "Musicians selling their souls at crossroads is a perpetual theme for example."

"Yeah, well since that awful year we have had tragedy upon tragedy. Unprecedented pandemics. Earthquakes – one happened just recently. The conditions have been perfect for the second coming to come and intervene for a few years now, so satanists have decided that it's necessary to cull female infants. They have tried desperately not to bring attention to what they are doing but the studies in numbers simply can't be ignored. They try to make it look as though the girls have simply disappeared or they try to make the deaths look like tragic accidents."

"So these street preachers have been right all along?" asked Judd.

"Yeah, if you believe the conspiracy theory."

"So why Pisces?" enquired Judd.

"It is believed that the first time around, the son of God: Jesus Christ, was born either in the month of February under the sign of Pisces or alternatively the month of June. So it seems that Satanists are taking no chances. Pisces is the sign of the fish. Wasn't Jesus the fisher of men? He performed the miracle of feeding the five thousand with fish too remember. It's a natural fit."

"OK, so that makes sense but what about June?"

"Personally, I actually think this one is a lot more compelling. We all know the story of the three wise men, right? But forget December 25th, that's just a convenient date that was chosen for Christmas day to fall on. Astrologers have pinpointed that a bright star, brighter than any ever seen before or since, led three wise men to baby Jesus two thousand years ago. But astrologers have discovered that this actually happened in June and not December."

"Well have we had such significant stars shine in recent years in the month of June?" asked Judd.

"Not exactly, but don't forget that the summer solstice happens every 21st June. I'd say any kids born on that day are especially in danger. On the day of the shortest night

Mercury, Venus, Mars, Jupiter and Saturn all line up in their distance from the sun. When this happens it can be a wondrous sight that fills the sky. However, the best views of this spectacle actually fall towards the middle and end of the month. I think these satanists really like to hedge their bets."

"So why a girl this time round?" asked Ray Talia, seemingly as intrigued as everyone else was.

"Hi. Sorry. Who's speaking now?"

"Hi. I'm, Ray."

"Hi Ray. Judd, Richie and Ray huh. I wonder, could you be the three wise men this time round?"

The three men looked at each other not quite knowing how to react.

"So why a girl?" asked Talia again.

"Why not?" said Kadence. "That's what the prophecy actually says, or one interpretation of it anyhow. If you take a look at the book of Revelation, you'll see mention of The Woman of the Apocalypse who escapes a dragon. This very dragon is thought to be Satan himself.

"The woman gives birth to a child but the child can be viewed as a clear representation for new life or a new age. Satan is cast out in the war of heavens but it's clear this dragon cannot defeat the woman. Hence why satanists are killing the young girls. They don't want to allow this second coming in a female form to defeat Satan."

"They're nuts," said Mercer.

"I tend to agree with you," said Kadence, "But whatever we may think it doesn't stop their beliefs and it doesn't stop their heinous actions. And maybe Crank is the perfect catalyst for something evil to take place. I told you those caverns are dark and perfect for any wicked activity."

"Thanks Kadence, you've been a great help," said Judd.

"You're very welcome, it's a shame that I'm not there with you. I feel that I could help some more."

"As valuable as your insight has been, Kadence, I wouldn't want you physically caught up with any of this."

"Yeah, leave it to us, the three wise men," said Talia.

But this type of adventure was becoming far too tempting for a psychic goth like Kadence. Ley Lines, pentagrams, Ouija boards, beliefs of the Messiah's second coming, such ingredients were cooking up an adrenalin rush like nothing she'd ever experienced before. There'd been one storm earlier but now a different type of perfect storm was brewing and she wanted to be firmly in the eye of it.

Once the phone exchange finished, Yasmin, sleepily groaned a question. "What the hell was that all that about?"

Kadence wasn't normally someone who was accustomed to telling lies. But this was an exceptional circumstance. "Your friend Judd wants us to go and meet him and his friends in Merseyside."

CHAPTER 27
HELLO

Earlier that morning.

Sleep had universally kicked in at the 'Big Brother and Sister' house.

Sensing a presence before him, Rufus, was first to stir from his slumber. As his eyes opened, he could see a white-bearded man looking straight at him.

"Father Christmas?"

"I'm sorry to disappoint you young fellow, it seems I may have awoken you from a pleasant dream about your childhood days. Castiel is the name and as I look around me, just like the bears from the Goldilocks tale, I'm interested to know who has been sleeping in my chair."

"Castiel?" asked Madonna, who was now also awake. "We found your record, Castiel and the Creatures of the Night."

"That record was made a long time ago my dear, as you can see, I've aged quite a bit to still be the lead singer of a Merseybeat band."

"Weird name for a band, Creatures of the Night?"

asked Elvis.

"It's how bands were named back then in Liverpool: Rory Storm and the Hurricanes, Gerry and the Pacemakers, Billy J Kramer and the Dakotas, even The Beatles were once known as Johnny and the Moondogs in a previous incarnation. I mean, what are Moondogs for Pete's sake? Werewolves? I don't think so do you? They were all simply fancy names chosen on trend that's all."

"OK, OK, we get it," said Elvis who was feeling a little irritated at Castiel's self-satisfying demeanour.

"So now you know my name I'd like to know all of yours, after all you are spread across my room."

No one rushed to answer. The reality was that they had broken into someone else's home and although not exactly feeling a profound sense of shame, they did all feel a bit like naughty children who had been caught with their hands in the biscuit tin.

Castiel was left to fill in the blanks for himself. "I think I can take an educated guess on what has happened here. I'm certain that there's a perfectly reasonable explanation for you breaking into my house and making yourselves comfortable. There was a dreadful storm last night wasn't there? You young guns needed to find some shelter and my humble abode must have presented itself to you as an ideal establishment for your needs. Of course, it was the storm that kept me away from returning to my own home last night, otherwise I would have welcomed you with open arms and maybe even dug out some hot chocolate for you."

"Well thanks for being so understanding, Castiel. My name's Rufus. Your summary of how we came to be here is pretty much spot on. However, the storm last night, as fierce as it was, didn't have much of a personal impact on me I have to say. When you've survived the Indian Ocean Tsunami of 2004 these kinds of storm seem like a trickle of rain in comparison." As Rufus spoke he fumbled for the gun that Judd had left in his safe-keeping, but his fingers were unable to connect with anything. He feared that it had been taken whilst he slept.

"Clearly you're a man of the world, Rufus, and a courageous one at that" said Castiel playing to Rufus's ego. "I can't help thinking that this recent storm was an aftershock of that dreadful earthquake in Asia. It's been a dreadful business altogether, the worst on record by all accounts. But again, not something that would phase you my friend, I'm sure."

"So what do you do now Mr. Castiel?" asked Madonna. "Now that you're no longer in the band?"

"Oh, I keep myself entertained, my dear. You can be sure of that."

There was a sudden sinister tone in the old man's voice and Madonna decided that she didn't want to delve any further. However, the ominous remark had the opposite effect on Paris. "So what's that pentagram all about on the door then?"

"You tell me, my dear. What do you see?"

"I dunno, it's a symbol of witchcraft, I guess. That's what I know pentagrams to usually be associated with."

The room felt an awkward silence as the recently found friends looked at one another, slightly embarrassed at Paris's line of questioning.

Castiel smiled. Although it was a smile that seemed to hold a level of menace to it. Or was that just the perception of everyone considering the circumstances? "I think you've been watching too many movies, my dear. If the pentagram is inverted it is indeed the Sigil of Baphomet,"

"The what?" interrupted Paris.

"The Sigil of Baphomet. In other words the sign of Satan's Church, but if it is not inverted it represents many good things in religions, such as Paganism or Christianity for example."

Paris stared inquisitively at the pentagram. "I don't know if it's inverted or not?"

"Well, let me assure you then that there's no need to worry, my dear."

A couple of others found themselves beginning to study the pentagram more intimately. The room fell into another awkward silence until their focus was interrupted by Castiel.

"So I'll seek my answer again. Who else do we have here scattered about my living room apart from Rufus and the inquisitive young lady."

Rufus did the honours. "Well you should know the young lady as Girl George, or Paris. Most of us here go by two names."

"Only my friend's call me Paris," interjected the tribute artist, who was still holding a sense of skepticism for the old man.

Rufus continued. "You can probably tell that some of us here are tribute artists by the way they're dressed. We also have Madonna and Elvis, and this is Isla, who isn't a tribute act at all though."

"Aah, tribute artists. You were at that event at the Liverpool Docks, I take it?"

"Yes that's right. I was the producer for the event, although I'm usually used to handling real stars, not their tribute acts."

"Really? Even though Elvis is no longer with us," said Castiel completely straight-faced.

Rufus turned a noticeable shade of red, but Castiel rescued the same man he'd embarrassed by continuing to speak. "Well we are very pleased to meet you all. I should also introduce you to my two companions, here we have Martha and Beatrix." Castiel was referring to the poker-faced looking women flanked either side of him.

"Identical twins, I see," acknowledged Rufus.

The two women didn't speak but simply nodded a single nod in creepy unison.

Two identical witches more like, thought Paris to herself.

"Why the Ouija board?" pressed Paris, like a dog with a bone.

"Have you been rooting through my personal things young lady?"

"Err, no it just kind of appeared."

Castiel smiled that smile again that seemed more sinister than sincere. "I'm just messing with you, my dear. No doubt you had to look for things in order to occupy your time. I've never used the Ouija board myself to be honest with you. It was already here when I purchased the house. Along with a book called *Paradise Lost,* an item that I presume has also presented itself to you."

Just then Elvis stood up which startled Castiel and his two funny-looking female companions, especially when his considerable size was now apparent. "Relax mate, I just need the bog."

Castiel managed a smile. "Of course, I'm sure you know where it is by now." Indeed Elvis did know where the toilet was and he made his way there not for the first time during his stay. As he emptied his bladder he began to share the same level of suspiciousness as Paris. This dude was weird. His band had a weird name, he sang in Latin for fuck's sake and those two old ladies definitely looked like a couple of witches if there was such a thing. And he too still wasn't convinced of the explanation of the pentagram. Inverted or not, who the fuck has one in their house?

He washed his hands and left the bathroom. He was soon presented with the staircase and he realised that no one had properly looked up there yet. Until now.

The height of the real Elvis has caused considerable debate over the years but it's generally accepted as being between six foot to six foot two inches. Keanu 'the King' Kennedy stood at six foot four inches tall and looked to weigh more than the real teenage Elvis did at his age. Therefore trying to inconspicuously walk up the stairs on light feet was always going to be a challenge. A single creak, coupled with the length of time that Elvis/Keanu was taking for him to pee, was enough for Castiel to discreetly signal to Beatrix to go and quietly investigate.

Once Elvis reached the top of the stairs there were no corridors or other rooms in sight, instead the stairway opened out into a single room that carried the length of the house.

His eyes marvelled at what he saw and began to walk across the room towards the epicentre of all that surrounded him.

That was until two bullets found his back.

He was a big and strong young man, but he was no match for unexpected gunshots.

The next sound that was heard downstairs was the full force of Elvis's muscular frame as it met the timber floorboards above.

"What the fuck was that?" asked Paris.

"You took the words right out of my mouth," said Rufus.

Suddenly, both Castiel and Martha each pulled a gun from their overcoats.

"It seems that Beatrix has found your friend Elvis snooping about where he really shouldn't have been snooping."

"What has she done to him?" demanded Rufus.

"You heard the gunshots, didn't you?" said Beatrix as she reappeared into view from the stairs. This was the first time that she had spoken and she was also pointing a gun.

"You bastards," said Rufus.

"Now you've taken the words out of my mouth," said Paris.

Castiel smiled as he held the gun. "Paris, you asked me about the pentagram and you failed to identify if it was inverted or not. Well, take a look at it now and follow the five points, in particular the upper two points of the star-like shape."

Paris did as she was asked. "So?"

"Can you picture a goat's head within the framework? A couple of horns perhaps?"

After a few seconds of studying the pentagram Paris replied "Yes."

"Well, now you have your answer."

CHAPTER 28
FAITH

The suspension on Mercer's car caused it to bounce here, there and everywhere as it found its way over the rough terrain leading to Castiel's house. Occasionally the car's occupants bounced along with it as the alloyed wheels dipped in and out of the various depth of holes on offer.

"Just park it here, Tank. I'm in danger of throwing up at this rate," said Mercer. "We can walk the rest of the way."

The remaining collection of gangster cars either followed suit bobbing up and down across the land or were parked up in the country lane, completely blocking the route for any forthcoming motorists. The car carrying Diego, Tilda and George Michael belonged in the former.

Judd led the way across the acre or so of land surrounding the building and suddenly everything began to look like a film set from a Guy Ritchie Movie. Hardened gangsters dominated the rural landscape as they marched on menacingly. All types of stereotypical characteristics were on show: heads were generally shaved to the scalp or hosting a sharp contrast of a mass of greased back hair;

whilst general attire was either leather jackets or smart suits. Either choice found them bulging with huge weighty or muscular frames placed within them. The scars of previous battles were evident on many faces and knuckles of the gangsters should anyone be able to get that close to observe. At present there didn't appear to be anyone else around the vicinity other than the visiting mob.

Judd was first to reach the house and he was able to push the door open with ease. Clearly, it hadn't been fixed since he'd damaged it to gain access the time before.

As he entered the house, followed by Mercer and Talia, he instantly became curious as to the quietness that presented itself. Curiosity soon gave way to a dreaded feeling of worry. "No one's here," he said.

"Perhaps they've gone for a walk?" said Talia. "It's not a bad location to get some air into your lungs from what I've seen."

"I'm not so sure. Rufus ain't much of a walker for a start," said Judd. "No, something doesn't feel right."

"I'm more concerned that my niece isn't here," said Mercer.

"I share your concerns, Richie," said Judd.

"I'm still holding you responsible until she's found safe and sound. Just you remember that, Stone."

"Fair enough. Believe me, I am well aware of that fact, Richie. The others will be taking really good care of her though, wherever they are. I can assure you of that."

"Well lad, forgive me if I don't feel assured."

"Perhaps the owner came back and chucked them out?" offered Tilda, who was by now also in the property. Diego and George Michael were hovering just outside the door.

"It's possible, I suppose," said Judd.

"If someone had broken into my house, I know I wouldn't be too happy," said Talia. Judd could only hope that the owner wouldn't have followed the same strategy that he knew Ray Talia would in such circumstances. Blow torches and other forms of torture sprang to mind.

"I don't like the look of that," said Tilda as she spotted the inverted pentagram on the back of door.

"What the fucking hell is that thing? This does nothing to help with my confidence levels regarding my niece, Judd lad."

Judd couldn't muster a suitable answer.

"Why don't you check upstairs?" said Tilda.

The three wise men looked at one another. Why hadn't any of them already thought of that by now?

Judd, already knowing the downstairs layout of the small abode, ran to the foot of the stairs and ventured up them properly for the very first time.

Once he reached the top, his brain registered a few incredibly chilling things that became evident in his new surroundings, but his eyes swiftly fell onto the motionless figure lying on the floor. He knew at once it was Elvis and ran as fast as he could to his recently found friend.

Blood was seeping through the back of Elvis's jacket and there was also a considerable pool of blood on the floor next to him.

Judd knelt by the young man and used all of his strength to turn him over. Next, he cradled Elvis's head in his arms hoping for a sign of life. Looking to the ceiling he found a rare need to reach out to a Faith he didn't usually seek. "Come on, he's just a kid."

Judd found himself searching Elvis's young and handsome face for even a flicker of hope. "Elvis, speak to me."

There was a positive response as Elvis found strength to open his eyes and speak, albeit in nothing more than a whisper. "Hey, Judd. You came back. I'm hurt, man." He was alive, but he was in bad shape.

As Tilda, Talia and Mercer reached upstairs they were shocked to unexpectedly find Judd cradling Elvis. Tilda naturally joined her friend and Elvis eager to offer any kind of assistance, whilst Mercer and Talia began to process their wider surroundings a little more robustly than Judd had been able to. Talia's response was quite apt and in character. "Fucking hell, what the fuck is this place?"

"I think this *is* Fucking Hell," answered Mercer, his eyes agape. "I knew I was destined to end up here one day but am I already here? I don't remember dying."

What greeted them was a collection of macabre and sinister objects. Straight ahead, facing them on the furthest wall from where they were standing, hung a large inverted cross.

Below that appeared to be what could only be described to any layperson as a witch's black cauldron.

Visions of varying body parts of newts and toads in a steaming broth filled each of their heads.

On either side of the inverted cross stood a mirror image of a goat-headed statue. The two statues possessed a man's body with ripped muscles to die for, but cloven hooves were present at the base of the legs, falling in line with the head of the creature.

Every wall was painted black in colour, although a mixture of satanic artwork and bookcases dominated the structure.

The odd book carried lettering large enough to read on its spine, and it was clear that they all represented similar dark themes of Satan, Lucifer, Black Magic and the like.

The artwork included a plain white canvas with the words Hail Satan written in bright red paint – or could it even have been blood?

A dark, antique looking coat stand stood in one of the corners of the disturbing room holding a small collection of black-coloured robes and cloaks.

A nearby shelf held a collection of silvery goblets which would have appeared impressively ornamental if it hadn't have been for the sinister circumstances.

"What happened, Elvis?" asked Judd.

"I dunno, my back was turned but my guess is that I've

been shot. I heard two gunshots before hitting the deck."

"No shit, Sherlock. Who did it?"

Elvis fought for his breath. "Like I say, my back was turned but it had to be Castiel. Either that or one of those freaky old biddies he dragged in with him."

"Castiel? The guy on the record we found?"

"Yeah, it's his house. He's a creepy looking fucker too in real life. He was as charming as they come but he obviously didn't like me snooping around up here."

Judd looked around more closely. "Well, I can see why he'd want all of this hidden. Do you have any idea where the others are?"

"I heard some raised voices but I couldn't make out any words. Then it soon went quiet."

"Any further gun shots?" asked Tilda.

"No," whispered Elvis, who then broke into a cough.

"That fucker Castiel has taken them somewhere then." concluded Judd. "I'm hopeful they are still alive."

Elvis continued to splutter. "OK, no more talking, buddy. We need to get you to a hospital."

"Don't bother with an ambulance," interjected Mercer. "It'll take them forever to find this place. I'll get a couple of the boys to drop him off at A and E. They'll be quick. May be worth you being a bit cagey about how you came about your injuries though Elvis, until we fathom this out."

"I tend to agree," said Judd.

"I feel I should go with him," offered Tilda.

"What's the point?" said Mercer. "You can't do nothing for him. He'll go straight to theatre and you'll be pacing the corridors readily available for the bizzies to interrogate. You stay with us; we don't know yet if a woman's touch may help us at some point."

Mercer was good to his word, Elvis was carried down the stairs by Barney and John, no mean feat considering his athletic build, and then the King of Rock and Roll was driven in style to the Royal Liverpool University Hospital.

On depositing Elvis's bleeding body to the Accident and Emergency department, Barney's only instruction before quickly departing the location was "Patch him up and make it good. When Elvis leaves this particular building he needs to be alive. And don't ask any stupid fucking questions while you do it."

Barney and John didn't know it, but on route to the hospital they had passed a mini clubman on the opposite side of the motorway. This mini clubman was getting closer to Castiel's weird residence as Judd discussed things with Mercer, Talia, Diego, George Michael and Tilda.

They decided to move back downstairs where the ambience was slightly less sinister, albeit the inverted pentagram was a constant reminder of something being very strange in this house.

Judd walked over to the record player and switched it on.

"This is no time for playing records, Judd lad," said Mercer. "My niece is still missing for fuck's sake."

"As are my friends. You're not the only one with concerns here, Richie. Just bear with me, I'm doing this for a reason" Judd reached for the record from earlier. "This record may have an answer for us. Look at the name of the band."

"Castiel and the Creatures of the Night. Never heard of them."

"Castiel is the owner of this weird place."

"That much I do know and I know he has something to do with the demise of my offspring. I also know that your friend Hunter knew him."

Judd didn't want to dwell on any part that Hunter may have played in all of this. Had he ever truly known his deceased friend? "I'm not going to play the whole record, but let's have a quick listen. I should have satisfied my curiosity about this when I listened to it the time before."

Judd removed the vinyl from the sleeve and placed it on to the turntable. He then raised the arm of the needle and placed it down towards the final grooves of the record, just before they met the circular label positioned at the centre of the disc. Next, he placed the index finger of his right hand onto the vinyl. He then began to spin the record anti-clockwise and gradually began to gather speed until the looped message when played backwards became audible.

The voice remained gravelly and sinister: *You make this music for me; I accept your gift. Only I can end days, don't let them be saved.*

"Do it again," said Mercer, genuinely interested. Judd span the record backwards once more.

You make this music for me; I accept your gift. Only I can end days, don't let them be saved.

"What the fuck does that mean?" asked Talia.

"I don't know what it means," replied Mercer. "It may well just be gibberish and purposely non-sensical. Rock bands have done it for decades. Some are so far up themselves that they try and claim that it's a satanic message to build their credibility, but most of the time they do it for a laugh, like a gimmick. It's a technique called backmasking."

"I know the Beatles did it a few times too," said Judd. "But we can all fathom why this sick dude Castiel would put a satanic message on his record."

"Except it wasn't Castiel," said a voice that had snuck into the vicinity.

The heads of Judd, Mercer, Talia, George and Tilda turned to see that two girls had entered the room along with Tank.

"Tank, who are these two?" asked Mercer.

"It's OK, Boss. I searched them before letting them in. They said they knew you and Judd. You've been chatting to them apparently."

"Well, I can see that's Yasmin," said Judd. "She works for me, so I'm assuming this must be Kadence."

"No, I'm Eva."

Yasmin screwed up her face and stared in disbelief at her girlfriend. "Eva?"

The girl with thick black hair and equally dark clothing suddenly appeared as stiff as a board. She seemed frozen to the spot, as if engulfed by another presence.

"You're Eva?" asked Judd.

"Yes," answered the girl.

"Judd, this is Kadence. I don't know what she's talking about."

"I think she's being channelled, Yasmin."

"Huh?"

"Eva was one of the names that came through on the Ouija board that we performed in this place. Hello Eva."

"Hello," Kadence's accent had switched to one of a Liverpudlian nature.

"Can you tell us a little more about what happened to you?

"I was Castiel's girlfriend. I lived with him here. Back then we were called all sorts of names and told that we were 'living over the brush' or 'living in sin', that type of thing. Living together out of wedlock was really frowned upon. But we didn't care what anyone said because we were so happy, and we could lock ourselves away here in relative seclusion.

"I wish that living with me had been the only sin that Castiel had been responsible for. Unfortunately, he made the record that you have there and he instantly changed.

"He was convinced that Castiel and the Creatures of the Night were going to be huge. He used to say that we would be bigger than Elvis Presley. And soon after, he was saying that we would be bigger than The Beatles. It really grieved him how successful The Beatles quickly became especially as they came out of Liverpool. He firmly believed that their crown belonged to him and his band.

"He wanted to do scary things with our music and he thought singing in Latin was a good technique, although of course it never caught on. Why would it? Everything went to his head but then when we played the record he changed all the more. That backward message you heard at the end of the record wasn't recorded at the studio by Castiel or anyone else from the band. I was there throughout the recording so I know. The first time we heard it Castiel was like a man possessed. He somehow instantly knew he had to play it backwards and the message was revealed to him. It was taken to be Satan himself appearing on the record. Castiel changed in a heartbeat swearing allegiance to Satan for evermore.

"But hearing the message had the opposite effect on me, I was terrified. When I refused to have any part in Castiel's enlightenment and his new way of thinking we got into an argument and Castiel turned extremely violent.

"So violent that he killed me. I became his first killing and he offered me as a sacrifice to Satan. Other victims of Castiel were to follow the same fate, but I was the woman he loved, so what better sacrifice could there have been?

"He killed me right there where you are all gathered. He used no weapons to slay me, only his fists and hands. His attack was frenzied, I didn't stand a chance. He only chose to cut my body and release my blood once he had carried me upstairs and chanted 'Hail Satan' as he stood over my dead body. Eventually he took me out to the garden and set fire to me.

"As I had more or less given up my family and friends to be with Castiel, I only became registered as a missing person by a couple of members of the Creatures of the Night. As you can imagine, without computers and the procedures that we have in place today, a missing person very seldom became any more than that back then. Castiel simply said that I'd left the home and hadn't provided a forwarding address.

"Since he killed me, I've watched things come and go in this evil house from the shadows. He turned this house from one that was so full of love into a place of pure evil. I've seen him recruit his disciples like those two twin witches he brought here today. They hang on his every word. It was one of those twisted women that shot your young friend. There's been many more recruited here over the years but the congregation became so vast that his church needed a new location. He practices Satanism here of course but ultimately he has his church in Crank Caverns.

"As I said earlier, he has killed more than me here, including sweet little children, the sick bastard. And he's killed many more up at Crank. Those caverns are the perfect location to carry out his acts of evil undetected."

Suddenly, Kadence's eyes rolled back into her head and her body spiralled into a temporary seizure before collapsing to the floor in a heap of exhaustion.

Yasmin instantly grew concerned and nestled her girlfriend in her arms. "Kadence, Kadence are you alright? Speak to me?"

Fortunately, Kadence soon began to come around, although she was clearly dazed from her ordeal. "I-I'm OK. What happened?"

"Don't you remember?" asked Yasmin.

"Not fully."

"You seemed to take on the persona of a lady who had been killed here. A lady called Eva."

"Have you ever channelled spirits before?" asked Judd.

"Yes, I have, but unfortunately I don't always have a choice about it."

"Well by doing so today you've been very helpful, girl," offered Mercer. "We now know all we needed to know about a guy called Castiel who is a murdering Satanist. I say we get up to Crank as soon as possible and tear apart this piece of shit limb by limb. He deserves a slow painful death. I wouldn't mind inflicting a bit of torture on him before his eyes close for the final time."

"Amen to that," said Talia.

"No," said Judd.

"No?" replied Talia. "What do you mean no? This

warped bastard deserves what's coming to him, Stone. What's wrong with you, it's not like you to wimp out."

"I'm not wimping out and I agree with both of you regarding what this lowlife deserves, but I'm just saying that now is not the right time."

"What do you mean?" said Mercer. "What if he gets away?"

"Judd's right," said Kadence, who by now was sitting in an upright position, still supported by Yasmin. "He's going nowhere other than Crank. Satanists carry out their procedures in the dark. In fact, he may not even be there until darkness falls."

"We just need to be patient," said Judd. "If we wait until dusk, we won't just take Castiel out we can take out his entire fucked up outfit. It makes me shudder to think about it but maybe Efan was one of his so-called disciples, if that's what we are calling them, and he was taking my Billie to Crank Caverns."

"And maybe other kids are on route?" said Kadence.

"I wouldn't be surprised," said Judd.

"Me neither actually," said Mercer, feeling the pain shoot through his heart as he contemplated the likelihood of what happened to his granddaughter. "OK, I agree we wait. We would have more chance of being able to save the kids once they are all there."

"OK, but if this nonce dares to show his face here again I'm smashing it in pronto," said Talia.

"You'd have to get in the queue, Ray," replied Mercer.

"Well, if we are staying here for a while, I want a drink and something to eat. I prefer to torture people on a full stomach, being hungry can cause me to rush things. Anyone know what's in the fridge?" asked Talia.

"I'll go and take a look," offered George Michael. Within a couple of minutes he returned.

"So what's on the menu?" asked Talia.

"An unskinned dead rabbit, but I'm not sure how fresh it is."

"I'll send some boys out to get pizza and beers," offered Mercer. "Just be prepared that the pizza may be cold and the beer may be warm depending on how close the shops are."

"We seem to be miles away from anywhere worthwhile," said Diego. "But pizza sounds good."

"Judd, you look very pensive," stated Yasmin.

"I'm just thinking about us biding our time."

"It was your idea," said Mercer.

"I know, I think it's the right thing to do if it means we have a better chance of rescuing as many kids as possible. The thing is it's highly likely that Crank is where he's taken Rufus and the others as well. I just hope I haven't left it too late to rescue them."

"Well, I've said it before and I'll say it again. If anything has happened to a single blonde hair on the head of my Isla, I'm still holding you personally responsible, Stone."

CHAPTER 29
RULES AND REGULATIONS

Part of the perpetual mystery of Crank Caverns is that it doesn't appear on any maps. This in itself has created mystery upon mystery over the passage of time.

But why would this be so?

You could certainly forgive the locals for not wanting to draw attention to the heinous legends that engulf the history of the area.

But maybe the 'cover up' goes even higher?

These questions and more certainly crossed Judd's mind as he led the collection of gangsters from two different cities up the slight incline of the dirt track marked as a 'Private Road'. The track began at the bend in the road where Crank Hill and Alder Lane met.

Once again, if anyone was witnessing the spectacle, they may believe that they were witnessing the filming of a Guy Ritchie movie, or maybe even one by Quentin Tarantino.

Kadence and Yasmin walked towards the rear of the procession, well-hidden and protected. Judd hadn't wanted them to accompany the gangsters and him at all and wished they'd stayed behind in the nearby Red Cat pub. However, he had to accept that Kadence was a valuable asset to have close by with her various insight and abilities, and she had personally convinced him as much. It seemed her methods of influence and persuasion were just as impressive as her spiritual and psychic capabilities. As for Yasmin, it seemed wherever Kadence went Yasmin would follow. Judd was genuinely pleased for his assistant, she deserved to be lucky in love.

The wind was fierce and biting as it soared over the identical hedges that flanked the ascent up the track, its formidable presence no doubt an aftermath of the previous night's storm.

At the top of the unkempt road sat what looked like an old farmhouse, although the signage designed to warn people to keep away claimed that the site held dangerous chemicals. This immediately caused suspicion in Judd's mind. Was it a chemical storage warehouse or a working farm? Surely it couldn't be both? He discussed his concerns with Mercer and Talia which resulted in a slight detour for about a third of the posse, whilst the others kept watch at the foot of the driveway to the farmhouse.

It was Judd who knocked on the door. "Let me do the talking."

There was no answer to Judd's knocking.

"Try again," urged Talia. Judd did what was requested.

Eventually a skinny, unkempt man answered the door, perfectly complementing the apparent state of the farm.

"Yeah?" It was not the most charming of welcomes.

"Got any eggs for sale?" asked Judd.

"Eggs?"

"Yeah, eggs. This is a farm ain't it? In fact, I was wondering if you had a farm shop, my friends and I are a little tired after our walk over the surrounding countryside. We're a recently formed ramblers club, you see, in fact this has been our very first walk as a group and I'm a little embarrassed to say that we all fell abysmally short on supplies. We've ran out of water and didn't even think to bring any chocolate bars or sandwiches, you know that sort of thing. So, do you have anything we could purchase?"

"No," said the man rudely and promptly began to shut the door. Judd prevented this from happening by forcing his foot into the doorway.

"Move your foot."

"We just want some refreshments."

"Didn't you see the sign back there? This ain't no farm we store harmful chemicals here. There's a pub half a mile down the road, they'll help you out. I ain't got no farm shop and I ain't got nothing for you, OK?"

"OK." Judd still didn't move his foot from the door.

"You don't look like any ramblers I've ever seen."

"And you don't look like a guy who stores chemicals. Where's your protective gear?" said an irritated Ray Talia unable to resist getting involved.

"My friend makes a good point," said Judd.

"I'm on my tea break so I've taken them off. Not that it's any of your business. Look, you're on private property, didn't you read the signs?"

"Yeah, I read them, but let's just say I don't like to follow rules and regulations much. Anyway, why don't you go and phone the police if we are trespassing and we'll wait here for them to arrive."

The man didn't move or speak.

"Don't want to involve the police, huh? Why's that then?" asked Judd.

"Get off my land or there'll be trouble."

Judd began to mock with laughter. "Do you hear that boys? If we don't move there'll be trouble. How's that then Mister?"

"I've got a whole lot of boys myself sitting in the back. You've got ten seconds until I call them."

"Could one of them boys sitting out back be a chap by the name of Castiel?" asked Judd.

The skinny guy narrowed his eyes. "What do you know about Castiel?"

"I'm more interested in what you know about him?" countered Judd.

"I'm going to count down from ten and then I want you gone from this property. 10-9-8-7, once I get to zero then you'll be sor…"

The man was unable to finish his sentence as the bullet of Ray's gun obliterated his skull.

"Fucking hell, Ray," said Judd. "There was no need for that."

"Bollocks, I just cut to the chase. He clearly knew Castiel and if he ain't directly involved in whatever warped set up is going on around here he was willing to protect it."

"Ray's right," said Mercer. "The cheeky bastard even had the audacity to threaten us." Mercer turned to a couple of his men. "Go in and see what's around, do a sweep of the place. You're all tooled up right?"

One of the heavies nodded.

"Good, my guess is he was bullshitting about his back-up because no one has come running out since the gunshot."

"Which means everyone is already most likely down at the caverns," said Talia. "It is getting dark quickly now so I reckon they're down there."

"This guy should have been as cooperative as the guy at the pub," said Mercer. "Then he'd still be alive."

"You didn't exactly give him much of a choice, Richie," said Judd.

"Of course I did, lad. I asked him for exclusive use of his car park or I'd smash his pub up."

"Some choice," said Judd.

Mercer prodded the dead man with his foot as if he was examining a piece of roadkill. "Well, this twat lying here bleeding all over the floor wouldn't have been so accommodating, would he? Besides, I left Teddy, Leslie and Ginger back there with the publican for company."

"Only so that he and his staff couldn't alert anyone that we had taken over the village and his pub," said Judd.

"One can't be too careful," said Talia.

"I know, I know. I just felt a bit guilty about it all. That one young barmaid looked terrified. I also don't think they are involved in any of this," said Judd.

"I don't think they are either," said Mercer. "But we don't want the police rocking up and spoiling the party, do we?"

"I guess not."

"They'd only complicate matters and get in the way."

The two men who had swept the property returned.

"Anything? asked Judd.

"Nothing," said one of the heavies. "But there are signs that the skinny dead guy has had company here recently. There's a heap of unwashed plates and cups, unless he's just a dirty bastard who never washes up."

"That could well be the case looking at the state of him," said Judd.

The other heavy spoke next. "So, although there were no other people in there, we did find some seriously weird shit."

"How do you mean, Cloughie?" asked Mercer.

"Let me guess, a pentagram?" interjected Judd.

"Yes," said Cloughie. "That was one thing we noticed but that wasn't anywhere near the worst of it."

"How do you mean?" asked Judd.

As tough as Cloughie undoubtedly was it was clear that he had been disturbed by whatever he had seen and he hesitated to speak. "There were jars of body parts, you know, organs like. Floating about in some type of liquid."

"Human?" asked Talia.

"Hard to say, maybe. They could be animals' parts I guess as they looked a bit on the small side. Still fucking weird though."

"I'll say its fucking weird," said Talia, as he drew

another kick into the lifeless corpse that he had created.

"Anyway, now this place has been eliminated from our enquiries let's move onto the caverns," declared Judd.

Talia kicked the corpse again before bending over to address it. "You must be the worst fucking look out in history." A final kick followed.

"You didn't have to hold us hostage like this, you know? If your friends are going to Crank Caverns in the name of all things good, they have my full support. I'm more than happy for you to make use of my car park."

"My boss doesn't like to take any chances, Lad," replied Leslie, just one of several shaven-headed members on the Mercer payroll. Leslie was a little more distinguishable than most as he was the only one who sported a thick handlebar moustache.

"Your boss fancies himself as bit of a gangster does he?" said a voice from an old man sitting at the bar.

The old man, the landlord, two barmaids and a couple of couples, one looking to be in their twenties the other in their forties, were all being held hostage by Leslie, Teddy and Ginger.

Tilda and George Michael looked a little uncomfortable that they were accompanying them but what could they do?

"Oh, Richie Mercer is a bonafide gangster alright, you'd do well to remember that old man. Pop down to Liverpool anytime you want if you need to see the evidence of his empire."

The old man obviously didn't scare easily. "Being a gangster may not be enough if he's heading over to the Caverns at this time of night," he said, before turning his attention to the pub landlord. "Fill up my tankard please, Harry."

Harry looked at Leslie for affirmation. "It's fine," said the heavy. "It could be a long night. In fact, can we have drinks all round, Harry? My boss will make sure that you're accordingly reimbursed." Leslie glanced at the barmaids and couples and it was easy to sense the fear on their faces. "You all need to relax. Just sit tight and if no-one tries any funny business, I promise you that nobody is gonna get hurt. There's just a small bit of business to do up at the Caverns and then we will be out of here."

"You seem very confident about the outcome at the Caverns."

"You know what, old man? You're really beginning to irritate me."

"The name's Leo."

"OK, you're beginning to irritate me, Leo."

Leo took a drink from his recently filled tankard and swiveled on his bar stool to face Leslie for the first time. "Look, mate. I don't mean any offence and I ain't suggesting that your boss can't handle himself, but this ain't Liverpool. This is Crank and Crank has a lot of legends associated with it, and all of them are as scary as hell."

"Even for a gangster?"

"Even for two gangsters?" asked Teddy. "Apparently Birmingham's finest has also joined forces with us."

"Even for an army of gangsters."

"Well, that's pretty much what is happening right now up at Crank Caverns," said Ginger. "There's an army of 'em gone up there and they mean business." Despite the name he went by, in actual fact, Ginger had dark hair. The nickname had been given to him as a kid due to his obsessive love of ginger nut biscuits. It had stuck with him ever since.

"So, tell us about these legends, Leo," said Teddy.

"No don't," said Harry, pouring the final drink for the hostages. He had thought it safe to assume 'same again.' "And what can I get you three fellows?" he asked nervously.

"Orange juice all round," came the unexpected response from Leslie. "We need to keep a clear head at times like this."

"And these two will have the same," said Ginger, referring to Tilda and George Michael.

"OK. Five orange juices coming up. Prudence, Polly, do you mind serving the drinks to our array of guests?"

"Sure," said Prudence, incidentally a girl who happened to have ginger hair. Polly's was dyed several colours with the dominant shade being pink.

"Why don't you want him to tell us about the legends?" Teddy asked Harry.

"Because I don't want them to define our village."

"If they're only legends we can take them with a pinch of salt, can't we?" said Leslie.

"I'm not going to argue with you," answered Harry.

"And that's very wise of you."

Leo laughed. "I'm gonna tell you, because frankly at my age I don't give a shit if you believe me or not. But listen, I've lived in this village all of my life and as you can imagine I've seen and heard a lot of things. Yeah, there are legends up here in Crank but I've seen stuff with my own two eyes and I've heard things with my own two ears. I know for a fact that there's a lot of stuff that goes on around here that is as real as the day is long.

"And this is why I fear for your friends. It may not feel like it now, but compared to them, you've drawn the long straw being sat here with us."

Prudence placed the last drink down which happened to be Leslie's orange juice. "Thank you, sweetheart, now sit down and make yourself comfy because old Leo over there is going to tell us a story or two to pass away the time."

Prudence felt obliged to sit down there and then next to Leslie because it would have looked strange if she hadn't opted to take the spare seat. Although Leslie was a scary city type, and as it seemed a gangster to boot, she still sensed that he wasn't going to hurt her.

Leo shifted the tweed cap on his head before beginning

his monologue.

"Now to weave this all together, I'll start off with the real stuff, throw in some of the legendary tales and then finish on some more real stuff, OK?"

"Fine," said Leslie. "A legend sandwich it is."

"Well first off, that boss of yours and his gangster cronies have got to get past a certain establishment before they can even get anywhere near the Caverns, and that may not be too easy."

"How do you mean?"

"Well, a lot of shit has gone on in those Caverns over the years, and I'll come onto that, but that building they need to pass has warning signs all the way along the route up to it."

"Why's that?" asked Tilda.

"They claim to be storing chemicals of some kind up there."

"Well chemicals can be hazardous," said Teddy. "Putting up warning signs just sounds like neighbourly common sense to me."

"It's bullshit, there's no hazardous storage of chemicals going on up there, it's just a bluff to keep people away. If chemicals were being stored up there it would mean the odd noisy chemical tanker trapesing through the village every now and then, right?"

"Yeah, I guess so," replied Teddy.

"Well, let me tell you that I've never seen a single tanker or lorry of any sort anywhere near that vicinity. However, I have seen dark-coloured cars with the windows blacked out head that way more often than not. Maybe even the odd transit van but no tankers. Not ever. It's all a cover for something else."

"Like what?"

"Well, I ain't too sure to be honest with you, but I'm sure it's got to be something sinister. Why else try and keep people at bay?"

"It could simply be a marijuana farm," said Teddy.

"Sounds like Leo here has already had some," laughed Ginger.

"Well let's see if your friends live to tell the tale because this is where the legends come in."

"Go on," said Leslie, actually becoming quite intrigued, much as the others were. The old man had quite the voice and demeanour for storytelling.

Leo went on to tell the exact same tale that Kadence had told Judd and the others. "Back in the eighteenth century four boys went down them there caverns. It's an eerie place but it's also a place that feeds off your curiosity and you can't help but want to enter it's labyrinth of darkness. And these four boys were as curious as Hell." Leo paused for another swig from his tankard, the time passing adding to the dramatic effect of the story telling.

"Because they were so small, they could get through all the various nooks and crannies quite easily, so they ventured deeper and deeper and it got darker and darker. The thing is, only one boy managed to get back out to tell the tale."

"What happened?" asked Leslie.

"The boy couldn't speak at first, but eventually he told of how he and his friends had been attacked."

"Who attacked them," asked Prudence."

"The boy said that little people lived down there."

"Little people?" asked Teddy? What, like dwarves?"

"Not exactly, much more vicious. Goblins perhaps?"

"Goblins, no way," said Leslie. "They don't exist, Leo. Come on lad, they are stuff of fairy tales."

"Maybe, maybe not, but the boy was adamant that evil little people were living down there. Maybe they still do. Anyway, this colony of little folk more than made up for their lack of size with the strength of an ox and the ferociousness of a rabid tiger.

"The boy claims that he literally saw his poor friends torn limb from limb."

"That's awful," said Prudence.

"That's not all, next they began to eat the raw flesh of the boys right there, right then. Can you imagine? A community of little savage cannibals that live in complete darkness at the centre of the caverns?"

"I didn't know any of this," said Prudence. "Did you Polly?" Polly just shook her head unable to find the words. She looked over to her kind boss, the landlord Harry, for any sign of affirmation to Leo's incredible tale. The look on his face told her that he had indeed heard of this awfulness before.

Tilda and George Michael looked at each other in disbelief, they too had been hanging onto every unbelievable word of Leo's.

"Anyway," continued Leo. "As I said, just this one kid managed to run for his life and get away, but he was reminded of just how lucky his escape had been because he had the deep scratch marks on his leg for days after."

"Scratch marks?" asked Prudence.

"Yeah, where one of the little bastards had grabbed his leg as he literally headed for the light at the end of the tunnel. Luckily, he made it but they so nearly got him."

Prudence looked terrified. Even the hardened Teddy, Leslie and Ginger began to look at one another seemingly a little unnerved by this grim tale.

"The story doesn't end there," continued Leo. "Two soldiers decided it was necessary to investigate the matter, so they went into the dark caverns. They could hear voices talking in the darkness but the language being spoken wasn't one they recognised. They pointed whatever they were using for light towards the areas where they thought they had heard the voices come from, and danced the beams all around where they sensed eyes spying on them. But they didn't reveal anything. Well almost anything."

"What do you mean?" asked George Michael.

"I mean the light didn't reveal any living being. But it did however shine on human bones and even a child's skull."

"Fucking hell," said Leslie, instantly apologising to Prudence for cursing in front of a lady.

"It's OK," said Prudence. "This is all as scary as fuck."

Leo paused again and this time drank a fair amount of beer from his tankard. Once he'd finished, he wiped froth away from his mouth with the back of his hand. "Wanna know more?" he said.

"I'm not sure," said Polly.

"Go for it," said Ginger.

"Yeah, go on," agreed Leslie.

"OK, well there's certainly plenty that goes on in these parts. Let me tell you about the White Rabbit."

"White rabbit. What like in Alice in Wonderland?" asked Teddy. "That was my favourite book as a kid."

"Didn't know you could read, Lad," mocked Leslie.

"Funny."

"A bit more sinister than that particular white rabbit," said Leo.

"Is this village some sort of animal sanctuary?" asked Ginger. "I mean, you're on about white rabbits and here we are sitting in a pub called the Red Cat!"

Leo didn't answer the question and instead continued to draw in his audience. "The tale of the white rabbit of Crank begins with an evil, nasty individual called 'Old Nick'."

"As in the Devil? Old Nick is one of the names for the Devil, right?" asked Ginger.

"Old Nick may as well have been the Devil himself that's for sure. He was a local farmer who inadvertently set the train of events leading to the death of a harmless large white rabbit that belonged to Jenny."

"Who was Jenny?" asked Tilda.

"Jenny was the six-year-old granddaughter of the old lady who lived at the foot of the hill of Crank," Leo pointed in the direction of the hill. "The ironic thing was, as nasty a piece of work that Old Nick was in his own right, he was convinced that he had been bewitched by that old lady. This was the seventeenth century, you see, and back then villagers were typically quick to believe that a socially outcast old lady must surely be a witch. And Old Nick done plenty himself to fuel the rumour. He had no good reason of course, but every village just had to have at least one witch in their midst back in those times.

"Now, one fateful night, Old Nick discussed his beliefs with his equally miserable pal, Dick Piers, and between them they set about breaking the witch's spell. They believed this could be achieved by drawing blood from the witch so they set about breaking into her cottage."

There was baited silence as Leo took another quick sup from his tankard. "Old Nick and Piers weren't the most sophisticated of intruders and with their clumsy entry they soon woke Jenny who was sleeping with her one and only friend in the whole wide world: her beloved white rabbit.

"Terrified, she grabbed her white rabbit and ran through the broken door out into the night. She darted up the hill making her way towards the chapel. Piers took exception to being outwitted and thought it necessary to turn on his heels and chase after her. He failed to catch Jenny but he did get hold of her rabbit and inexcusably kicked the poor creature to death."

"That's terrible," said Prudence.

"That's not all," continued Leo. "The next morning a local monk went to the chapel and found the lifeless body of a child. Jenny had died from fright, exhaustion and most likely of all heartbreak from the previous night's happenings."

"Poor kid," said Leslie. "I'd like to have got my hands on those pair of bastards."

"Don't worry, my friend. Karma was not far away. Exactly a month to the day after Jenny's burial, Dick Piers, found himself confronted by an angry white rabbit. He looked into the eyes of the creature in sheer disbelief as he realised it was the very same white rabbit that he had kicked to death those few weeks before.

"The spineless cretin turned and ran into the night consumed by fear. His body was found the next day at the foot of Billinge Hill. It was rumoured that he had taken his own life, but who really knows for sure?

"And the story doesn't end there. As the days followed, Old Nick then began to feel eyes upon him at every turn he made. He would turn starkly expecting to discover who his stalker was but every time his eyes met with nothing. Until one day the white rabbit decided to show himself and torment him further. The vengeful rabbit chased Old Nick across the nearby fields until the evil old fool died of exhaustion and fright. A similar ending to that of poor Jenny."

"Old Nick and Dick Piers deserved everything they got," said Prudence.

"Aye," agreed Leo. "I can't disagree with that. The trouble is that white rabbit got a taste for revenge, remember the whole village had been guilty of branding the old lady a witch. Maybe she was after all and this is how this white rabbit of Jenny's became a surefire prophecy of doom?"

"Prophecy of doom? How do you mean?" asked Leslie.

"Long since the deaths of Old Nick and Piers, it has been known that if you walk the lanes of Crank and a white rabbit crosses your path then it is a certain sign that your time will shortly be over. There are declarations upon declarations of local people who have reported seeing a white rabbit only to find within a few days they have passed away. This is why even to this day the villagers grow crops to pacify the white rabbit of Crank. Since growing the crops and offering them to the white rabbit to eat at will he no longer seems to appear to prophesies any deaths."

"Like an offering to a god?" said Tilda.

"Aye, exactly like that," said Leo.

"Shit, I never knew any of this," said Prudence.

"Me neither," said Polly.

"Your parents would know, for sure," said Leo. "I guess folk like to protect their young these days from such dreadful tales."

"Well we're not protected from the tales any more, are we?" said Polly.

"You'll be OK. As long as the rabbit keeps getting his belly full of crop," said Leo. "Haven't you two girls ever noticed how this village has a wonderfully low crime rate and a below average occurrence of mortalities?"

"Err, not really," said Prudence.

"Something you take for granted, huh. Let me tell you, for decades now the villagers have believed that if we keep the rabbit happy, he comes out at night and protects us while we sleep. That way folk never have to wake unexpectedly and face any type of shock that poor Jenny did that fateful night. However, while the rabbit may be keeping the village safe, only God alone knows what goes on at those caverns over the way."

"God or perhaps Satan," offered Leslie.

"Aye, I think you've hit the nail on the head there, son. Them caverns exist for Satan's pleasure."

To access the area to the Caverns, there was a need to follow a dip at the end of the lane. As Judd approached the area, he was curious as to why he was stepping on a never-ending carpet of half-eaten, weird looking off-white-coloured vegetables, something that resembled a hybrid of a carrot with a turnip. Of course, he hadn't yet been educated on the tale of the white rabbit.

The dip was shielded by bushes. Judd carefully pulled back a branch of foliage to assess if they were also shielding the enemy, but there wasn't anything of life in sight. The settlement must have been further on.

As Judd descended and led the others to the lower part of the dip, he looked upwards and high to the left where he noticed the shell of a derelict house. Now Judd was able to better understand why they had passed a couple of gothic stone gate posts positioned just before a row of bushes.

The land of what would have once been the gardens of the house appeared surprisingly flat considering all the bumps and hills that lay all about them. There was no fence or wall in position to hide the garden. What seemed particularly curious was the fact that the land had clearly been maintained and kept well by someone, whereas the house had seemingly been left to rot serving no apparent purpose.

At present, the garden resembled a travelling circus. Except, the inhabitants of the cages that were scattered about were human rather than performing elephants, tigers or lions. Judd's heart sank when he could make out that one large cage was housing a collection of eighties tribute acts along with his old pal Rufus.

He wanted to go and rescue them there and then, but when the screams of children could be heard up ahead, Judd realised that he needed to plough on. The adults would simply have to wait.

At least the crying noises of the children pinpointed to where the hive of activity most likely was occurring. The lay of the land fortunately allowed Judd and the gangsters to form an undetected circle behind the grassy banks that looked down onto and around the Cavern.

Remaining undetected they were able to gain sight into the pits of the mini-valley that preceded the entrances to the Cavern. Two openings sat side by side, separated only by a huge limestone rock. The entrances fell dark very quickly and seeing deep inside them from their current position was impossible. What could be seen however was the scattering of graffiti on the rocks, including an arrowed sign pointing into the cave to 'Narnia', clearly a joke by some unsuspecting soul who may well have paid for his or hers take on artistic comedy.

It soon became disturbingly apparent as to where the cries of the children had been coming from. A number of cages holding a collection of terrified and confused pre-school girls came into view, and worryingly, what appeared to be a sacrificial slab was positioned nearby.

Judd moved his head to get a better panoramic view but soon pulled it back like a tortoise into his shell when a guard looked up and he feared that their eyes had connected. As nothing seemed to follow, Judd, concluded that he hadn't been spotted after all.

Judd's view was good enough and he could see that a fire was raging in order to provide both light and heat.

However, the fire must also have been shielding another cage of infant girls because they began to come into view one by one from behind the flames. Adults were leading them into one of the two entrances of the cavern.

The girls looked terrified.

Some were kicking and screaming as they were carried like an effervescent rugby ball under the arms of evil rugby players. Some who were able to walk did so passively, totally consumed by fear it would seem.

Light entering the tunnel was provided with a mixture of modern-day torches and flaming fire lanterns, the type that would have been used centuries before.

Curiously, a line of girls was being led out of the other opening of the Cavern, making it more of an exit in fact, and they appeared well-behaved and completely void of fear. It was as if after entering the cavern through one opening, and eventually coming back out again from the other, some kind of transformation was taking place.

Talia turned to Judd. "We've got to act now and save those poor little kiddies."

"Save them from what?" said Mercer. "Look at the ones coming out of the Cavern, they seem fine."

"But clearly, they've been taken from their homes. This is no place for kids," countered Talia.

"I won't disagree with you on that point," answered Mercer.

"The trouble is, if we steam in now, we could put the

kids in danger," said Judd.

"Well, we certainly haven't come all this way to do nothing have we?" said Talia. "Come on, does this look right to you?"

"I think Ray's right, Judd. I hate to think of any collateral damage, especially with kids as young as this, but this doesn't look like the kind of thing that we can just stand by and watch."

"Who's to say the adults are not a bunch of nonces, either?" said Talia.

Judd was in a state of indecision contemplating what to do for the best. With children being involved he wasn't completely comfortable at leaning towards his usual gung-ho attitude. He looked over at the lines of children again and noticed that the traffic had come to a natural end. Those that were going in were in and those that were coming out were out. "OK, let's do it."

And with that he was the first to stand up and run down the hill towards the collection of adults scattered about the place.

Those that were in the Caverns would have to be dealt with later.

The disciples were certainly taken by surprise as gangsters sped down every slope and appeared from every nook and cranny of the grass verges. Unsurprisingly, when it came to a fist fight they didn't stand a chance, even less so with such a well-timed ambush. They were completely out of their depth against a collective of England's most seasoned gangsters and one particularly hard bastard known as Judd Stone.

Diego slotted into a nice little niche of cracking the skulls of disciples together, while Judd easily picked off any optimistic assailant with ease.

As blood spilled out of broken noses amongst the noise of shattered teeth and broken limbs, all in favour of the gangsters of course, a most unexpected thing happened.

The girls that had walked blissfully out of the cavern, the ones that at first seemed more pacified than those going in, began to defend the disciples by jumping on the backs of the gangsters. Others were kicking shins. Hard. Or hanging onto legs like child vices. Some were viciously biting like rabid animals.

The gangsters didn't know how to react, battering kids wasn't their style and their hesitance and distraction caused some of the conscious disciples to attempt to engage in a much fairer fight.

And then the inevitable happened when you have a psychopath such as Ray Talia in your ranks.

Gun shots were fired which took out the remaining standing disciples and they fell lifeless amongst the bloody and broken bodies that were either unconscious or writhing in agony. This bought more than enough time to gather up the vicious children and lock them back in the cage, but not before their bitemarks had been sorely felt.

"Fucking little bastards," said Mercer.

"There's definitely something happening to them girls when they enter that cavern," said Judd.

"Then let's venture in and find out what," said Mercer.

Judd didn't hesitate and led the way once again followed closely by Mercer, Talia and a healthy handful of gangsters. It made sense to keep a few behind to watch over those disciples that may gain consciousness.

Judd looked at his large friend and feared he may find navigating underground a little too challenging. "You OK to stay back, Diego? They could do with your muscle if it kicked off here again."

"No problem," replied Diego.

"Kadence, you stay here too, I think it will be safer," said Judd.

"I thought we'd been through this?"

"OK, OK. Yasmin, you stay then."

"Where Kadence goes, I go, anyway, you know how tough a cookie I am. Don't patronise us just because we're female, we can look after ourselves."

"Besides, we have just laid into this lot too you know," stated Kadence.

"There's no time to argue," said Mercer.

"OK, OK, but you ladies stay at the back," conceded Judd.

Led only by the light of the inbuilt torches of mobile phones they stumbled along the tunnel not quite knowing where they were heading. Furthermore, the jagged surface of the dark cavern often proved tricky underfoot.

Echoing sounds of dripping water added to the eerie setting and venturing further and further underground made for an ever-increasing feeling of coldness.

It took a while but eventually the prize was in reach.

Voices could be heard, albeit not fully audible considering the distance the crew were currently positioned, but there was clearly a gathering of sorts nearby. Light from up ahead also began to gradually enter the darkness.

"Turn your torches off, guys," instructed Judd. "We don't want these warped bastards to know we are on to them."

"Do as he says," said Mercer and Talia almost in unison.

Judd continued to lead the way but his gait became more measured as each carefully placed step brought them closer to the action.

Deciding that they were close enough for now, he held out a hand to halt the entourage and then signalled to line up against the jagged wall. They could then be in a position to better assess what lay ahead whilst remaining out of view from the congregation of disciples.

"What are we waiting for?" whispered Talia. "Let's just steam in and wreck these fuckers."

"Ray, my dear friend, patience is a virtue," whispered Mercer. "Judd knows what he is doing, we want to protect as many kids as possible remember. We don't want any of them getting caught up in the crossfire if we can help it."

"If they are anything like those little bastards that just attacked us, I'm not so sure," answered Talia.

"Let's just watch for a bit," said Judd.

From the shadows of darkness, they could now see that the heart of the cavern opened up into a huge open space, in contrast to much of the claustrophobic journey that they had just experienced through the tunnels.

There were a number of controlled fires scattered around the area to provide light and heat.

The faint voices that could be heard earlier were now much more clearer and seemed to resemble a chorus of Gregorian chants.

Ahead of the lines of children and disciples stood something that resembled an altar shrouded in a dark cloth. An inverted cross was placed upon it.

Standing at the altar was a man wearing a black habit. He was flanked either side by an identical looking elderly lady. It was Castiel and the evil twins, Martha and Beatrix.

Most of the disciples were facing the altar, down on their knees with their heads bowed. Others either dragged the unwilling girls one by one to the altar or calmly escorted the more complicit children.

Castiel spoke in a loud voice and appeared to say something in Latin before compelling each child to take a bite of a black vegetable, similar to the ones Judd had noticed on route to the caverns, but strikingly contrasting in pigment.

The young girls were then forced to wash down the rotten vegetable with a drink of cloudy liquid.

"What the fuck is going on here?" asked Talia. "It's supposed to be bread and red wine, not vegetables and scrumpy! I should know being the good catholic that I am."

Judd didn't feel it necessary to disagree with Talia's self-appraisal of being a good catholic but instead went on to offer an explanation of what he thought they were seeing. "I think what we are witnessing is a Black Mass, Gentlemen. And I wouldn't be surprised if that's animal urine being served up rather than scrumpy cider."

"The sick, evil bastards," said Talia.

"Amen to that," said Mercer.

As each child turned from the altar their state of behaviour was consistent beyond consistent.

They were zombie-like in their state of complicit calm, but as each child unknowingly turned towards Judd and the others, it looked as if flames of fire raged in the girl's eyes for a few moments.

"They are literally the flames of hell in those little girls' eyes," said Mercer.

"I tend to agree," said Judd. "It seems that any designs to offer little girls to Satan via slaughter or sacrifice have now been traded by making them Satan's slaves instead."

"It's not only Black Masses we are witnessing, it's black magic," said Mercer.

"It certainly looks that way," agreed Judd again. "I think it's time that we put an end to this madness and save any more little girls from being sent to a life of hell."

"About fucking time, too," said Talia.

The speed at which they came out of the shadows took the unsuspecting disciples by surprise, especially as so many of them were knelt on the floor facing away from the ambush.

Just like their counterparts outside of the caverns, those disciples inside were no match for the gangsters as the breaking of bones and screams of pain echoed and bounced around the natural jagged walls.

With an ironic look of disgust on his face, Castiel watched on shouting out phrases in Latin in between castings of aspersions and threats such as 'Satan will make sure you pay for this."

But when he realised that the gangsters were getting closer to him and it seemed that no true form of Satan himself was to appear any time soon, he turned on his heels and made his way down an entrance that stood at the rear of the sinister area.

Mercer spotted Castiel's retreat and headed straight after him.

Perhaps Castiel would regret his decision never to allow guns into the Black Mass area of the caverns. He had always considered it a disrespectful slur to the presence of Satan.

Beatrix and Martha spotted an adjacent opening and ran a lot sprightlier than their years may have suggested. Yasmin and Kadence looked at one another. Kadence nodded to Yasmin's "Let's get them old hags."

Although Castiel ran like a coward through the darkness, he still ultimately believed that he would be protected by the master of Hell himself, Satan. This feeling of protection and narcissist self-worth overwhelmed him even when he realised that the route he had taken had led to a dead end.

Once Mercer caught up with him, Castiel turned to face the gangster and screamed at him in an almost mad-like state. "You can't defeat me; I am Satan's warrior. You will feel Satan's wrath through me."

"And I'm Richie Mercer, Liverpool's top gangster and I don't need anyone to help me kick the shit out of you, lad."

"You can never, ever defeat me you fool."

"Well, we'll find out soon enough which one of us is telling the truth won't we, lad. But before we do, you need to tell me about a little girl who went missing a few years ago. I want to know what happened to her, and don't bother sugar coating it Mr. Crowley, because the end of your miserable, warped life will feel all the more pleasurable as I snuff it out."

"Do you know how many little girls I've offered to Satan over the years? What makes this girl so special that I'll remember her?"

"Because she was my granddaughter and she was

therefore very, very special. If you can tell me that she's still alive and hidden away somewhere, you may just get away with me maiming you."

"How long ago are we talking about?"

"More than a decade."

An inane smile spread across Castiel's face. "That's just too bad for you. It's only recently that I've changed my strategy in serving the master. It got very time consuming and messy killing all those young girls. You see, I could never truly know which of them was the actual second coming of Christ in a female form. Any of those girls could have been sent to walk the earth. Nowadays I just turn them into slaves of Satan instead of killing them, it's a far more productive process. And just imagine if I strike lucky enough by turning the second coming into a slave of Satan's. However, unfortunately for you, if I did come across your granddaughter, I will definitely have killed her."

"You're one warped fuck aren't you, lad. Yes, of course she was special but she wasn't any second coming. None of them are you stupid prick."

"Such naivety."

Mercer pulled a picture from his pocket and he stepped closer to Castiel. "Take a look at this picture. If you ever came across her you had better tell me now."

Castiel reluctantly did as he was asked. "I hate to disappoint you but she could be any of the girls I've had to deal with. I don't remember her."

"Then take a closer fucking look." Mercer thrust the photo into Castiel's face.

"No, sorry. I still don't remember her."

Mercer's patience wore thin and he headbutted Castiel.

Castiel staggered and attempted to fight back, still believing that he had the power of Satan behind him. Mercer blocked the High Priest's punch with ease and countered with a strike so hard that Castiel fell to the floor.

Lying on the cold surface, Castiel looked through

watery eyes and saw an image begin to appear. He smiled and then it turned into laughter.

"What you laughing at you prick", said an exasperated Mercer as he stuck the boot into Castiel's ribs.

"He's here. He's here to save me."

Mercer quickly took a look behind him and then back at his victim. "There's nothing there, you dumb fuck. Looks like you hit your head on the way down, Lad."

Castiel continued to look just beyond Mercer and the image became clearer. His laughing ceased abruptly and his face changed to one of confusion followed by dreaded fear.

Castiel was looking straight at a large white rabbit.

Still on the floor, Castiel, began to scurry away, but in reality there was nowhere for him to go.

Mercer took another peak over his shoulder as Castiel's eyes clearly seemed to be fixed on something behind him. Again, Mercer, couldn't see anything.

But Castiel could, all too well.

The face of the rabbit began to change. One to a face that he hadn't seen in years.

But there was no mistaking who it was. It was the face of Eva.

Castiel was stunned into a state of paralysis.

"Enough of this," said Mercer, still oblivious to what was happening to Castiel. He decided that the High Priest was worthy of the deepest insult and humiliation possible and promptly stripped him of his robe. "Fuck me, you've got three nipples, you freak. You really are a weirdo, ain't ya, Lad?... Wait a minute, I've heard about this kind of thing. You have a single mark in the centre of your chest to resemble a witch's teat. It's for Satan himself to suckle at, isn't it? Well I'll soon put an end to that." Mercer took out a blade, bent over the quivering Castiel and promptly sliced off his third nipple. Castiel let out a scream and writhed in agony.

Now in closer proximity to the half-naked Castiel,

Mercer, spotted something around his neck. Mercer yanked it from him to take a closer look and quickly discovered it to be a silver necklace with two charms hanging from it. A gold figure of a teddy bear and the other being the initial 'S' with diamonds snaking around the shape of the letter.

Mercer recognised it straight away and rage instantly consumed him. Seeing his granddaughter's necklace had at last brought some realisation of her fate, but it wasn't the happy ending that he had been hoping for.

And that cheeky piece of shit quivering in front of him had had the nerve to wear it like some kind of trophy.

Mercer forced open Castiel's mouth and sliced out his tongue. "Well, it's not like you say your prayers now is it, Lad? Even though you're gonna need them."

Jack The Ripper himself would have been proud of what Mercer did next.

Mercer didn't stop slashing Castiel even when he was long dead. Each frenzied stab and slice that he placed on Castiel's pathetic and lifeless body was as much an act of therapy for Mercer as it was an act of revenge.

The crème de la crème of the slaughter was the carving of not one but two letter Ss in memory of Mercer's daughter and granddaughter. Both inflicted while Castiel had still been alive.

Meanwhile, the battle of the females was taking shape in the adjacent tunnel following Yasmin's rugby tackle on Beatrix which sent her crashing hard to the ground. The old woman's torch had skimmed along the floor following the impact and it had landed favourably for Yasmin to see what she was doing within its well-placed beam.

Yasmin grabbed the old bitch's grey hair and used it as a method to smash her head over and over into the ground. Beatrix soon lost consciousness. Content that the old bag was no longer a contender, Yasmin, turned to her girlfriend to discover Kadence was not having quite the same amount of success in defeating the other old lady.

Just as the speed of the old ladies' sprints had been deceptive, so too was the amount of fight in Martha. Beatrix would most likely have been just as handy, but Yasmin hadn't left any opportunity for her to fight back. Perhaps working for the perpetual and capable brawler Judd Stone all this time had its benefits!

Amongst the trading of kicks and punches, Kadence, managed to grab hold of Martha's hair which brought her face down to Kadence's ascending knee. It connected perfectly.

Yasmin, keen to help out her girlfriend, followed up with a kick into the old lady's stomach which saw her physically lifted from the floor.

Suddenly though, Yasmin, felt a weight on her back. Despite her beating, Beatrix, had regained consciousness and screaming like a banshee had jumped on Yasmin, riding her like a rodeo bull.

Yasmin realised that the point of the tunnel where they had caught up with the two evil twins had been fairly narrow so she decided to run backwards knowing that Beatrix would connect with the wall first before she herself would.

The plan worked, and Beatrix loosened her grip on Yasmin with the impact of the stone connecting with her. Severely winded, the old woman slid down the wall unable to offer much movement.

At the same time Kadence grabbed the hair of Martha once again and using all her strength spun her round and round before eventually letting her go. The momentum of the swing sent Martha crashing into the same wall as her sister and she ended up crumpled next to her. They both seemed to be deeply unconsciousness.

"Come on Yas, let's leave the old witches to rot in their own blood."

Yasmin and Kadence hit a high five and walked away from the scene victorious in battle.

It seemed a longer departure walking down the tunnel

instead of running along it, but they had still almost made it back to the main area when the evil old twins eventually began to stir.

"Martha, we need to put a curse on them two little bitches."

"Once I can walk again, I'll consider it."

Suddenly, Beatrix let out a scream.

"What's wrong?"

"I think a bastard rat just bit me. Ouch, there it goes again. The rat must be the size of a dog!"

Then Martha screamed. "I've been bitten too," she said.

Then the bites began to be accompanied by the sound of giggling.

"What's going on, Beatrix?"

But before Beatrix could answer her sister, a swarm of little people were upon them eating their raw flesh.

The screams of the two evil twin sisters as they lost their lives funnelled down the tunnel to Yasmin and Kadence just as they stepped out from it into the main altar area.

Mercer was already back there too, less his jacket which he'd left at the scene, such was the saturation of Castiel's blood on it.

"Did you hear those screams, Yas?" asked Kadence.

"Yes, I did. Pretty blood-curdling too. That couldn't have been what we did to them, surely. Could it?"

"No way. There must be something else in those tunnels. I suggest we get out of here."

Judd now came into view and he didn't look too pleased. "You two never leave my sight again, understand?"

Yasmin, as contrary as ever, simply rolled her eyes. "Whatever."

"We won't, Judd, we promise," said Kadence being a whole lot more diplomatic.

"OK, good. Now if any of these scumbags scattered

around here are still alive, we need to gather them up and take them with us until we decide what to do with them once and for all," said Judd.

"I have a few ideas," said Talia.

The gangsters rounded up the blood-soaked disciples and began to shepherd them down the tunnel to lead them back to the outside world. The disciples realised that any attempt to fight back would be futile.

Suddenly, a creaking sound began to occur from above them.

Judd was first to react and looking up he soon began to sense what was happening. Especially when the sound escalated to that of a rumble. "Hurry up, the roof is going to cave in." No sooner had he voiced his prediction when a fall of rocks collapsed and crumbled behind them, landing on a number of disciples and clearly blocking access to the rear, including the alter which was now splintered into pieces. Ironically, the inverted cross had found its way to stick out of the mass rubble.

"Well, that's a few less twats that we need to round up then," said Talia.

Somewhat miraculously, the children present had managed to escape from the tumble of rocks completely unharmed and on the right side of the rock fall. There was a mixture of terrified kids who were glad to have been 'rescued' but some had already been subjected to the Black Mass by Castiel.

"We're not going with you," stated one of the transitioned girls, belying their years in confidence and ability to articulate. Talia didn't hesitate in cocking a gun at her head. "You will do exactly what we say and just because you're a kid don't think I won't put a bullet in your skull."

Funnily enough, even those children who had encountered the Black Mass transition suddenly became compliant.

As they walked onwards across the craggy surface, Judd

almost obsessively continued to assess the rocks for any potential fall whilst the gangsters rigourously kept an eye on the captives. Every now and then the pleasure of throwing the odd punch or a kick at the Satanists proved too much temptation and as such, the journey back to the outside world passed by uneventfully. The disciples knew any resistance would have been unwise and the threat of guns at the ready had also been enough of a deterrent.

On their return it took a moment for their eyes to adjust from the darkness of the cavern, only to find the sight of high flames lapping at the air. The gangsters that had stayed back from entering the Caverns had started a funeral pyre to get rid of the countless dead bodies that had been perceived to be in the way.

"Well, I guess that saves The Undertaker a job," said Mercer to no-one in particular.

Those that were still alive had been kettled together and were then joined by those that had just been led out of the cavern so they could be held captive as a collective.

"All OK, Diego?" asked Judd.

"Yeah, mate. How about you?"

"Yeah, good."

Kadence and Yasmin nurtured and comforted the children who had been lucky enough to escape Castiel's Black Mass whilst the others were thrown into the cage with the others who had been captured earlier. They were almost feral, snarling and reaching through the bars keen to get out and form an attack at the gangsters.

"What are we gonna do with these kids," asked Mercer.

"I really don't know," said Judd. "But one thing's for sure, we dare not let them out of that cage."

"Amen to that," said Talia. "If they weren't so young, I'd waste them all, which is precisely what we should do to these evil fuckwits," he said pointing to the disciples.

"Nah, too messy, Lad" said Mercer, somewhat ironically considering the fate that he had not long bestowed upon Castiel. "The thing is though, we do need to do something with them."

"I have an idea," said Judd. "Follow me."

Judd led Mercer and Talia, along with a handful of gangsters who were shepherding the disciples and their hanging heads, through the meandering paths of dirt and patches of grass. Once at the top of the dip he led the entourage further into the gardens of a derelict house and eventually to the cage where a collection of eighties tribute acts were being held.

Both the site and sight were surreal. It looked like someone had placed these people in a cage to form a small collection of eighties pop stars.

Judd removed the metal bar that was holding the latch and door at bay and not before time released his friends.

Madonna left first and promptly hugged him, grateful to be seemingly free from the nightmare.

The others soon followed and were equally as grateful to have been released.

The disciples were swiftly marshalled to trade places with them and were duly locked soundly in the cage out of harm's way.

Isla, Mercer's niece, ran to her uncle and she hugged him. The tough gangster allowed a rare sight of human emotion to be seen as he hugged her back and kissed her on her blonde head. "Are you OK?" asked Mercer. "Do I need to take care of anyone here?" Regardless of any recent camaraderie, he was still prepared to make someone pay if his niece had been mistreated.

"No, Uncle Richie, honestly. These are my friends."

"And him?" said Mercer nodding towards Judd.

"Yeah, him too."

"Are you sure?"

"Yeah, Uncle Richie. I'm sure."

"OK," he hugged his niece again.

"So, what now," asked Rufus.

"Well, I don't know about anyone else but I need a drink," said Paris

"Me too," said Madonna.

"Then to the village pub it is," said Mercer.

"And what about these fuckers in the cages?" said Talia.

"Well, they're not going anywhere, are they?" said Mercer. "Come on Ray, I'll buy you a drink."

"Only if I buy you one back."

CHAPTER 30
I KNEW YOU WERE WAITING FOR ME

Harry wasn't sure if he should be relieved or terrified when he witnessed the influx of gangsters enter his pub.

Incidentally, Judd was most definitely pleasantly surprised to hear The Beatles track "Revolution" being played over the pub's juke box.

"Line them up, Lad," ordered Mercer, pulling a wedge of notes from his coat jacket and placing it down on the bar. "This should more than cover it, and there's a little something extra in there for your trouble over the past few hours."

"This will definitely help cover things," said Ray Talia also placing a wad of cash on the bar.

Harry sensed a slight tension between Talia and Mercer and quickly assessed them as being one another's nemesis. Clearly Talia wasn't going to be outshone by Mercer's generous offer.

Harry then observed Mercer smile at Talia's childish behaviour, but would the Liverpudlian have done anything different to the Brummie? Probably not.

As for Harry himself, he suddenly felt as if the

inconvenience had all been worth it and for the first time that evening he finally began to relax.

After pouring the first two ales he thought it proper and wise to present them in perfect synchronisation to Mercer and Talia. Although it was Mercer who was first to grab his pint of freshly poured nectar. "Cheers."

"Cheers," said Talia, following suit and clinking glasses with his counterpart.

Meanwhile, Prudence and Polly were helping Harry with the largest round they'd ever had to pour and distribute.

Judd was next to grab a pint of ale and then turned to the two head gangsters. "When you two have finished your dick measuring contest you can clink my glass too. Cheers."

"Cheers," replied Mercer and Talia. Whether any of the three men liked it or not, an unspoken bond had inadvertently been forged over the past few hours.

Judd reflected on his first acrimonious meeting with Mercer and how he had used a story about Geezer Butler's mysterious book and witchcraft to try and gain a slight advantage over the gangster. Now of course he figured such an advantage could have only been marginal, for Mercer had clearly proved that even things of a supernatural nature could never unnerve him. As for Talia, he already knew nothing could frighten that psychopath.

"A gin and tonic for my niece please?" said Mercer to Polly. "The rest of my boys can wait for their beer."

"And so can mine," said Talia. "And make sure both you and your pretty colleague get one for yourselves."

"Right away, sir," said Polly to Mercer followed by a "Thank you, sir," to Talia.

By this time, Harry had noticed that young kids were also in the bar and didn't deem it appropriate. "Can you take them through to the back, please?" he asked Yasmin. "There's a kids corner in there anyway with a few toys and colouring books."

"Yeah, no problem," said Yasmin, and she and Kadence expertly chaperoned the children to a more appropriate environment.

When Harry then noticed that Madonna and Boy George had joined George Michael he knew once and for all that this was a night that he wasn't going to forget. Little did he know that if things had gone a little better, he would have had Elvis Presley making an appearance as well!

"Keep them coming, bartenders," said Mercer. "Money is no object."

Instead of keeping up with Mercer, this time, Talia, swiftly downed the remainder of his pint and said something a little more unexpected. "I'm just popping out for a bit. I just need to clear my head a little."

Judd and Mercer just shrugged at one another as Talia walked away.

"Fancy another?" asked Mercer.

"It would be rude not too," replied Judd with a smile.

As it turned out, the evening became a memorable experience and fortunately for some very good reasons despite the original circumstances that had led to a swarm of gangsters invading Crank. As the hours passed by, it was almost as if a celebration unfolded in honour of defeating Castiel and his Satanic cult.

Eventually, Talia returned more hyperactive than ever, shaking off Judd's questioning of why he smelt of petrol.

The alcohol continued to flow into the night. Prudence and Polly led the dancing as the eighties cover acts took turns on the karaoke and even Tilda paired up with George Michael for a dream-come-true rendition of "I Knew You Were Waiting For Me."

Things then evolved incredibly in the music department, including the wondrous sight of gangsters taking a turn on the karaoke. Ironically these most hardened of men belted out tracks by the likes of Steps and the Spice Girls, and some even managed to sing the songs pretty well!

The young girls slept soundly through all of the joviality, as each of the adult female contingent took a turn of checking in on them. Although Kadence did find enough time to deliver a song bang on topic with a more than passable rendition of "White Rabbit" by Jefferson Airplane.

Throughout the night, Rufus, also kept people typically entertained with a steady flow of bullshits.

It was only when the next morning came and Harry offered to cook everyone breakfast that Judd woke out of his hungover slumber. His head was a little sore but inwardly he was quite content as he reminisced about last night's fun.

But then his thought process starkly changed as he suddenly remembered something. "Shit, those kids have been locked in cages all night! Harry, can I use your phone?"

CHAPTER 31
HERE COMES THE RAIN

"This must be her," said Judd to Tilda as a barely roadworthy car approaching them began to slow down. Once safely parked away from the bend in the road, the engine was switched off and the driver's door opened. Out stepped a small, skinny figure with oversized spectacles which presented a slightly comedic contrast to the shape of her face.

Judd had arranged to meet at the small parking area situated at the bend in Alder Road. In truth, it wasn't an official parking area, it was more of a convenient plot of unremarkable land that was large enough to host vehicles and people had used it as such over the years. It also sat at the foot of the dirt track that led to Crank Caverns.

"Mr. Stone, I presume," said the small lady as she reached out a hand to Judd. "Reverend Coral Richards of Rainford Parish at your service." Judd willingly shook the hand of the eccentric vicar, taking care not to squeeze too hard.

"Pleased to meet you, Reverend Richards. Thanks so much for coming at such short notice. This is my friend,

Tilda."

"Tilda, what a lovely name. I'm pleased to meet you too."

"Likewise," replied Tilda also shaking hands.

Judd had decided to bring Tilda along as he figured that her presence would appear as a much less threatening encounter to both the vicar and the children whom he planned to release.

"I picked up a sense of urgency on the phone, Mr. Stone."

"Please, call me Judd, and yes, your senses have served you well."

"OK, Judd it is. So, what is it that I can do for you, Judd?"

"I need you to walk with me up towards Crank Caverns, please? Is that OK?"

"Yes, but may I know the reason?" answered Reverend Richards.

"Am I correct in thinking that there aren't any churches in Crank itself, but your parish covers this area?"

"That is correct. There aren't any churches in Crank, not anymore, hasn't been for some time in fact. And yes, I represent the Church of England element of God's flock in these parts, not that I'd close my door to anyone in need, of course, Judd."

"That's good, the last part about your door being open I mean. I'll be honest with you Reverend Richards; you were the second number that I called."

"Oh?"

"I initially dialled the Catholic church in Rainford but I didn't get an answer."

"What's this about, Judd?"

"I phoned the Catholic church as I know that they can perform exorcisms. Forgive me, but I wasn't sure if the Church of England can as well."

"We can, yes."

"That's good, although I'm not sure that it is an

exorcism that is needed as such, but more of a reversal of what's been imposed on some young girls. Something forced on them by a satanic high priest...I know this sounds a bit far-fetched, Reverend, but believe me, there really is a genuine need for your services."

"I'd like to help, but the thing is it's not quite as easy as you may think, Judd."

"How do you mean? I thought you said that you can perform an exorcism?"

"Yes I can, but only with the strict and express permission of the Bishop."

Judd ran his fingers through his hair, a regular characteristic he would demonstrate when thinking things through or feeling slightly agitated. "I don't think we have time for all that. These girls have already spent one cold night locked in cages."

"There can be no other way, Judd. I have to have permission from the Bishop."

"And in the meantime let innocent children die? I'm sorry to be so blunt, but please, you must let me take you to these girls. Surely God wouldn't let a piece of bureaucratic procedure get in the way of freeing children from the influence of Satan."

Reverend Richard looked at Tilda. "Is he always this persuasive?"

"Yes, but usually not quite so diplomatic," answered Tilda.

"This is him being diplomatic?" The pint-sized vicar turned on her heels and opened the door to her car.

"Hey, you can't go," said Judd.

She returned clutching an item. "Relax, I can't perform an exorcism without my Bible now, can I?"

Judd breathed a sigh of relief. "Thank you, Reverend. For a moment I thought you were running out on us there."

"I'm not promising anything just yet, Judd, it all depends what I can achieve in reality. But it seems apparent that we should go and take a look at these young girls."

"We could save time if we drive to the top of the dirt track, but then we will still have to take the footpath as most of the route is inaccessible by car."

"OK then, hop in."

Judd took the passenger seat whilst Tilda occupied the back.

Reverend Richards turned the key to start the engine and then crunched the gears as she found reverse.

"Sorry about that, I'm always a little nervous when I have passengers."

Judd found himself hoping that her driving skills wouldn't be a reflection of how well she could perform an exorcism!

As it turned out, Reverend Richards, managed to steer the car into the entrance of the dirt track with little bother, but a reduction in speed may have helped the car's suspension from having to wrestle so acutely with the bumps and potholes on its ascent.

As they travelled along the short but bumpy journey, Judd, brought Reverend Richards up to speed as quickly as possible on what he had witnessed Castiel do with the Black Masses and the seemingly change of persona of the children.

"It could be some sort of hypnotic trance that he's applied to the girls," offered Reverend Richards. "I'm not quite sure what he's done but unless a spirit has entered their body an exorcism won't solve the problem."

"You mean a spirit like a demonic possession?" enquired Tilda, as her head made contact with the roof of the car.

"Exactly that. However, if it is the Devil himself that has entered them, then I'm not sure I have the necessary capability to free them of his hold."

In spite of not knowing exactly what waited ahead of them, Reverend Richards thankfully brought the car to a halt for everyone's sake, albeit a little abruptly.

Judd remained focused on getting to the girls and freeing them.

They stepped out of the car and made their way over the uneven terrain until it flattened out to the first cage, the one that had initially held Rufus, Isla and the eighties tribute acts.

As they approached the cage, on sight of the Holy book under the arm of the funny looking bespectacled woman and her dog collar, some of the young girls cowered away. Others displayed a more telling act of defiance as they hissed and spat through the bars of the cage.

Reverend Coral Richards looked to the sky and addressed her God. "Lord, give me the power to understand what has happened to these children. Allow me the wisdom to know if it is indeed the fallen angel that has usurped their being and soul."

Suddenly, a crack of lightning appeared in what was until now a calm sky. Judd figured that it was either a dramatic coincidence, or God was indeed answering his loyal servant. Equally, he feared that in stark contrast it could be the wrath of Satan himself.

Rain began to fall, not heavily, but enough to notice a small soaking on clothing and small sprinkles of water dancing majestically on the ground.

The young girls' hissing and snarling increased and by now they were frantically shaking the bars of the cage, manically attempting to free themselves or reach between the bars to get to the three uninvited adults who stood before them.

Reverend Richards responded by making the sign of the cross in mid-air and speaking as emphatically as she possibly could. "Blessed are you, Lord, all-powerful God, who in Christ, the living water of salvation, blessed and transformed us." She repeated the sentence again, and then again, and then again.

Still the rain fell from the sky.

The roof of the cage served to shelter the children who were huddled more centrally, but those who had forced their way to reach through the bars began to noticeably change. Their manic aggressiveness gave way to a much more gentler persona and they appeared to now be frightened and confused. Some even began to cry and asked to be let out of the cage.

"Open the cage," said Reverend Richards.

"Are you sure, some of these kids still look like they'll tear us apart," said Tilda.

"Some yes, but not all of them, some wish to be released."

"It could be a trick," said Judd.

"Trust me," said Reverend Richards. "I assume that you do or you wouldn't have asked me to get involved. Now, unlock the cage and release them. Please."

Judd did as he was asked and Reverend Richards repeated the same Biblical words that she had spoken earlier: "Blessed are you, Lord, all-powerful God, who in Christ, the living water of salvation, blessed and transformed us."

The children ran out of the cage, either intent on attack or simply glad to be free, but within seconds they all seemed like normal children. Each and every one of them now devoid of any demonic possession or similar. Reverend Richards collapsed to the ground, exhausted.

"You blessed the rain," said Tilda. "You made the rain into Holy water."

"I think so," said Reverend Richards fighting for breath. "It's all I could think to do. As the rainwater touched them it transitioned them back to being normal little girls."

"Water of salvation, blessed and transformed. That's pretty amazing," said Judd.

"You say they went through a Black Mass?" asked Reverend Richards.

"Yes," said Judd. "At least, that's what I think it looked like. Rotten vegetables and suspected urine seemed to be served up to the children, while an inverted cross stood nearby."

Still gasping for breath, Reverend Richards reached under her cassock and pulled out her mobile phone."

"What are you doing?" asked Judd.

"I just want to make sure things are all OK. I have a much more useful phone number for my catholic counterpart in Rainford than you do... Hello, is that you Father Fitzgerald... great... Yes it's me, Coral Richards. Don't ask any questions, I just need you to trust me. I need your help... go to the Red Cat pub and bless as many bottles of red wine as you can. I have some young folk here who require communion. I'll be bringing them to you shortly. Bye for now." She hung up. "Now let me get my breath back and then lead me to the second cage that needs my attention."

"I certainly will," answered Judd who was able to look down inro the valley where the cages and Funeral Pyres were scattered. "I'll need to take you down there," he said pointing in the necessary direction. Judd could just about make out the images of the young children moving about in the one cage, but the other cages seemed totally void of life.

Judd reached out for the reverend's hand and helped her to her feet. After a couple of moments bending over with her hands on her knees Reverend Richards was ready. Straightening herself up she said, "OK, let's go. I'll do the exact same thing with the young girls that are down there."

"You'll be glad to know that it's mainly downhill," said Judd. "Just watch your step, it could get slippy with all this rain. I notice it's getting heavier albeit the sky is remaining as blue as can be."

Reverend Richards nodded.

Once Judd had led the way to the area in question, on closer inspection he could see exactly why there hadn't been any movement in the cages without young girls in them.

At first, he thought the smell of cooking flesh was purely attributed to the funeral pyre, but inside the cages there was a horrific scene of smouldering body mass and bones. Fortunately, the flames had been burning long enough to disguise the most gruesome sights that come with the burning of human bodies.

Now it was all too clear why Ray Talia had gone missing the night before only to return smelling of petrol.

CHAPTER 32
SWEET CHILD O'MINE

Primrose Neves took a final drag of her umpteenth cigarette of the morning and threw it amongst all the others in her backyard before killing its burning ember with the sole of her slider. She had kidded herself that by breaking her smoking chastity of six years or so, that a return to smoking would somehow help her deal with the fact that her only daughter was missing.

At least she was somehow managing to hold it together though. Well one of them needed to. Her poor hubby Kirk had been a broken man these past few days barely able to function or even speak.

Primrose figured that she should go back inside and check on him. Again.

"Fancy a cup of tea, love?" she asked gently as she leant against the doorframe that stood between the living room and the kitchen.

Kirk nodded and managed to whisper a single word: "Please."

Cigarettes and tea had kept them both going to a certain degree, although the hope of ever seeing their daughter again was fading by the hour. Not that either of them had dared to mention it to the other. Saying it may make it true.

Primrose filled the kettle with water, turned off the cold water tap and returned the kettle to its cradle. Next, she flicked the switch so that the electric current could begin the boiling process.

She returned to her husband as she waited for the kettle to boil and sat on the sofa that provided a view to the outside world. She had stared out of that window religiously since the disappearance, willing her daughter to come home and nonchalantly skip up the path totally oblivious to the worry that she had caused. In truth, her daughter hadn't even been walking for that long.

As yet the return of her little girl sadly hadn't happened, but she did begin to notice something occurring outside the house.

"Who's that?" she said to Kirk as her eyes met the appearance of a huge bald head resting on huge shoulders.

The figure rose above the hedge indicating that he had stepped out from a shielded parked car. Primrose could tell from his movements that he was now walking to the other side of the shielded vehicle and she assumed that he was opening the door for someone else to step out. Her assumption was correct and it soon became apparent that the first scary looking man needed to open the door for a second one, because the latter seemed to be carrying something in his arms.

Both figures came fully into view as they walked up the Neves' garden path and Primrose could now see that whatever was being carried by the second man was wrapped in a blanket.

"Fuck me, they're coming here," said Primrose.

"Perhaps they are undercover cops?" said Kirk who had by now also clocked them.

"Maybe, but wouldn't they have arrived with Jacinda?" Jacinda was the Family Liaison Officer who had been assigned to them by their local police force. Jacinda had been extremely supportive, but unfortunately the police on the whole had struggled to find any leads for their missing daughter.

The doorbell rang.

"Kirk, I'm not answering the door to those big scary looking bastards."

Kirk didn't reply to his wife but he duly got up from his armchair and headed to the front door. In truth he was past caring if he was about to get his head kicked in for something as yet unknown. Primrose decided that she may as well follow him.

"Can I help you lads?" said Kirk once he'd opened the door.

"On the contrary, mate. I think we can help you," came the reply from one of the men. Suddenly, whatever was wrapped in the blanket was carefully handed to Primrose by a pair of huge and tattooed hands. "She's slept like a baby, bless her, but then again, she ain't much older than a baby by the looks of her. It'd be a shame to wake her."

Primrose could hardly believe her eyes. "It's Lori, Kirk, It's our Lori, she's back with us."

"Yeah, I can see that, thank you guys." Then Kirk realised what he was saying. These two meatheads were considerably bigger than him but he wasn't going to hesitate in chinning at least one of them depending on how the remainder of the conversation went. "How come you had her in the first place. Was it you that took her?"

"No mate, I promise you. We are simply returning all the girls to their rightful owners."

"Girls?" said Primrose. "There's more than Lori that's been missing? What the fuck has been going on?"

"All you need to know Mrs. Neves is that all the girls, including your daughter, are now perfectly safe following a very carefully executed intervention."

"And please be reassured that those that took her have been made to pay for their impertinence and excessive taking of liberties," said the other large man. "They won't be able to do anything like this ever again."

"So you rescued her? Them? Lori?"

"We did, well a few of us did. The main thing is, is that your daughter is absolutely fine."

Lori began to stir out of her slumber. She smiled at the man who had been holding her. "Hi Sparky, this is my mommy."

"I know honey. You're safe now."

"Mommy, Sparky is my friend."

Primrose could only smile as joyful tears welled in her eyes.

This same scenario was happening all over England as the gangsters of Birmingham and Liverpool safely returned missing daughters to their parents.

CHAPTER 33
DON'T YOU (FORGET ABOUT ME)

"So I guess this is the end of our little adventure and we all go back to our normal lives," said Judd.

"Whatever normal means?" replied Madonna.

Judd hugged her first. "You take care now Pop Princess."

"I will, you too."

"I've discovered that the docks didn't suffer much damage in the fire after all and there was nothing sinister involved," said Rufus. "Perhaps I could organize a Beatles Festival next year? We all still love Liverpool, right?"

All eyes fell on Rufus.

"Even me as the world's biggest Beatles anorak needs a bit of time before we can even consider that one," said Judd.

"Just a thought," said Rufus.

Judd approached Paris. "Paris, it's been really good to have met you albeit in the most craziest of circumstances."

"You too, Judd. I hope to see you again," replied Paris slowly releasing herself from Judd's hug.

"Elvis, we gonna high five or shake hands?"

"Fuck that, Judd. We have a bonafide bromance going on. Just don't squeeze too hard I haven't quite healed yet." Judd and Elvis hugged.

Incidentally, as Mercer's men had taken Elvis to the hospital it had been Talia's men who had collected him and brought him back for the brief reunion.

"George, Andrew, George. Hey, what can I say."

George and Judd hugged one another and slapped backs. "I'll see you again, Judd, as I'm definitely keeping in touch with this lady," said George looking towards Tilda.

"You'd better," said Tilda.

"I'll look forward to it," said Judd. "But perhaps don't ask me to be your Andrew Ridgeley again, huh?"

"Deal. I shouldn't need to now anyway as my pal George, Andrew, you know who I mean, is on the mend."

"That's good. It's still so confusing with you two," laughed Judd.

"And Elvis, I'm glad you are on the mend too. It's great news," said George Michael.

Elvis winked in grateful acknowledgement and gave a thumbs up.

"Do I get a hug?" asked Tilda.

"You know you will," laughed George Michael. After hugging her friend, Tilda briefly turned to Kadence. "Hey Kadence, can I have chat with you later. It's about something that happened to me and George here in Liverpool. Something very weird."

"Sure. If it's weird I'll know, right?" smiled Kadence.

"Err, kind of but I didn't mean it like that."

"I know, I'm only joking. Anyway, let me guess, something happened on Bold Street, right?"

"Right," answered George Michael looking slightly astonished. "How did you know?"

"I'll tell you both properly later. Just know this, time time travel is a real thing, right? You won't have been the first."

Next, Judd carried on with his goodbyes but paused a

moment when he came face to face with Isla, desperately searching for the right words. He still wasn't sure that he found them. "Isla, some say that things are meant for a reason even when it's unclear at the time as to what that reasoning could be. I truly believe that my life has been richer for meeting you and dare I say it even Uncle Richie here. I'm just so sorry that we might have put you through a whole lot of crap to get us here. Also, I'm genuinely sorry about Tatiana."

"Thanks Judd, you're a good guy underneath it all. I can't say I'm sorry for your pal Hunter, though."

"I wouldn't expect you to be. Anyway, he's no longer considered to have ever been a pal of mine. Or Diego's or Rufus's for that matter. Good riddance to bad rubbish, aye. Take care Isla, if you're ever in Birmingham make sure to look me up. I promise you that next time it'll be a lot more straightforward." Judd and Isla hugged.

Judd looked at Mercer who was hard to read. "Don't even think about hugging me, lad."

Judd smiled. "I wouldn't dream of it, but I hope a handshake is customary for you."

Mercer didn't crack a smile but after a moment's pause, he took Judd's hand and shook it. It was one of those handshakes where the squeeze indicated a power struggle. For once in his life, Judd, willingly conceded the subliminal contest.

"You know if my niece here hadn't have vouched for you, you'd be with your scumbag friend Hunter, don't you? This could have all turned out very differently for you, Judd. But. Without this little adventure as you call it, I would never have found closure for my daughter and granddaughter. You can perhaps understand why I stop short of thanking you, but I'm content to recognise that we have discovered a mutual respect between us, Judd."

"Richie, I'm truly sorry for the loss of your girls. Believe me, if you hadn't have got to Castiel first I would have gladly delivered his just rewards on your behalf."

"Understood, but regarding putting that bastard straight into Hell that pleasure just had to be all mine."

"There's been a lot of means justifying ends, I guess," answered Judd.

"Revenge is always a sweet dish to serve up," interjected Ray Talia.

"Amen, to that," said Rufus.

"What would you know about it," asked Judd. Rufus was just about to open his mouth to speak when Judd thought now wasn't the time to tolerate another legendary bullshit. "It's OK, Rufus, tell me later. I'm sure everyone wants to get off."

"Before you go Rufus, I think there's something you could do for me, in way of making amends," said Mercer. "After all, it was your idea to put that festival on in Liverpool which led to the inconvenience that we all found ourselves to be in over the past day or two."

Rufus gulped, he realised what a man like Richie Mercer was capable of. What on earth did he want him to do? "Anything, Mr. Mercer. You just name it, sir."

"It's my birthday next month and I'd like you to bring this little collection of tribute acts together one more time. Just for me."

Inwardly, Rufus breathed a sigh of relief. "I'm sure that can be arranged. Where did you have in mind?"

"Somewhere in Liverpool of course, maybe one of my own clubs in fact. I like to party in style."

"Hold on a minute," interjected Talia. "It's my birthday next month too and I've been a lot more inconvenienced than you have, Mercer. I had to bring my boys all the way up north to help out with this little project. I think the main gratitude should fall to me."

Mercer's face remained unreadable. "Ray, I have a certain amount of gratitude for you. It was an interesting and successful collaboration between our two outfits, but don't push it. And in the nicest possible way when are you fucking off back to Birmingham?"

"When we are good and ready," replied a defiant Ray Talia. "Although to be honest with you, I need to smell the fresh air of Birmingham again sooner rather than later."

"Err, maybe you could have a joint birthday celebration," offered Rufus keen to retain the peace. "I mean, I think you two gentlemen deserve to be entertained and celebrated in equal measure.

Everyone waited with bated breath, surely this compromise wasn't going to materialise. But then it was Mercer who surprised everyone first.

"Fine by me, I can welcome you to Liverpool one more time I suppose in honour of our recent collaboration, Ray."

"No fucking way, you can come to Birmingham."

Mercer laughed. "I don't think so. I tell you what, if you don't want to travel as far as this again, we'll go for somewhere in between. I suggest a venue in Stoke-On-Trent."

"I ain't going any further than Wolverhampton."

Judd felt obliged to interject. "Hold on boys. Do you really think that your gangster counterparts in Stoke-On-Trent and Wolverhampton are just going to let you walk into their patch and have a party? That would be a blood bath and a war that none of us wants to see."

"He has a point," said Mercer.

"I guess he does," agreed Talia.

"You need somewhere neutral and gangster free," said Rufus. "I can offer you Shrewsbury, I have a cousin in Shrewsbury who has a very nice and large venue indeed. It would be perfect for your birthdays and I'd say it's roughly half-way between Liverpool and Birmingham." Rufus closed his eyes daring to hope that his suggestion would bring the solution. He opened his eyes to see the remarkable sight of Richie Mercer and Ray Talia shaking hands.

"See you in Shrewsbury, Ray."

"You will indeed, Richie."

"Now that you two have finished your latest dick measuring contest can we all go about our business," said Judd.

"Not quite," said Mercer. "Rufus, I have one more condition.

"Go on," answered Rufus, gulping once more, looking nervous of what this condition could possibly be.

"I want someone else on the bill as the headline act, and I don't want you to disappoint me, Rufus."

"Who?" asked Rufus. He only hoped that he could deliver the request.

"A Black Sabbath tribute act."

"I agree," said Talia unexpectedly. "Birmingham will be duly represented if we have Sabbath playing."

Rufus appeared relieved once more. "I can do that, no problem," he said. Suddenly, Rufus became interrupted as his phone rang. "Sorry, I just need to get this." Mercer and Talia looked at one another, neither seemingly impressed at Rufus's insolence at accepting the call in their presence. It turned out to be a video call.

"Hi Rufus, how's my favourite promoter?" came the familiar voice from the phone speakers.

"Hey, I know that voice," said Madonna. "Surely it can't be?"

Paris stepped behind Rufus to take a peek who was on the video call. "Fucking hell, it is!"

Judd moved next to gain a look over Rufus's shoulder. "Well I never, it is them! Rufus does actually know a global superstar."

"Here, let me see," said Diego, but he had no chance of getting in with his huge frame.

"Hey," said Rufus. "I'm glad you called. Listen, I have two friends here with me and they are having a joint birthday party, next month. I was wondering if you could help out…"

CHAPTER 34
BROKEN LAND

"I think he's missed you," said Errol, as Mr. Mustard jumped excitably all over and around Judd when he entered his Rotunda apartment.

"And I've missed him too, haven't I, boy? Yes I have," said Judd in an uncharacteristic coochie-coo voice, crouching down on one knee to make it easier to connect with his dog. Mr. Mustard was still bouncing about excitedly on his hind legs. "Thanks for having him, Errol, you too Slim. Yasmin told me she'd called on you boys when she had to come and join me on my adventures up north."

"You're welcome," answered Slim. "Yeah, you're welcome," followed Errol. "We had fun with the little fellow to be honest. And please be assured Judd, neither of us have broken your internet connection gambling online. We're both doing OK, on that score. No pun intended."

"Glad to hear it, boys. Since having Billie, I haven't even put an each way roll-up on the horses."

"That's great news," answered Errol. "Takes some willpower no doubt, although as I recall you had a decent win not long before she was born. Went out on a high, huh?"

"I guess so," smiled Judd. "But I've consciously not been tempted to blow it all again."

"Nice one," said Slim.

"Keep things that way, my friend," said Errol.

Judd's friendship with Errol and Slim had arrived from attending the same support group for gambling addiction. They'd kept in touch ever since and they were part of another good circle of friends for Judd, just as Rufus and Diego had been.

Naturally Hunter had been permanently scratched from Judd's friends list, something that would have happened even if he had managed to make it out alive from Richie Mercer's attention. It turned Judd's stomach to think what his former friend had been mixed up in.

"Give me a few days and I'll get you both a beer for your trouble," said Judd.

"I'll hold you to that," said Slim.

"Me too," said Errol. "Now I think we should leave you with your dog. See you soon."

"See ya, thanks again. I'll be in touch."

No sooner had Errol and Slim closed the door behind them when a video call came through Judd's phone, which was now fully charged once again.

He signalled to Mr. Mustard to calm down a little and answered the call. "Brooke, this is an unexpected surprise."

"Someone has been pestering me to speak to her daddy." Next Brooke's face was replaced with Billie's."

"Hey Billie, how's my little girl then?"

"Hello Daddy," Billie's ability to speak was well advanced for her tender age. Like a lot of kids, however, she still struggled with pronouncing the odd word correctly. "Take me to cimena, please Daddy."

"Cimena, you mean cinema right? Mind you, when I was your age I called it the pictures," smiled Judd. "Of course, we can go to the cinema, Billie. What we gonna see?"

Billie just shrugged.

"OK, shall Daddy choose the film?"

Billie nodded with a big smile spread across her pretty little face.

"Shall we take Mommy too?" again Billie nodded. Then Brooke's face appeared back on the screen and Judd sensed he'd said the wrong thing. "Sorry Brooke, I got a bit ahead of myself there, I guess. When shall I pick her up?"

"You can pick *us* up, tomorrow at one. We can have a bite to eat before we go and see the new Disney thing that everyone's raving about."

Now it was Judd that was beaming with a smile. "It's a date, thanks Brooke."

"Don't read too much into this Judd, I just like Disney cartoons, right?" said Brooke gently.

"Of course, see you tomorrow. See you tomorrow, Billie."

"Bye Daddy, see you tomorrow. Love you."

"Love you too, Honey."

Judd continued to smile as the phone went dead. He wanted nothing more than to get back with Brooke and return to living as a family again, but he dared not build up his hopes too much. Nevertheless, this was an unfamiliar offer from Brooke to tag along with him and Billie and he had just realised that it wasn't even on one of his allocated days to have access to his daughter. This could only be interpreted as a positive sign regarding his relationship with Brooke, and one thing was for sure. Tomorrow was going to be the best day he had experienced for a long time.

Just as Judd was feeling over the moon about reconnecting with Brooke, Mr. Mustard, who had been waiting patiently was poised to jump excitedly all over his owner again. Unfortunately, the faithful dog was forced to cry out a slight whimper when his master's phone kicked in again with another video call. "Sorry boy, looks like I'm popular today…Hello?" he said answering the call. Instead of one face appearing on the screen he was greeted by two faces: Father Fitzgerald and Reverend Richards.

"Hello, Judd," said Father Fitzgerald whilst Reverend Richards gave a friendly wave. "Judd, I fancy myself as a bit of a private detective myself and after the experience in Crank I set about doing a bit of my own research."

"It's very interesting findings," said Reverend Richards.

"Go on," said Judd.

"I'll be honest with you," continued Father Fitzgerald. "The way that we were able to bring those kids back from the brink of evil seemed to go a little more smoothly than I'd have expected."

"I can echo that," said Reverend Richards.

"What do you mean? Perhaps you should have as much faith in yourselves as you do in your God. You performed an exorcism, didn't you? Father Fitzgerald, you gave the children blessed communion wine, and Reverend Richards, what about I saw of you in action? You both performed exorcisms, of sorts anyhow?"

"Of sorts," said Father Fitzgerald, but without express permission from either of our religious authorities. We broke all protocol. For that reason alone, it troubled me that it worked so well."

"Good defeated evil it's as simple as that, surely. Perhaps you don't need centuries of outdated bureaucracy to perform such acts. Everything evolves over time. Wait, you said troubled as in the past tense. So you're not troubled anymore?"

"I am a little but I think I may have a rational explanation. I can't be sure if I've worked things out correctly but it is plausible."

"Go on."

"It took a lot of research and digging about but I discovered that a Castiel Masson belonged to the International Society of Hypnotherapists. That was until he was expelled five years ago for 'unethical' practices of hypnosis."

"The same Castiel Masson that I've had the brief displeasure of knowing?"

"It's not a common name," interjected Reverend Richards. "It would explain why he needed children to be of a certain age, a child's mind from the age of three is more in touch with their imaginations than any adult can ever be. Therefore, the power of hypnotic suggestion is more easier placed in such a child, whereas a baby on the other hand cannot be hypnotised."

"Hence the shift from a King Herod type baby slaughter to a more practical solution: Hypnosis."

"Exactly," said Father Fitzgerald. "It seems even the child who is destined to be the second coming could be hypnotised according to Castiel's beliefs."

"And let's be honest, his ego would suggest as much," said Reverend Richards.

"It does makes sense. I was glad for the reduction in the deaths of young girls but I was puzzled as to why. Castiel was a narcissist, there's no doubt about that, but are you sure that your own modest egos aren't playing down the intervention that you both delivered?" asked Judd.

"We can never be sure but I believe that the reversal of the Black Mass that Castiel delivered was the perfect antidote to bring the hypnotised child back to their natural state. We can only hope that there aren't more already out there. So good did triumph over evil but perhaps with a more scientific explanation than a spiritual one."

"But Reverend Richards, I saw you turn falling rain into Holy water."

"Did I though? The touch of water on the children's skin, perhaps only when coupled with my words from the Bible, may have been enough to reverse their hypnotic state."

"I think you're doing yourself a huge disservice," said Judd.

"Maybe, but like Father Fitzgerald says, we can never

be sure, and hypnosis is a thing, right?"

Judd paused for a minute as he processed the information. "So do you think it could have been a form of mind control? The kids were set up to perform as products of experiments similar to MK Ultra programmes?"

"It's possible," said Father Fitzgerald. "Who knows what carnage these kids could have inflicted as their physical strength grew."

"I've experienced stuff like this before," said Judd. "Mind control. I know from first-hand experience that people can be programmed to carry out acts of heinous crimes based on what would seem to be a totally unremarkable trigger to the likes of me and you. But to a programmed assassin a single innocuous word or signal can set them on a path of destruction to imminently kill a particular target. I'd hoped that I'd never come across that type of thing again."

"Like I said, we will most likely never be sure, but the good news is, Judd, is that it has all been put to a stop. Whatever was being planned may well have materialised into something catastrophic. Thankfully, the girls we do know of are now back to normal so they are free to make their own decisions in life. Hopefully steered by the influence of God and not by the influence of evil."

"Thank you for your call, Father Fitzgerald and Reverend Richards. And once again thank you for your help up in Crank, whether you were instruments of divine interventions, exorcisms or simply reversing a hypnotic state from the children. I'll always be grateful."

"God bless you Judd," said Reverend Richards.

"May the Lord be with you," said Father Fitzgerald.

"Goodbye, both."

Judd looked over at Mr. Mustard who by now had settled down in the comforting knowledge that his owner was home. "Well, well, well. Life is certainly what happens when making other plans, hey boy?"

Judd walked over to the window of his apartment and looked out across the Bull Ring Shopping Centre. He spotted a very animated manic street preacher amongst the hordes of shoppers, not one of them taking any notice of him, and Judd allowed himself a wry smile. He turned to Mr. Mustard again. "It's so much easier being a dog, Muzzy. You just have to devote your love to one person, lick your balls every now and again, enjoy your walks in the park and get served up uncomplicated food that you appreciate in a heartbeat. There are no bigger questions for you to think about that can drive you crazy if you let it, is there boy? For a dog, you already know the meaning of life and don't need to question any of it."

Judd moved away from the window and headed towards his drinks cabinet. After the last few days he needed a drink and a period of relaxation. He took a glass tumbler, placed it down and then reached for a bottle of single malt whisky. He unscrewed the gold coloured top and half-filled the tumbler. He'd have to forgo the ice, but neat single malt whisky would do just nicely.

Judd took a small sip and the warm and welcoming flavour of Scottish peat danced on his tastebuds. A second satisfying sip was inevitable before placing the tumbler down again in order to head over to his vinyl collection.

Judd was far from anal, but he did like his records and CDs positioned in alphabetic order. He subconsciously and briefly found himself glancing at the 'C' section but there would be nothing attributed to Castiel and the Creatures of the Night here.

Instantly applying his attention to searching through the 'L' section he quickly discovered his album of choice, an original copy of *Double Fantasy* by John Lennon and Yoko Ono, the final album released in the former's lifetime. Judd pushed the recent memories of Castiel's record collection from his mind as he took the vinyl from its sleeve, fired up his turntable, placed the needle on the opening grooves of the record and waited for the hissing and scratchy noises to give way to the opening chimes of "(Just Like) Starting Over".

Once the music kicked in proper, Judd, reclaimed his glass of whisky and eased into the sofa to savour every moment.

It had indeed been a crazy few days.

He tapped the empty seat next to him signaling for his faithful dog to come and join him, which Mr. Mustard willingly did, resting his head on the lap of his owner.

Judd's philosophical juices were flowing following the experiences of the last few days coupled with the conversation he had not long had with his new-found friends of the clergy.

As he listened to the lyrics of one of his favourite songs, and certainly one of Lennon's most poignant considering the circumstances of it's release, it wasn't so much starting over that Judd needed to experience. It was instead more of a case of trying to get back to some kind of normality.

Some beers with the lads, that's what Liverpool was meant to have been. So that was something that he needed to see through soon. Just a regular drink with the boys, starting with Errol and Slim. He certainly shouldn't leave it so long again until he meets with Diego and Rufus again either.

He needed some regular detective work too, just bread and butter stuff, nothing exciting.

But, actually… maybe there was a glimpse of hope of starting over again. With Brooke. "One day at a time, Stone. Just take each day at a time," he told himself…

Judd timed the final drops of his glass of whisky with the closing of side one of *Double Fantasy* and the track 'Beautiful Boy (Darling Boy)." It made him think of Billie. His beautiful girl, darling girl.

Now slightly re-energised, in order to start to get back to reality he felt that a good place to start would be to take a look at his emails. He knew there'd be a few that would be work related and he was happy to accept that his short break was over. Not that his trip to Liverpool had felt much like a holiday.

Judd fired up his laptop which was in easy reaching distance and replaced Mr. Mustard's head with it on his lap, but the dog stayed close by and he sighed a sleepy sigh.

Judd waited for the sequencing of starter screens to pass by and then he opened up his email app. As he waited for them to load, he kept an eye on the increasing number count of unopened emails: 246, 247, 248 emails were waiting, and he was still counting when for some reason his eyes fixated on a particular email from an unknown source, yet the name in the address bar was recognisable to him for some reason. Cullis.

Judd wasted no time in clicking on it to reveal the text.

Dear Mr. Stone,

My name is Father Cullis... Father Cullis?... More contact from the church. Judd searched his mind, he knew that name. Was he a friend of Father Fitzgerald perhaps? Then it dawned on him. It was the Priest who had recently been murdered. Judd continued to read with a spiked interest....

...and I am writing to you as I understand that you are a very credible private detective, but more importantly, I also understand that you are a man with a very open mind who has experienced things that many other private detectives would not have the capacity to even begin to comprehend.

I don't kid myself that you are a religious man but I do believe that if a priest is taking the time to write to you about a subject that for many may seem outlandish, I have every confidence that you will take me seriously. Please read on...

Judd did just that.

And it was all in there.

Without even meeting him in person, Father Cullis had possessed the wisdom to entrust Judd Stone with a significant amount of privileged knowledge. This being that a second coming was nigh in the form of female and that there were followers of Satan intent on preventing this prophecy from emerging and having any positive influence on our broken land.

Father Cullis explained how he hoped to stamp out this evil but feared he wouldn't have the resource, capability or sadly length of life to achieve his goal. Father Cullis had prophesied his own death.

Therefore, he reached out to a certain private detective whose work he was remarkably familiar with.

Yes, Father Cullis had reached out to Judd Stone, the man who had captured serial killers. The man who had researched the power of mind control and brain washing. The man who once had a friend with telekinetic powers and this same friend had been married to a woman who could speak to the dead. Father Cullis knew that Judd Stone was a man who had experienced the 27 club phenomenon and who had also undergone past life regressions.

Father Cullis had considered Judd Stone to be a unique man. A man who had encountered all of these thought-provoking experiences whilst being equipped with the investigative skills of a private detective.

And perhaps most importantly, Judd Stone, could independently work outside of the constraints of the church to defeat Castiel and his satanic cult. Yes, even Castiel had been named.

"In the name of God I am passing the baton on to you, my friend," the email had said. *"And may God's strength and love be with you."*

Well, Father Cullis certainly hadn't been wrong in his assessments, it was just ironic that reading the email hadn't been an altogether necessary ingredient in defeating Castiel. Though it would have been helpful to have discovered it sooner rather than now that was for sure.

Judd sat back in his chair slightly a gasp. Now even

more information needed to be processed. Father Cullis had been correct; Judd wasn't a religious man but he suddenly felt compelled to access the search engine. He typed in a single comment, one he wasn't sure of the exact words but one he was confident would serve in getting him what he needed. "The Lord moves in mysterious ways' were the words that he typed.

A few suggestions came up on the first page, it was quickly obvious, and somewhat surprising, that such an exact phrase didn't appear in the Bible. Perhaps the most popular suggestion would do.

It did.

"For my thoughts are not your thoughts, neither are your ways my ways," declares the Lord. "As the heavens are higher than the earth, so are my ways higher than your ways and my thoughts than your thoughts. ISAIAH Chapter 55 verse 8 and 9."

"Wow, Muzzy. That's pretty mind-blowing stuff."

Judd then clicked on the King James Version and discovered that the verse was strikingly similar.

This led him to stumbling across information about a book by King James called *Daemonologie,* which Judd quickly interpreted that a modern translation would surely lead to the more contemporary *Demonology.* Judd was amazed to quickly discover how this particular publication helped pave the way to the injustice of the Pendle Witch trials.

Judd addressed his dog again in order to speak his thoughts. "It seems lots of things can move in mysterious ways and a lot of things can have connections, Muzzy. Who was it who once said that there was no such thing as a coincidence? Well I now know that the most darkest side of witchcraft, or Satanism, or whatever it is has recently been snuffed out, all because of dots being joined for whatever reasons and by whatever hand. But Muzzy, now my head hurts. This is all too overwhelming for me to process."

Muzzy looked at his master with loving eyes to acknowledge his master but made no sound.

Judd smiled and shut the lid on his laptop. "Work can wait for another day methinks. I'll put the second side of *Double Fantasy* on."

And soon Judd was back to finding his more familiar inspiration by listening to the music of John Lennon.

THE END

ABOUT THE AUTHOR

Martin Tracey is an author who likes to push the boundaries of reality. He lives in Birmingham, England and is married with two daughters. His passions include The Beatles and Wolverhampton Wanderers.

JUDD STONE WILL RETURN IN BOOK FIVE OF THE SERIES.

MIND GUERRILLA

When a high-end escort is discovered murdered in her plush waterside apartment, so begins the hunt for a serial killer known as *The Crucifier* due to the unusual slaying and positioning of his victims.

In parallel there remains the need to locate a dangerous and elusive doomsday cult.

DCI William Chamberlain and DI Judd Stone have an acute thirst for justice on both accounts.

Stone is an ex-football hooligan turned cop. Riddled with guilt and anger, he is used to getting results – albeit somewhat unconventionally.

Chamberlain suffers from Multiple Sclerosis, but curiously, as his health deteriorates, his ability to perform acts of telekinesis increases. When faced with life or death, Chamberlain progresses from manipulating physical matter to controlling minds and sets in motion a dramatic chain of events.

But why do things spiral out of control, placing an unknown high-profile target in danger?

Assistance comes from the most unlikely of sources but who is also working against the wheels of justice?

And just what is the connection between *The Crucifier*, the cult and the high-profile target?

With Spaghetti Western overtones, the chase from Liverpool to London and through both Birmingham UK and Alabama, finds both detectives having to confront their darkest demons in pursuit of the sweet taste of revenge.

CLUB 27

DCI Judd Stone is heading for rock bottom. He breaks the rules, he gambles and he's begun to play around.

An unlikely lifeline is thrown Judd's way when he finds himself catapulted into trying to prevent Rock and Pop sensation Phoenix from becoming the next member of the infamous 27 club – the name given to the list of iconic musicians who die at the age of 27.

Judd's quest is not made easier when Phoenix's lifestyle is even more self-destructive than his own - but how can Judd possibly protect someone from themselves?

And who else could be conspiring to benefit from Phoenix's death? A crazed fan? Birmingham's ruthless Gangsters? A Secret Society? Or maybe even those who Phoenix believes to be closest to her?

And when Phoenix embarks on an unprecedented tour performing at some of the most wondrous places of the world, the stakes to protect her become even higher.

This sensational follow up to the award-winning *Mind Guerrilla* will have you rooting for the irrepressible Judd Stone all over again.

LUNAR

Amidst ancient stories of prowling werewolves, the Lunar Society would meet under the light of a full moon to change the face of industry and enlightenment forever.

When the discovery of a human skeleton at one of their old haunts coincides with the disappearance of a talented female prodigy, Private Investigator Judd Stone is certain that the two are connected.

Travelling as far afield as Prague and as close as his native city of Birmingham, Judd includes past life regressions in an attempt to unlock the explosive age-old mystery and rescue the missing girl.

With a cloud descending over the treasured legacy of the Lunar Society, Judd quickly finds himself embroiled in a shockingly dark underworld of organized crime. So dark in fact he will need a lot more than the light of a full moon to escape with his life.

Printed in Great Britain
by Amazon